Praise For **JINX**

"*Jinx* is filled with real magic, not just the magic young Jinx learns, but the magic of a great book."
—JOHN STEPHENS, *New York Times* bestselling author of *The Emerald Atlas*

"Complex characters, compelling fun, a marvelously dastardly villain, all steeped in a tasty stew of mystery and magic. What more could a reader ask for?"
—BRUCE COVILLE

"A truly wonderful book."
—SARAH PRINEAS, author of *The Magic Thief*

"Blackwood fills her tale with drama and delightfully funny dialogue."—*Publishers Weekly* (starred review)

"Blackwood puts her central three characters through a string of suspenseful, scary situations before delivering a properly balanced closing set of resolutions, revelations and road signs to future episodes."
—*Kirkus Reviews* (starred review)

SAGE BLACKWOOD

JINX'S FIRE

KATHERINE TEGEN BOOKS

An Imprint of HarperCollins Publishers

Jinx's Fire
Copyright © 2015 by Karen Schwabach
All rights reserved. Printed in the United States of America.
No part of this book may be used or reproduced in any manner whatsoever
without written permission except in the case of brief quotations embodied in critical
articles and reviews. For information address HarperCollins Children's Books, a
division of HarperCollins Publishers, 195 Broadway, New York, NY 10007.
www.harpercollinschildrens.com

Library of Congress Cataloging-in-Publication Data
Blackwood, Sage.
    Jinx's fire / Sage Blackwood. — First edition.
        pages   cm
    Sequel to: Jinx's magic.
    Summary: "Jinx travels throughout the Urwald to unite its people and creatures
against encroaching threats"— Provided by publisher.
    ISBN 978-0-06-212996-3 (hardback)
    [1. Magic—Fiction.   2. Wizards—Fiction.   3. Orphans—Fiction.   4. Forests
and forestry—Fiction.   5. Fantasy.]   I. Title.
PZ7.B5345Jj   2015   2014022688
[Fic]—dc23   CIP
                                                                              AC

Typography by Carla Weise
15 16 17 18 19   CG/RRDH   10 9 8 7 6 5 4 3 2 1
❖
First Edition

To
Aaron Schwabach
&
Qienyuan Zhou

with

warm blue

&

deep green

Contents

TO KEYLAND

THE EDGELAND

...ONE CANYON

Butterwood
Clearing

Cold Oats
Clearing

THE STORM STRIP

Witch
Seymour's
Cottage

Wanderer's
Bridge

Blacksmiths
Clearing

Entrance to
Salt City

...LD

Bonesocket from Afar

Sticking to the path won't always take you where you need to go. So Jinx left it, and pushed his way through an elderberry thicket. He crept silently toward the edge of Bone Canyon. He hid in the shadow of a hemlock and looked across at the steep cliffs of Bonesocket Island, and the high walls of the castle, and the spindly bridge of bones that climbed to the Bonemaster's domain.

A few days ago he had seen his friend Elfwyn, a distant figure in a red cloak and hood, walking along the edge of the island. She hadn't seen him.

A twig snapped behind Jinx. He turned quickly. The Bonemaster had a nasty habit of sneaking up on people. But no one was there.

Jinx searched the undergrowth for thoughts or knowledge—he could see such things, if they were close enough. He found nothing. If someone was stalking him, they were keeping their distance.

He left the tree and moved closer to the edge. This was difficult. Heights made him uncomfortable. And he still couldn't see any sign of Elfwyn.

She had gone to spy on the Bonemaster—and be his apprentice—over a year ago. Just thinking about it caused a thick, sick twist in Jinx's stomach. It was bad enough to think of *anybody* being at the Bonemaster's nonexistent mercy. But Elfwyn's truth-telling curse made it a hundred times more dangerous for her.

Another twig snapped, closer this time. And Jinx sensed thoughts and emotions. He reached for the fire inside him, ready to cast a spell. Too late. A hairy, clawed hand gripped his shoulder.

Jinx spun, fists raised. It was only Malthus.

"You sca—startled me," said Jinx.

"My apologies." Malthus nodded toward the island. "Werewolves handle these matters very differently, you know."

Jinx stepped away from the canyon's edge. "I'm worried about her. She thinks she can fool the Bonemaster. But with her curse, he can make her tell him anything. How's she supposed to fool him when she can't keep a secret?"

"You weren't thinking of going over there, I hope," said the werewolf.

"I would if I thought I could get her out of there. But she doesn't even want to leave."

"And the Bonemaster would kill you," said Malthus.

Jinx didn't answer, because it wasn't a particularly heroic thought, but it was true. The Bonemaster used to think Jinx was just Simon Magus's not-too-bright apprentice. He didn't think that now.

"You think he recognizes you as the other wick? The flame that balances the ice?" the werewolf asked.

"I don't know." Jinx shrugged. "I'm not really sure what all that means anyway. But he doesn't think I'm just something he can use to get at Simon. Of course, he's already *gotten* at Simon."

"If the Bonemaster knows he's a wick, if he knows you're the other wick . . ." The werewolf tapped a fang thoughtfully. "He may . . . do something."

"To Elfwyn?" said Jinx, alarmed.

"To you. Elfwyn is not important in the scheme of things."

"Then I don't care about the scheme of things," said Jinx.

"You and the Bonemaster are both connected to the Paths. He may try to reach you through them."

"The Paths of Fire and Ice?" said Jinx. "I thought you

said they were separate. I'm fire and he's ice and the paths don't touch."

"I hope I was right," said Malthus. "Have you spoken to the elves again?"

"No," said Jinx, edging away slightly. He could see the green-gold hunger in Malthus's thoughts, and though he knew that the werewolf was determined not to eat him, he also knew it was always a struggle. "Was I supposed to?"

"No. Elves are to be avoided." The werewolf took out his notebook, wrote something down, and chewed the tip of his pencil thoughtfully. "You grow more powerful."

"I guess."

"Time is running short."

"For what?"

"Once the Bonemaster recognizes the source of both your power and his, he will act against you. Have you found out what he's done with the wizard Simon?"

The last time Jinx had seen Simon, he had appeared to be frozen into a giant slab of ice in an upstairs room at Bonesocket. According to Elfwyn, though, he wasn't *really* there. But where he *really* was, she didn't know. Neither did Jinx.

"You said Simon doesn't matter," said Jinx accusingly.

"I may have been mistaken." The werewolf straightened his gold-rimmed spectacles with the end of his pencil. "Simon may matter very much. Further research is needed.

Unfortunately, I lack resources."

"What kind of resources?" Jinx was still looking across at the island, in case Elfwyn appeared, and also trying to keep an eye on Malthus, in case the werewolf suddenly decided to eat him.

"Books," said Malthus. "I have too few books. Particularly, I lack books in Qunthk."

Jinx was surprised. "You read Qunthk?"

"Passably," said the werewolf, also surprised. "Do you?"

"Yeah," said Jinx. "It's a monster of a language. No offense."

"None taken," said Malthus. "Might you have read anything that speaks of the Paths of Fire and Ice?"

"You mean the Eldritch Tome?" said Jinx. "I *think* it talks about them. We're—"

"You've seen the Eldritch Tome?" An avid red-gold excitement from Malthus.

"You know about it?"

"Only as a legend. I had no idea it still existed."

"Well, we, um—" He was about to say *have it*, but the werewolf's hunger was rather nervous-making. Jinx edged away from him, closer to the Doorway that would take him home. "I really have to go now."

Malthus looked disappointed. "I, too, must depart."

Jinx watched Malthus slide down into a wolf-shape and then lope away.

Once upon a time, it would have taken Jinx a day and a half to get home from here. But not now. Jinx had made a doorpath. The doorpaths had been his friend Wendell's idea. Jinx had made them using KnIP, Knowledge Is Power, the magic he'd learned in Samara. He could see the Doorway now, a hole in the scenery through which another scene leaked. He stepped into it, and was standing in a hollow oak a hundred yards from Simon's clearing.

He sighed, and went home. Home wasn't quite what it used to be.

According to Simon's wife, Sophie, you could learn a lot from sharing your house with sixty-seven other people. When Jinx asked her what, exactly? she said, "Patience and diplomacy. And perhaps a bit of tact."

From which Jinx gathered that she thought he was lacking in all of those things.

At least there was the south wing.

Years ago, when he'd first come to live with Simon, Jinx hadn't been allowed into the south wing. Now Jinx didn't let other people in there. And he used the same excuse Simon had—there were dangerous things in there. Which was true.

But the south wing also hid things, like Simon's workroom, and the KnIP door that led to the desert world of Samara.

Sophie sat at Simon's workbench, with three books open in front of her. The first was the Eldritch Tome. In the second book, she was writing out a translation of the Qunthk text into Samaran, and also into Urwish. In the third book, she jotted down what she thought it actually meant.

She kept the green bottle containing her husband's lifeforce in front of her as she worked.

Jinx leaned his elbows on the workbench and tried to look at what she was writing. "Malthus wants to see the Eldritch Tome."

"That werewolf friend of yours?"

"I'm not sure he's a friend, exactly. Friends shouldn't have to make an effort not to eat you. He said—" Jinx picked up the bottle and gazed into it. Long ago, the Bonemaster had trapped Simon's lifeforce in the bottle. It appeared as a tiny Simon. And lately the tiny Simon had stopped moving.

"Malthus said that Simon might matter a lot," Jinx finished.

"Well of course he does," said Sophie.

"Not the way werewolves think. To them, it's the pack that matters. He thinks Simon's got something to do with the Paths of Fire and Ice."

"Ah." Sophie's thoughts were suddenly guarded, a dense blue-brown cage of worry.

"So I was wondering if Malthus could borrow the tome."

"Perhaps when I'm finished studying it," said Sophie.

"He knows stuff," said Jinx. "He might be able to help us."

"I'm not letting this book out of my sight until I'm finished with it," said Sophie with iron finality. "Does Simon look different to you?"

"No," said Jinx. Except that he used to be about six feet tall, he didn't add.

"You don't think he's . . . fading?"

Jinx waved a finger behind the bottle. "I can't see through him."

"But he's losing color."

"I don't think so," said Jinx.

They both stared into the bottle. They did this sometimes. They just sat there mutually, mopingly missing Simon. And this was despite the fact that Simon was, when you got right down to it, not a very nice person.

The thing was, he was *their* not very nice person.

"Have you had any more of those visions?" said Sophie.

"No," said Jinx. "Just that same dream again, where I'm walking along a path between walls of ice. And I always have this feeling that I'm looking for Simon. But he hasn't said anything since that first time."

"If Malthus is right and you're a—flame, was it?—it

seems odd that you dream you're walking the Path of Ice instead of the Path of Fire."

"Well, who'd want to walk a path of fire?" said Jinx. "Anyway, if the Bonemaster put Simon somewhere with his spell, maybe I have to use the Path of Ice to get him back because that's what the Bonemaster used to put him there. Because the Bonemaster's the wick of ice, and I'm the wick of fire. According to Malthus."

Sophie glanced from Simon to the Eldritch Tome. The cloud of worry around her head darkened. Jinx decided not to tell her what else Malthus had said . . . that the Bone-master was likely to attack Jinx.

He craned to read over her shoulder. "Did you find something else about the paths?"

"Yes. It's a bit different from what your werewolf friend says." Sophie flipped a page. Jinx squinted to read the tiny words.

Where the paths meet, the paths part. Let ice
touch fire, let fire breach ice.

"So it sounds like they aren't really parallel," said Jinx. "They join somewhere?"

"Maybe." Sophie closed the book with a sudden thump, as if she didn't want Jinx to read what came next. "Isn't it time we checked on Reven?"

Jinx made a mental note to look at the tome later.

The Free
and Independent Nation

Jinx's former friend Reven was supposedly the right-ful king of Keyland. But the *wrongful* king of Keyland wasn't interested in giving up his throne. Jinx was keeping an eye on Reven through the Farseeing Window.

The north tower room had at least a dozen people living in it. They crowded around to watch as Jinx cleared away an armload of cats. He laid a tiny golden bird, an aviot, on the windowsill. He thought of the bespelled aviot he'd hidden in Reven's boot.

The view in the Farseeing Window swirled and dove and then showed Reven, sitting on a high seat—a throne, Jinx supposed, but it looked like it was made of branches.

Jinx could see that Reven was speaking to a crowd. Most of them wore swords. They were Reven's army, which he'd raised to rebel against his uncle, King Bluetooth of Keyland. And they were in the Urwald.

"We need to find out exactly where they are," said Sophie.

"All I know is it's somewhere in the east," said Jinx. "The trees say the Terror is back in the Urwald. That's what they call him."

You couldn't hear anything through the Farseeing Window. It wasn't that informative, really. Jinx closed the spell and turned the window back into a window.

Down below, in Simon's clearing, people were hilling potatoes.

A man came up the path, out of the forest. He was a stout man, bald on top except for a chicken. He had another chicken under each arm, and a goat trotting at his heels.

Jinx hurried downstairs and outside to greet him.

Witch Seymour set down the chickens, and nodded at Jinx. "One's been walking for two straight weeks. And the paths are not what they once were. I hope I can rely upon your hospitality, as one magician to another."

"Sure," said Jinx. "Um, are you staying long?"

"One must," said Witch Seymour. "Is it too much to hope there might be a cool drink available?"

Jinx led the witch into the house, goat, chickens, and all. The kitchen was full of people—the kitchen was *always* full of people.

Jinx introduced Witch Seymour to Sophie. Someone poured the witch a mug of cider. Witch Seymour took a long swig, wiped his mustache on the back of his hand, and looked around.

"One had heard something about this," he said. "Where did all these people come from?"

"Cold Oats Clearing," said Hilda, a girl a couple of years older than Jinx. She and her small cousin, Silas, had fled that clearing after it was destroyed.

"Gooseberry Clearing," said a girl.

"Badwater Clearing," said Nick, who was hovering near Hilda. Badwater Clearing had been destroyed by the Bonemaster a few months ago.

"What's happening in the east?" said Jinx. "Have you been attacked by the Bonemaster too?"

"The Bonemaster?" said Witch Seymour, raising his eyebrows. "Certainly not. I've been attacked by your good friend, the King of Nowhere."

"Reven? Really?"

Even though Jinx would have liked to think of Reven as evil, it was hard to imagine him attacking Witch Seymour.

"Oh, *he* didn't attack me," said Witch Seymour, pushing his mug forward for a refill. "No, indeed. Quite the gentleman is our King of Nowhere. Just passing through, you understand, and won't have a wisp of one's thatch harmed."

"Then why—"

"But he's just one man, isn't he, Whitlock?" said Witch Seymour, addressing the goat, which had curled up at his feet. "He gives his orders, and then off he goes, and his army moves in."

"Oh." Jinx thought of the soldiers he'd seen in the Farseeing Window.

"Hordes of nasty Keylish ruffians," said the witch. "One knows when one is beaten, I hope. One heard something was happening here. Some sort of banding together. Solidarity and safety."

"This is the free and independent nation of the Urwald," said small Silas proudly.

The witch looked around in surprise. "It is?"

"Yes!" said Silas. Several people nodded, and Jinx felt a surge of pride. He'd gotten that across to them, anyway. The Urwald was a country. Although some of them were still a bit confused on the point and thought that Simon's kitchen was a country.

"Then someone's invading your country," said the witch.

"It's your country too," said Jinx. "How big is this army, exactly?"

"Thousands," said Witch Seymour. "One didn't have time to count, in fact, while one's cupboards were being emptied onto the floor and one's furniture broken up for firewood. They carried off most of my hens, and I fear the worst. Speaking of cupboards, is there any chance of a bite?"

Instantly three people set about finding food for the witch. That was one good thing about having a houseful of people. They mostly helped each other. Well, a lot of the time, anyway. When they weren't quarreling.

"Did you actually talk to Reven?" said Jinx. "What's he doing?"

"You think he'd tell one that?" said the witch. "He's a king, isn't he, Whitlock? Or thinks he is. Kings are regrettably lacking in any tendency to gossip. But one surmises he's hiding from King Bluetooth of Keyland, the gentleman he's trying to depose."

"Hiding a whole army in the Urwald?" said Jinx.

"The Urwald is big enough to hide any number of armies," said the witch.

"Why didn't you do magic?" said Cottawilda, Jinx's ex-wicked stepmother.

"Because," said Witch Seymour, "magic has limits. There were at least eighty ruffians, and they dropped in unexpectedly."

"I thought you said there were thousands," someone muttered.

"What good is it to be a magician, then?" said Cotta-wilda.

"Let's stick to the point," said Sophie. "Where are these ruffians now?"

Witch Seymour shrugged. "One didn't ask for their addresses. One was too busy running for one's life."

"Haven't the trees told you where this king is?" a woman asked Jinx.

"Yes, go ask the trees," Cottawilda ordered.

"They've told me," said Jinx, mustering patience. "He's in the east somewhere. He's not cutting down trees. If he were, they'd know exactly where he was."

"I expect," said a woman, "he'll try to get himself a clearing, won't he? No one likes to be in among the trees where monsters might get you."

"Oh, that reminds me," said Witch Seymour. "The folk in Blacksmiths' Clearing are making a stand. They want to know if you're with them. They heard some rumor about a nation. They want to know if they're in it."

"Of course they're in it," said Hilda.

"We all are," said Nick. "Anyone who's Urwish. And Sophie of course."

Hilda and Nick had been among the first people to really understand what Jinx meant about the Urwald being a country.

"Making a stand?" said Sophie. "You mean fighting?"

"Of course I mean fighting." Witch Seymour put his hands behind his head and leaned back in his chair. "There've been battles."

"I was afraid it would come to that," said Sophie. "But we haven't seen any fighting in the Window."

"Nonetheless," said the witch.

"Then we need to fight back," said Jinx.

Witch Seymour looked around the kitchen. "Did one mention how *many* soldiers there are? And they have swords."

"We have axes," said Jinx.

"Enough axes?" said the witch. "And where do axes come from, pray tell?"

"And that's why Reven is attacking the blacksmiths," said Sophie. "We need to protect them. I should go talk to them."

"*I* should go," said Jinx. "And I'm going to talk to Reven, too."

"Why does it always have to be you?" demanded Inga. "You could get hurt, you know, going so far away among strange people."

Jinx clenched his teeth in annoyance. Inga, who came from Jinx's home clearing and had once held his face down in pig muck when he was little, was thinking pink fluffy thoughts at him. He supposed he should be grateful, because at least it proved that Jinx wasn't someone it was impossible to think pink fluffy thoughts about. But being Inga's, these pink fluffy thoughts were overlaid with flat grayness. All her thoughts were. Inga was grayly afraid and incurious and just generally, well, flat.

Besides, Inga was at least four inches taller than him. Maybe she entertained some idea that she could still hold Jinx facedown in pig muck if she wanted to. She couldn't, of course. Jinx was a lot stronger than he used to be, and he could do magic now, and anyway there was no way he'd ever let himself, Inga, and pig muck be in the same place again.

Sophie shook her head. "You can't go. You're too—"

Jinx shot her a look, and to his relief she stopped. No one *else* in the room thought Jinx was too young. Reaching the age of fourteen in the Urwald took considerable skill, sense, and luck.

"I should go, because I can make a ward to protect Blacksmiths' Clearing," he said. "And because Reven might listen to me."

It was decided that Hilda and Nick would go with him, because they could use the doorpaths. Not everyone could. No matter how many times Jinx explained how to use a KnIP spell, some people still didn't *know* the Doorways were there.

Sophie could use them, too, but she was also the only one who could keep the houseful of Urwalders from quarreling. So she had to stay behind.

❧ ❧ ❧

Late that night, when he had Simon's workroom to him-self, Jinx opened the Eldritch Tome to see what Sophie had been hiding from him.

It was a passage he'd read before.

Let life equal death, and let living leaf equal cold stone. Take leaf to life, and dearth to death, and seal the whole at the nadir of all things.

Jinx had never been able to make anything of this. Had Sophie? He pushed a cat off her notebooks and looked.

In her first notebook, Sophie had translated this into Samaran, and Urwish, and then into Old Urwish, probably to see if it made sense in any of them.

Jinx looked at her second notebook, to see what she thought it meant.

She'd written

Life = death = meeting of paths? Fire and ice?

Lifeforce/deathforce?

Living leaf = cold stone = repetition of above?

Dearth/death = ????

Jinx had a sudden memory. He picked up a pencil and wrote in the margin

I once met an elf named Dearth.

He knew what "nadir" meant. It meant the absolute lowest possible point. He thought of what Malthus had told him . . . that the Paths of Fire and Ice went down, much further than the roots of the Urwald. He turned the page to see what Sophie thought.

On the next page, Sophie had written

seal = Simon????

A Journey by Doorpath

Jinx went to the bottom of the staircase. "Sophie!"

She appeared at the top. "There's no need to bellow, dear."

"What does this mean?" He waved the open notebook at her.

"What does what mean?" she asked, starting down the stairs.

"What does 'seal equals Simon' mean? 'Seal the whole at the nadir of all things'—you think that has something to do with Simon?"

Sophie took the notebook and went into the workroom. "I was just trying to think what that ridiculously abstruse passage might mean. Because of what came before, I thought it was talking about the Paths of Fire and Ice. And you did say that the Bonemaster had trapped Simon in something that looked like ice or glass."

"But not at the nadir of all things!" said Jinx, feeling panicky. How many times could he lose Simon? "Simon was in a room at Bonesocket."

"Or *appeared* to be," said Sophie. "But—"

"What about 'seal'?" Jinx demanded. "Why seal?"

"Well—" Sophie frowned at the notebook, and Jinx could see her thoughts struggling with each other. She wasn't happy about this. "It does sound like the tome might be talking about connecting the Path of Fire to the Path of Ice. And it could be that Simon's been put in place to form the connection."

That didn't sound good at all. "How the—"

"Language, Jinx."

Jinx gritted his teeth. *Simon* had never said "Language, Jinx." Simon considered swearing a useful skill. "How could the Bonemaster do that?"

"I don't know," said Sophie. "But the two paths seem to symbolize lifeforce and deathforce—"

"I think they kind of *are* lifeforce and deathforce."

"—and Simon's done both kinds of magic. So it might be that he was naturally able to touch both paths." She shook her head. "I just don't know."

"Malthus might know," said Jinx. "If we loaned him—"

"We're not loaning the Eldritch Tome to anyone," said Sophie. "It's the only thing that can help us find Simon."

❧ ❧ ❧

Everyone followed Jinx out to the tree they called the Doorway Oak. It had rotted from the middle over the centuries so that it was like a small room, surrounded by a C-shape of tree trunk. Inside, if you *knew* they were there, you could see the overlapping arches of the dozen Doorways that Jinx had made so far.

There were doorpaths to the clearings that had been destroyed by the Bonemaster—Cold Oats Clearing, Badwater Clearing, and Jinx's quondam home, Gooseberry Clearing. Those places were all thoroughly planted in beets, pumpkins, and potatoes now, to feed the people in Simon's clearing.

There was no doorpath to Blacksmiths' Clearing. Jinx hadn't bothered to make one because the only time he'd ever been there, they'd kicked him out.

Knowledge was the power that made a KnIP spell. Making the doorpaths required an enormous amount. Fortunately, Jinx could use other people's.

He stepped into the trunk. The Urwalders crowded in as close as they could. The golden wires of their knowledge twisted and looped all around them. Jinx drew on it for power, and *knew* that Blacksmiths' Clearing was right in front of him. A new Doorway opened, and he stepped through. Nick and Hilda were right behind him.

❧ ❧ ❧

Everyone in Blacksmiths' Clearing seemed big and grimy. And jumpy.

"That magician boy!" a woman said. "The one who turns people into stones! He's come back."

"I didn't turn anyone into a stone," said Jinx irritably. "I turned one guy into a tree." And it had sort of been an accident. Largely.

The blacksmiths gathered round, their arms folded. And this was the thing—they were all blacksmiths. Men and women and all of the children except the very smallest. They had scorched eyebrows and smoke-colored faces.

"Witch Seymour told us you wanted to know if the rest of the Urwalders are with you," said Nick.

"We came to tell you that they are," said Hilda.

"Doesn't look like it," said a girl. She looked around her. "Seems like we're all alone here."

"We've come to help," said Nick.

Expressions of pure skepticism greeted this announcement.

But the girl stuck her hand out. "Glad to hear it. Name's Maud."

They introduced themselves.

"We've been making weapons," said Maud. She had brass-colored braids and a way of tilting her head back when she spoke so that Jinx's view of her was mostly nostrils. "But we've run out of iron. We've had to turn our hoes and shovels into axes."

"We'd make swords if we knew how to use 'em," said a man. "But we don't, so it's axes. They've attacked us three times so far. We fight 'em off. But there's been folks killed."

Grim, tight, gray clouds around the blacksmiths' heads. Packed into boxes the blacksmiths didn't want to open.

"How many—" Nick began.

"They don't want to talk about it," said Jinx.

"Six," said Maud.

"So far," said a woman.

"So how are you going to help?" said Maud. "Can you turn the invaders into trees?"

"No," Jinx admitted. It had taken all the Urwald's power, plus really losing his temper, just to do that once. "But I can put up a ward."

A purple cloud of disappointment from the blacksmiths— was that all?

"What's a ward?" said Maud.

"It's a magic shield," said Hilda. "It will keep out anyone Jinx tells it to."

The blacksmiths looked doubtful, but nodded. "If that's the best you can do," said a woman, with what Jinx thought of as typical Urwish gratitude.

Jinx walked the perimeter of the clearing, building the ward spell high and deep, arching it into a dome overhead, sending it far underground. He did it with the trees' help. He used their power, and they used his.

When he got back to where he'd started from, the smiths were all staring at him, more disappointed than ever. "That's it?" said a man.

Hilda and Nick smiled. "You might try walking out of the clearing, sir," said Hilda.

The man hmphed and strode toward the forest. He clanged against the ward and fell to the ground.

"What good's that?" he said, picking himself up. "We're trapped in our own clearing."

Patience, Jinx thought. And diplomacy. "I have to tell the ward who to let through."

He taught the ward to recognize every man, woman, and child in the clearing—and himself, Hilda, and Nick. He could add other people later.

"Well, I suppose that'll be some help," said a woman.

"Are you kidding?" said Maud. "It's great! Wait'll those dastards try to invade our clearing again. Now if only we could get more iron."

"The Wanderers'll bring more," said the woman. "You folks staying for dinner?"

They ended up staying the night. The blacksmiths served them a kind of stew made of turnips and porcupine.

"How many axes can you make?" Hilda asked, over dinner.

"None, until we get more iron," said Maud. "We're waiting for the Wanderers to bring it."

In the morning, Jinx made doorpaths to some of the other eastern clearings. He left Nick and Hilda to go and do the explaining; Jinx had been thrown out of most of these clearings in the past and he didn't want to waste time reforming his reputation.

He needed to find Reven.

"He's in the Storm Strip," said Maud.

"Then what's he need a clearing for?" said Jinx. "The blowdown went on for miles. That's plenty of space."

"He wants *our* clearing because we're blacksmiths. Blacksmiths means weapons." Maud rubbed her nose thoughtfully. "I suppose he wants to be closer to Keyland, too. He can't get from the Storm Strip to Keyland in a day's march. You want me to take you to their camp?"

"No, thanks," said Jinx. "It's better if I go alone." Now that he was closer, the trees would tell him exactly where to find the Terror.

"They're a few miles down the strip, west by south-west." Maud pointed. "But you're going to have to go down the path—"

"No, I'll just cut straight through the woods," said Jinx. "Thanks."

"You shouldn't go off the path," said Maud. "There's

all kinds of dangerous things."

"I know," said Jinx.

Of course he knew there were dangerous things in the forest. He was one of them.

～～～

Jinx remembered the storm that had formed the Storm Strip. He'd been caught out in it, and nearly killed. Great blasts of wind had brought down all the trees in some places, but left the younger, more flexible trees standing in others.

The trees explained to Jinx as he walked along—here, there had been a sudden harsh wind that had lasted for a mile and uprooted everything—there, a lightning strike had set a fire that the rain had doused.

It's like a lot of new clearings, Jinx couldn't help thinking. He knew the forest would take a different view.

He had to climb over heaps of fallen trees. Once a startled lynx leapt out from among the tree trunks and snarled at him—probably protecting kittens, Jinx thought as he backed away.

Where the tree trunks lay deepest, burying the ground, there were no saplings or seedlings. We really could have new clearings here, Jinx thought.

Why did you let Reven back into the Urwald? Jinx asked the trees.

Let. We did not "let" the Terror in. The Restless go where they will.

Before, said Jinx, *you used a wind to blow him into Bone Canyon.*

Perhaps. The trees had never exactly admitted to this. *But the wind was already blowing.*

But you could've done something, said Jinx. *Summoned monsters or something. I know you can summon monsters.*

The trees murmured and rippled. They didn't like to admit this, either. *There is less strength now,* they said. *Less power. It is more difficult. The lifeforce ebbs away, and so the Restless invade.*

Jinx was about to ask them what they meant, when he heard voices up ahead. He paused, and remembered the acting lessons his Samaran friend Satya had given him. He had to look—no, he had to *be*—completely confident. He walked on, as if he belonged here, among the Keylanders cooking in front of tents and log huts.

The further he walked, the more tents and cabins there were. And the more soldiers. Some were drilling, practicing deadly sword thrusts. They looked very efficient.

He tried to count people in clusters—ten here, twenty there. Hundreds. He lost count. Hundreds of swords and axes. There were no logs underfoot here—they'd all been cleared away and used to make walls between the camp and the forest.

"Hey! Enemy in the camp!"

Men ran at him, brandishing swords. Jinx was still

struggling to put a ward around himself—it was slow work, with no trees nearby to give him power—when they surrounded him. They grabbed his arms and pulled them behind him. Swords bristled at Jinx from all sides. Above them was a crowd of hostile faces.

"I know this boy!" a man said. "He turned my boss into a tree and then he made axes rain down from the sky!"

Jinx recognized him as one of the Keylish lumberjacks he'd caught cutting trees in the Urwald.

"I've come to see Reven," said Jinx.

"Who?" said one of the hostile faces.

"He means the king," said another.

"Let him say it, then," said someone else. "Make him say 'king.'"

Jinx shrugged. "'King.' I'm here to see King Raymond, who told me his name was Reven."

"Well, you ain't going to see him," said the soldier who had spoken first. "You know what we do to woodrats who wander into our camp?"

"Hey, who's that? I know that voice." A new face appeared above the tangle of swords. "I know that boy. He's a friend of my stepdaughter's. And I don't care for the word *woodrat*."

The man who'd said *woodrat* muttered something that might have been an apology, but not to Jinx.

"Hello, Helgur," said Jinx, surprised. What was

Elfwyn's stepfather doing in the enemy camp?

Helgur gave Jinx a curt nod. "This boy is a friend of the king. My stepdaughter brought him and the king to visit my wife once. If he says he wants to see the king, it's probably all right."

The sword points didn't go away. The hostile faces muttered.

"If you gentlemen don't care to take the word of a 'woodrat,'" said Helgur, "send to the king and ask him yourself."

More muttering.

"We'll do that," someone said finally.

"Just don't any of you let your guard down," said the lumberjack. "The boy's a very dangerous magician."

"What are you doing here?" Jinx asked Helgur.

"Visiting," said Helgur. His thoughts were boxed in and uncertain. He seemed to feel he'd given Jinx all the help he could, and was not sure whether he regretted it. So Jinx stood surrounded by sword points for what seemed like hours.

At last a tall man with bushy black eyebrows came striding up. "The king says, what's the boy's name?"

"Jinx," said Jinx.

"The king said he'd see the boy if the boy's name was Jinx," said Bushy Eyebrows.

In Reven's Fort

Jinx was hustled forward, still surrounded by sword points, which made for very uncomfortable walking. They came to a large square fort made of logs. A gate in the fort stood open, and Jinx and all the sword points went through.

Reven was sitting on the throne of branches Jinx had seen through the Farseeing Window. A double line of men with swords formed an avenue in front of him. Jinx was brought to the foot of the avenue and given a push.

"Kneel," Bushy Eyebrows commanded.

"That's not necessary, Darnley," said Reven.

"Kneel before King Raymond," Darnley continued,

"who slew the wild ogre, and bested the mighty Bonemaster, and walked with wizards but lived to tell the tale!"

Several hands were pushing down on Jinx's shoulders, and he struggled to stay upright.

Reven stood. "Let go of him."

The hands vanished.

Jinx wanted to say *Walked with wizards?!* But the words caught in his throat. He hadn't ever talked to a king before. Of course he'd talked to Reven, and even punched him a few times. But it was clear that if he were to try to punch the man standing at the other end of the avenue, Jinx would be dead before his fist connected. And although this person looked exactly like Reven, he also looked like a king.

He didn't have a crown, or velvet clothes, or any of that sort of kingly accoutrement. What he had was a manner.

"Um," said Jinx.

"Welcome, Jinx." Reven smiled. "It is good of you to visit us."

"Am I allowed to come close enough to talk?" said Jinx. And to see your thoughts?

"Please approach." Reven climbed back onto his throne.

Jinx walked down the avenue of soldiers to the foot of the throne. It was high enough that Jinx had to look up at Reven. Jinx gritted his teeth and told himself not to be awed by any of this pageantry. This was the Urwald. Kings didn't belong here.

Now he could see Reven's thoughts—blue and green squares of calculation, and a little flash of trepidation. Reven wasn't afraid of Jinx, was he? No. But he was slightly worried.

"What exactly do you think you're doing here?" said Jinx.

"Leading a rebellion against the usurper King Bluetooth of Keyland. You know that, Jinx."

"And why are you doing that in the Urwald?"

"Because the Urwald provides convenient cover for my soldiers, of course, as we plan our next attack."

"Convenient? You're a good fifty miles into the Urwald," said Jinx.

"Excuse me, my lord king," said a man standing beside the throne. "I don't much care for this boy's tone, hey."

"I think it would be for me to object, Sir Thrip," said Reven coldly. "If objection were necessary. It is not. Urwalders are as they are."

"Sir Thrip?" Jinx stared. "You have Sir *Thrip* with you? Where's the other one? Badgersomething?"

"Lord Badgertoe fell nobly at the Battle of Edgeland," said Reven. The soldiers in the avenue put their hands to their hearts and bowed their heads briefly.

"Badgertoe stuck me in the neck with a knife. And this guy"—Jinx nodded at Sir Thrip—"cut your face with a sword, remember?"

"There was some initial misunderstanding," said Reven. "But—"

"You still have the scar," said Jinx.

The king stood up. "I would fain speak to my friend alone," he told his attendants.

He stepped down from the throne, and strode majestically down the avenue of soldiers. Jinx followed him.

Reven walked across the fort without saying anything. At the far side, out of earshot of his men, he sat down on a log and gestured for Jinx to do the same.

Jinx shook his head angrily.

"How is the lady Elfwyn?" said Reven.

And it really was Reven talking. Not the king. Jinx blinked.

"She's fine," he lied.

"And the good wizard Simon?"

"Fine," Jinx lied again. "Look, Reven—"

"And he knows you're here?"

"Of course," said Jinx.

"We'd like cooperation," said Reven. "We aren't here to make war on Urwalders."

"If you're not making war on us, then why are you so far into the Urwald? And what about Blacksmiths' Clearing? And Witch Seymour's cottage?"

Reven frowned. "I visited the good witch two weeks ago. His cottage is fine."

"No it's not," said Jinx. "Because after you left, your soldiers ransacked the place and he had to run for his life."

"Are you sure?"

"Yup," said Jinx.

"That is not acceptable," said Reven. "I told them to leave him alone. If he tells me who was responsible, I'll—"

"*You* were responsible," said Jinx. "Because they're your soldiers. And that's not even the point, Reven. The point is that you shouldn't be in the Urwald."

Reven sighed. He stood up, unsheathed his sword, and tossed it casually into the air. He caught the hilt with one finger, twirled it around his wrist several times, and then slid it back into the sheath. Jinx tried not to look as if he wished he could do that.

"I told you, good Jinx. I need to be here to stage my assault on King Bluetooth. Surely you can't approve of King Bluetooth. He makes magicians dance in red-hot iron shoes, you'll recall."

"And now that you're here, he's likely to come into the Urwald looking for you."

"That would be regrettable," said Reven.

"And there have been six people killed in Blacksmiths' Clearing."

"The Blacksmiths' Clearing people are armed," said Reven. "And very reluctant to come to terms. We are leaving them alone for the nonce."

"You're going to have to," said Jinx, thinking of the ward he's put up. "So after you stage your assault or whatever on King Bluetooth, you'll leave?"

Reven's eyes gleamed. "No man can see the future."

"He can have a pretty good idea of what he thinks he's going to do, though," said Jinx. "I'll tell you what it looks like from my—from our point of view. From our point of view it looks like you're invading the free and independent nation of the Urwald. It looks like war. Against us."

"'The free and independent nation of the Urwald'?" Reven raised an eyebrow. "That's what you came up with? It's a bit unwieldy."

Jinx waved that aside angrily. "We want the attacks on the eastern clearings to stop. If you attack them, you're fighting all of us."

"Really? Have you discussed this with the people in Lady Elfwyn's clearing?" said Reven. "They seem willing to make terms."

"Butterwood Clearing? What was Helgur doing here?"

"Arranging the sale of cheese and butter. The good folk of Butterwood Clearing have found it quite profitable to cooperate with us." Reven smiled. The kingly manner was back. "Consider the facts, Jinx. The Urwald is unde-fendable. It's a vast expanse of land with a few thousand people at most. You're woefully unequipped to deflect an attack from even one side—and that, you understand, may not be what you're facing."

"What's that supposed to mean?"

"You may find yourself in a situation," said Reven, "where my protection and assistance could be useful to you."

Jinx made a very rude suggestion about Reven's protection and assistance.

"I can understand your feeling that way," said Reven. "But—"

"There's more of us than you think," said Jinx. "And I should tell you we have the werewolves on our side."

"I'll bear it in mind," said Reven. "It won't make much difference to us, as I doubt we would have found the werewolves particularly friendly to us anyway. But forsooth"—he looked around at the open expanse of the Storm Strip—"we find that monsters tend to stay away from treeless places. In times to come, there may be less space left for werewolves and their ilk."

"What do you mean by that? Are you talking about cutting down trees?"

"You'll admit it would solve many problems," said Reven. "Of course, I'm prepared to offer some concessions in return for your cooperation. An area where you and whatever people you're speaking for—and whatever werewolves—could continue to live in—well, I won't say harmony, because I'm familiar with the Urwald's ways. But certainly I can see setting aside a reservation of ten miles square—"

"Are you out of your mind?" said Jinx. "You're talking about destroying the Urwald!"

"Preserving it," said Reven.

"What you're talking about would kill most of the people in the Urwald. Which, incidentally, is millions of people, not thousands."

Reven looked confused for a moment, and then smiled. "Is this your old notion that trees are people? They can't fight, Jinx."

"You're forgetting that we can do magic," said Jinx.

"I noticed something about your magic, while we were traveling together. It seemed to me to be very strong where trees were, and rather weak where trees weren't. And when I questioned the lady Elfwyn, she said that she'd noticed the same thing."

"You shouldn't ask questions of Elfwyn," said Jinx. "It's not nice."

"Speaking of not nice." Reven unbuttoned his belt pocket, and drew out something that glittered. He tossed it to Jinx. "Yours, I believe?"

Jinx caught the tiny golden bird in both hands—the aviot.

"My boot heel came off, and that was inside," said Reven. "I kept it, in hopes it might bring you here. Of course, I've been leaving it home whenever I went out to do anything that might upset you."

Reven stood up, and nodded to some guards who were, Jinx realized, standing closer than he'd thought. The drawn sword must have been a signal. "I feel we both understand each other better as a result of this conversa-tion, don't you?"

"Oh, much," said Jinx sarcastically.

"Then let me have my guards escort you to your accom-modations, and perhaps bring you some refreshment."

"Thanks, but no," said Jinx. "I'm leaving."

The guards were quite close now, and there were a lot of them. They spread out, surrounding Jinx and Reven.

Uh oh. Jinx hadn't thought that Reven would try to harm him. Or, let's face it, kill him. Reven, in Jinx's experi-ence, generally felt that he could find more useful things to do with people than kill them.

"Not leaving just yet, I think," said Reven. "After all, you do have some people and werewolves at your command, and quite a bit of magical power when you're near trees. As you said, you could make things inconvenient for us."

The soldiers had formed a square, several men deep, around Jinx and Reven.

"I can't have you running around loose," said Reven. "And keeping you here is probably the best way to control Simon."

"You don't think he'll attack you to get me back?" said Jinx.

"Not if he thinks you might be harmed."

The fire inside Jinx wasn't enough. He could freeze the clothing of the guards in front of him—but not the ones behind him. The same went for setting their clothes on fire—he'd be killed before he could do any real damage. Reven was perfectly right—Jinx was too far away from the trees to use the Urwald's power.

Jinx could see the soldiers' different colored thoughts, and the red and gold worship of Reven—what was it with this king stuff, anyway? And he could see the woven golden wires of their knowledge. Oh, plenty of knowledge. More than enough.

But it was too far away to reach. To use it, Jinx would have to walk toward them. And their swords. And then use KnIP before those swords could get him.

He wasn't sure he could do KnIP that fast. Well, he was about to find out.

He ducked his head, charged at the guards, seized their knowledge, and *knew* as hard as he could that the hollow tree near Simon's clearing was right in front of him.

Someone grabbed his arm. He struggled, broke free, and fell forward into the gap that appeared before him.

From the sawdusty floor of the Doorway Oak, he looked back at the astonished faces of the soldiers and—just for a second, before he got control of his royal expression—Reven, as they stared at the space where Jinx had disappeared.

Jinx laughed.

But a moment later something Reven had said sunk in.

You're woefully unequipped to deflect an attack from even one side—and that, you understand, may not be what you're facing.

What exactly had Reven meant by that?

The Wanderers' Code

When Jinx got home there were Wanderers in Simon's clearing.

"There's nowhere for us to camp," said Quenild, the chief Wanderer.

"Yeah, sorry about that," said Jinx. "We had to plant more onions."

"And someone's moved in with the goats and chickens."

"Yeah, Witch Seymour." Jinx looked at the shed. The witch had added a window, with blue-checked curtains, and built a chimney.

"I'm afraid we're a little overcrowded," said Sophie.

Tolliver, a Wanderer boy about Jinx's age, pulled up

a carrot from a patch at his feet and gave it to his donkey.

Jinx looked at the Wanderers' carts. "Is that sugarplum syrup?"

"Yup. Bought it out west," said Tolliver.

Jinx thought of all the people they had to feed. "How much do you want for it?"

"A hundred and eighty pennies a barrel," said Tolliver promptly.

"What?" Jinx turned to Quenild, who was more sane.

"That's the Keyland price," she said. "We bought it for trade to Keyland." She turned to Sophie. "We had trouble getting here. The paths are overgrown."

She and Sophie wandered away. Jinx wondered if Sophie would explain that the trees were taking back the paths because they felt the Restless weren't honoring the Ancient Treaty. Probably not. Even most Urwalders didn't believe Jinx when he said that. He heard the front door of the house open.

"What's the price of sugarplum syrup *here*?" he asked Tolliver.

"Same as the Keyland price."

"How much did *you* pay for it?" Jinx demanded.

"That's our business."

"Keylanders will really pay that much for sugarplum syrup?"

"Sure. Sugarplum trees only grow in the Urwald," said

Tolliver. "They need the shade."

A new thought crossed Jinx's mind. "What else do you get from the Urwald?" He peered into the cart.

Tolliver gleamed suspicion. "Why do you want to know?"

"I just wondered what we're good for."

"Glass," said Tolliver. "And sugarplum syrup. That's about it."

"Glass?" You hardly ever saw any glass in the Urwald. Magicians had windows and bottles, but no one else did.

"Sure. We buy it raw from the trolls. Take it to Key-land to be worked."

Jinx thought about this. "Glass comes from the Glass Mountains?"

"Wow," said Tolliver. "You're smarter than you look."

Jinx decided to be diplomatic and let that pass. "You didn't bring any iron."

"What do you want iron for?" said Tolliver.

"The people in Blacksmiths' Clearing need iron. To make axes." He hurried on, before Tolliver could say *wow* again. "They need all they can get. We're practically at war with Keyland."

"You're at war with Bragwood too," said Tolliver. "We're getting out of here."

"What do you mean?"

Tolliver waved an arm in a generally westward direction.

"You're being invaded by Rufus the Ruthless."

"Excuse me," said a voice.

Jinx looked up and saw his best friend, Wendell, standing beside the wagon, idly feeding Biscuit another carrot.

"Hey! When did you get here?" Jinx felt instantly more cheerful. He hardly ever got to see Wendell, who had been his roommate at the Temple of Knowledge. Wendell had hated life in the Temple, and was now much happier working as a guide for foreign merchants in Samara.

"This morning. Satya's here too. She's in working on the map."

"Oh good. I want the Wanderers to look at it," said Jinx.

"Mind speaking Urwish?" said Tolliver, annoyed.

"Sorry," said Jinx. "You remember Wendell, right?"

"Sure. Appeared out of nowhere with his hair burned off," said Tolliver. "Didn't really notice him much because you were busy bleeding all over the dry goods."

Wendell smiled and nodded, taking Tolliver in stride. "Where does the iron come from?"

"Ask your Urwish friend here. He ought to know."

"Let's assume I don't," said Jinx.

"It comes from mines in the west," said Tolliver.

"The west of the Urwald?" said Jinx. "We have iron mines?"

"Just small, no-'count iron mines," said Tolliver. "They

hardly produce anything. But if there's Wanderers making the trip anyway, we bring it on over to the Blacksmiths. We didn't go this time because the paths were overgrown."

There was an uncomfortable shift in Tolliver's thoughts. Jinx could see Tolliver was lying. So there was some other reason for not bringing the iron. What?

"Can you show us where the mines are?" said Jinx. "Come inside and look at the map."

As far as Jinx knew, no one had ever made a map of the Urwald before. It had been Sophie's idea.

Satya was doing the mapping. Satya didn't speak Urwish, although (or maybe because) she tried very hard to learn. That was all right, Jinx thought: He didn't speak map.

The Urwald was big. That much they could all agree on. The rest was complicated, and had to be drawn in in pencil and argued over.

The map was spread out on the kitchen table, and Sophie, various Urwalders, and the Wanderers gathered around it. Satya was sitting at the south edge, pencil ready.

She was dressed all in black, which made Jinx think she must have just come from some mission that required slipping unseen through the night streets of Samara. Satya was a scholar at the Temple of Knowledge in Samara, mainly so she could steal knowledge and pass it on to the illegal Mistletoe Alliance.

Sophie, too, was a member of the Mistletoe Alliance, although she'd had to flee Samara for her life.

Satya had managed to recover the Crimson Grimoire, a book that Jinx had accidentally left in Samara. But on the way, she'd let the Mistletoe Alliance make a copy of it. Jinx supposed this was okay. The important thing was to keep the book out of the hands of the Bonemaster, who could use it to entrap more people's lives in bottles.

Jinx looked at the map. Simon's clearing was very close to the center of the Urwald. A day's journey to the west was Gooseberry Clearing, where Jinx had been born. Satya had drawn a black square to show that it had been destroyed by the Bonemaster. Cold Oats Clearing, a week's journey to the east, was another black square.

To the north was Bone Canyon. Satya had drawn Bonesocket as a tiny castle on an island.

There was another black square for Badwater Clearing. It had been blasted and burned eight months ago. Since then, there had been no more clearings destroyed. And not so much as a whisper of a rumor about what the Bone-master was up to. Jinx did not find this reassuring.

Dots marked the other clearings . . . which were mostly in the east, because Jinx, who had traveled more of the Urwald than most people, hadn't seen much of the west. All he could point out to Satya in the west was Dame Glam-mer's cottage, another path that went to Bone Canyon, and, further south, the Glass Mountains, where the trolls lived.

Now that the Wanderers were here, they could get more information.

"Where are the iron mines?" Jinx asked.

"Right here." Tolliver pointed to a spot in the far west. "There's a clearing nearby"—he pointed—"called Deadfall Clearing. Nice name." He looked over the map. "You've got the paths all wrong. And that's not where Blacksmiths' Clearing is."

"I've been there," said Jinx.

"Well, when everyone else goes there it's ten miles south of where you found it," said Tolliver.

He grabbed the pencil from Satya (she scowled) and drew a new Blacksmiths' Clearing.

"Erase that," he told Satya, pinning the old Black-smiths' Clearing with his pinky.

Jinx translated.

"I understood," said Satya, in Samaran. "This boy is very rude."

"He kind of takes pride in it," said Jinx.

"And you might as well divide everything right here," said Tolliver.

He dragged the pencil hard down the middle of the map, making a thick gray line from north to south.

"Hey!" said Satya. "You just made a mess of the whole thing!"

Jinx obligingly translated this.

"That's where King Rufus and the Woodland King have agreed to split the Urwald," said Tolliver.

"Who's King Rufus?" Satya asked Jinx.

"The king of Bragwood," said Jinx. He turned to Tolliver. "Who's the Woodland King?"

"That's what they're calling that Keylish guy, the one who's trying to overthrow King Bluetooth."

"You mean Reven?" said Jinx. "He's not a Woodland King, he's a woodland invader! And nobody can divide the Urwald. It's ours."

Angry murmurs of agreement from the Urwalders.

"Tough. They've done it," said Tolliver.

"You'll be getting refugees from the west soon, I think," said Quenild.

Jinx looked around the crowded kitchen. "Here?"

"'Course," said Tolliver. "Here's where everyone knows about. Well, you told us to tell them you were starting an Urwish nation—"

"I didn't tell you to tell them all to come here!"

"They will, though, because it's where they've heard about," said Tolliver.

"This is where your nation is," said Quenild.

"The whole Urwald is our nation!"

"Your nation is as much as you can defend," said Tolliver. "I'd've thought even *you* would know that."

"The Bragwood king is the one they call Rufus the Ruthless?" said Sophie.

"Yup," said Tolliver. "So you may not get so many refugees as all that."

"You've got to help us," said Jinx. "We need all the iron we can get for the blacksmiths to work into weapons. We've got to arm all the clearings so they can fight back."

There was a heavy silence. The Wanderers looked at each other. They looked at Quenild.

"We can't do that," said Quenild.

"Why not?"

"It is forbidden by the Wanderers' code."

"What's the Wanderers' code?"

"Our law," said Quenild. "All Wanderers are bound to follow it. We can't help anyone who's arming for war."

"But this isn't a war of conquest," said Sophie, her voice calm, although Jinx could see her thoughts were angry. "The Urwalders are defending their own homes. They have a right to do that, surely?"

"Since both Keyland and Bragwood claim the Urwald," said Quenild, "some people would call your war a revolt."

"It's not *our war*," said Jinx. "It's Reven's stupid war. He's invading us."

Quenild shrugged. "That's not for me to say. I'm sorry to tell you that we don't Wander through nations at war. You may not see us again until this is over."

"If you're still around when it's over," said Tolliver. There was a worried purple cloud. His thoughts struggled with each other.

"Which you don't think is flippin' likely," said Jinx. "I thought you guys were on our side!"

There were purple and green puffs of regret among the Wanderers. They all looked to their chief, Quenild. Tolliver gritted his teeth.

Jinx was furious. And there was a time when he would have stalked off angrily, calling Reven every name he could think of and throwing in one or two for the Wanderers. But he couldn't do that now. People were looking at him the way the Wanderers looked to Quenild.

"Right," he said. "So now we know that. Thanks."

More ripples of regret. None of the Wanderers would look at the Urwalders directly.

Then Tolliver stepped forward and grabbed a pencil. "You'll have to get it yourself. It's no good your going straight to the iron mines," he said. "Iron ore is just a bunch of rocks. You'll need to go to the Bloomeries. That's where they smelt the ore into iron."

He leaned over the map and sketched. "Bone Canyon continues down this way, and then it opens up here, and the Bloomeries are here, beside the river. The path comes up here—"

Jinx looked at the map. He didn't *know* any of the

places Tolliver was drawing, and that meant he couldn't make a doorpath. "Isn't it shorter to walk down Bone Canyon?"

He *knew* Bone Canyon.

"About the same," said Tolliver. "But you wouldn't be able to take carts into the canyon."

"We don't have any carts," said Jinx.

"Then how are you going to carry the iron?"

"We'll figure something out," said Jinx.

The West

What Jinx wanted to be doing was to find out what the Bonemaster had done to Simon. But the problem of iron for the blacksmiths had to be dealt with first.

"The Bone Canyon doorpath might take you a little closer to the Bloomeries," said Sophie. "But you ought to go and warn Dame Glammer that there's an invasion coming."

"*You* could do that," said Jinx. Dame Glammer made him uncomfortable, and anyway, he wanted to get started. If the blacksmiths didn't get iron soon, the Urwalders couldn't defend themselves.

"All right," said Sophie. "Perhaps I'll be able to

convince her to come and stay with us."

Jinx hoped not.

He'd made a doorpath to the witch's cottage months ago. Dame Glammer had quickly understood how door-paths worked, and had hopped in and out of the Doorway easily in her butter churn—but she didn't like having it so close to her cottage, and she'd asked Jinx to take it away again.

"I can't," Jinx admitted. "KnIP spells can't be undone."

"Magic that can't be undone is better left undone," the witch had said. "Otherwise we're soon in over our heads, aren't we, dearie?"

Jinx shrugged. He'd been in over his head for ages.

Now he watched Sophie vanish inside the Doorway Oak as she went off to visit Dame Glammer. He wor-ried . . . Sophie sometimes seemed to trust the witch too much. Jinx knew for a fact that Dame Glammer talked to the Bonemaster.

Wendell, Hilda, and Nick were coming with Jinx. Wendell didn't have any guiding jobs scheduled at the moment.

Satya had to go back to the Temple of Knowledge—she could never be away for long, for fear the preceptors might notice. If they guessed where she'd gone, she was toast. If they guessed that she was involved in the Mistletoe Alli-ance, she was toast. There were a lot of ways for Satya to potentially become toast, which was probably why, Jinx reflected, she spent a lot of time in a state of barely controlled terror.

But you had to admire the fact that she never let being terrified stop her.

She came as far as the Doorway Oak to say good-bye to them. Most particularly to Wendell. Jinx turned away while they did this.

The thing Jinx wondered about—well, sticking your face at someone—was, wasn't it awfully awkward? He'd given the matter quite a bit of thought, and as far as he could see there was no safe way to go about it. What if the person you were sticking your face at screamed? Or bit you?

He supposed he could ask Wendell how it was done, but that would mean admitting he didn't already know.

After a rather squirmingly long time, Satya left. Jinx, Wendell, Nick, and Hilda stepped into the Doorway Oak and out onto the edge of Bone Canyon. It was not the place where Jinx sometimes went to look at Bonesocket, but a place further west, where he, Reven, and Elfwyn had entered the canyon two years ago on their way to see the Bonemaster.

Climbing down to the canyon floor, Jinx felt the loss of the trees' comforting murmur. He looked upriver toward Bonesocket, which was out of sight around several bends. Elfwyn was up there. He hoped she was all right. And the Bonemaster was up there. Jinx wondered what the evil wizard was planning. When and how would he come after Jinx?

And what had he done to Simon?

They headed off in the opposite direction. The canyon was flattest next to the creek, which rushed along in the deep channel it had cut through a rock slab, so they walked there.

Jinx's magic wasn't nearly as strong this far from the trees.

It took them a week to reach the western end, where the canyon walls gradually became lower, and the river burbled away into the forest. The Bloomeries were a cluster of squat stone ovens. Jinx touched one. It was cold.

"Where are the people?" said Wendell.

"I guess they're in Deadfall Clearing," said Jinx.

There was a path into the forest. Jinx was relieved to feel the trees' lifeforce around him once again. It didn't feel quite as strong as usual, and that struck him as odd. Anyway the murmur of the trees' voices welcomed him.

It was only a mile to Deadfall Clearing.

It was one of the poorer ones—it reminded Jinx of Gooseberry Clearing: huts that were almost all roof, and leaky roof at that. At the far side of the clearing, people were digging and hoeing.

Hilda and Nick stopped abruptly.

"Ouch," said Nick, rubbing his nose.

Hilda turned to Jinx. "There's a ward spell, sir." She always called him *sir* for some reason.

Jinx touched the ward. It was there all right, but with a little concentration, he was able to pass his hand through it, like a thin wall of jelly. He felt into the spell with his mind, and told it to let them in.

They walked into the clearing.

"Hey, what are you doing here?" A woman came toward them brandishing a hoe. "Invaders!"

People came running, wielding hoes and shovels. Jinx tried to draw up a ward around himself and his friends. But the Urwald's power felt all wriggly and hard-to-reach. This had never happened before! Jinx and his companions raised their hands. The people surrounded them.

"How did you get through our ward?" the woman with the hoe demanded.

"I'm a magician. It wasn't a very strong ward," said Jinx. He could see from the Deadfallers' thoughts that they were likely to attack any moment. He fumbled for the fire inside him.

"It's a perfectly fine ward," said the woman. "It's always worked till now. It keeps out werewolves and everything."

"Werewolves don't come into clearings," said Nick.

"It's part of the Truce of the Path," said Jinx. Malthus had told him this.

"Rubbish!" said the woman. "If it weren't for our ward, we'd be overrun with werewolves. I know that for a fact."

"What are you doing here?" a man demanded. "We don't need magicians. We're under the protection of the very powerful wizard Angstwurm Magus, for your information."

"I never heard of him." Jinx still had his hands in the air. "We just came for some iron, that's all."

"We sell our iron to the Wanderers," said the woman.

"They're not coming," said Jinx. "And we need—"

"Rubbish! They always come. What would you know about it?"

"They *are* nearly a month late," said the man, frowning.

Jinx was relieved to see doubt scribbling across his mind. The man lowered his shovel and, one by one, the other people did the same.

Slowly, in case they changed their minds, Jinx put his hands down. "They're not coming," he said, "because they don't trade with nations at war."

Utter confusion.

"War?"

"Nations?"

"What?"

Jinx took a deep breath. "King Rufus of Bragwood—"

"Never heard of him."

"—has declared war against the free and independent nation of the Urwald—"

"Never heard of it."

"—and we've come to take your iron for—"

The weapons came back up. "Our iron is ours! And we already pay tribute to a wizard. We don't need more magicians."

Jinx gritted his teeth. "Listen, you idi—"

Hilda grabbed his arm. "Shut up, sir. Please."

Jinx stared at her. Hilda had never said such a thing to him before.

Hilda turned to the woman with the hoe. "Ma'am, you seem like a sensible woman. Could I talk to you for a moment, please?"

Everyone watched them walk away.

"She told me to shut up," said Jinx. He still couldn't believe it.

"Yes, it was very shocking of her," said Wendell.

After a few minutes the woman swung her arm in a come-here gesture. The Deadfallers went off out of earshot, and talked, argued, and shouted in the best Urwish fashion.

Then they came back.

"Right," said the woman, whom Hilda introduced as Griselda. "We've decided we believe you about the war. A couple people remember hearing about this King Roofless before."

Jinx glanced at Hilda to see if she was going to let him talk. "Do you believe us about the Wanderers?"

"We're not sure," said Oswald. "But they've never been late before—"

"Is it Quenild's group?" said Jinx.

Oswald frowned. "Yes."

"They've skipped you," said Jinx. "They were at our place a week ago, headed east."

The Deadfallers considered this.

"Yes," said Oswald at last. "I see."

Jinx sighed with relief. "Good. Now, we've come to take your iron—"

Nick, Wendell, and Hilda all grabbed him. Jinx shrugged them off. "I do know how to talk to people, you know. I've been working on diplomacy."

"Maybe you could work on it some more," Wendell suggested, in Samaran. He switched to Urwish. "He means we'll *buy* the iron, of course, if you're willing to sell. How much are the Wanderers paying you?"

"Thirteen pennies a hundredweight," said Griselda promptly.

Jinx could see that this was a lie, but he didn't feel like having everyone tell him to shut up again.

"The blacksmiths are probably paying twice that," said

Wendell. "So they'll be glad to give you eighteen."

Confusion, calculation, discussion.

"If we get eighteen, then Angstwurm gets nine . . ."

"Wait a minute, you mean you pay that wizard—" Jinx began, and Wendell grabbed his arm.

"They're paying half what they earn to a wizard!" Jinx told Wendell in Samaran. "That's extortion."

"Maybe we could worry about that later," said Wendell.

One of the Deadfallers shot a suspicious glance at the sound of a foreign language. Wendell gave her a friendly nod.

"They have to see the advantage to themselves, or they're not going to help us," said Wendell.

"But the Urwald is their country!"

"They don't know it yet," said Wendell. "You have to be patient with them."

"I *am* flippin'—"

Hilda turned around. "They've decided to do it, sir. As long as it's all right with the wizard."

"Why's it any of his—"

"I don't know, sir. It's just the way they do things here. And they want to know how we're going to transport the iron—are we going to send carts?"

"Of course not," said Jinx. "I'm going to use their knowledge to make a doorpath."

"I think we'd better not explain that to them just now," said Hilda.

~ ᴗ ✔

The Deadfall Clearing people pulled stone blocks from holes at the bottom of the ovens, and hauled out rough, ash-covered lumps of iron.

"How do we know how much those weigh?" said Jinx.

"I'll handle this," said Wendell quickly.

"Yes, and we'll explain to them about the doorpaths," said Nick.

Hilda nodded emphatically.

"Fine." Jinx stalked off, feeling put upon. If it weren't for him, none of them would even be here. Nobody would be trying to unite the Urwald, or getting iron for the blacksmiths, who would probably have been overrun by Reven's army because nobody would have built a ward for them. . . .

Well, they obviously felt they didn't need him. Let them talk things over, and once they finally worked their way around to where they needed a doorpath to transport the iron, well, then perhaps they'd remember that nobody but Jinx could make one.

Fretting and fuming, he marched along the path to Deadfall Clearing.

He didn't want to go there either. He sat down in a bed of thick moss, leaned against a birch tree, and let the Urwald's calming lifeforce wash over him.

But it didn't. Or not like it usually did. Instead of being

a long, green murmur of life that reached downward and outward forever, it seemed to burble, blop, stop, and start. There
were interruptions. It was as if the Urwald had hiccups.

What's going on? he asked.

The question wasn't specific enough for the trees. He
tried again. *Something's happening to the Urwald's lifeforce,* he
said. *It's not as . . . whole as it should be. It's not as strong.*

It drifts downward, said the trees. *The lifeforce ebbs away.
Flows down. No, not flowing. Drawn. Pulled.*

By what? said Jinx. *Or who?*

Deep paths. Deep forces. Ice.

Jinx didn't like the sound of that at all. *Is this why
you're having trouble summoning monsters? Why you couldn't stop
Reven? Does this have something to do with the Bonemaster?*

"Ho. Pretty confident, are we? Sitting down and rest-
ing off the path?"

Jinx looked up at a man in a white robe. Or, well,
probably it had been white once. He had a pointy hat.
Underneath that he had a square face and a square, grayish-
brown beard. And square, smug thoughts.

"I bet you're Angstwurm," said Jinx.

The Price of Iron

"Angstwurm *Magus*," said the wizard. "And you're that overreaching, jumped-up apprentice I keep hearing about, aren't you? The one who wants to be a king?"

"No," said Jinx, getting to his feet. "I'm Jinx."

"That's the chap I mean."

"And I don't want to be a king!"

"Supreme ruler, then. Emperor."

"I don't—" Jinx began hotly.

"What's become of Simon Magus, eh? We've all been wondering."

"So have I," said Jinx. "And I don't want to be an emperor."

"Oh, come now." The wizard made a *tut-tut* noise. "You've obviously done something with him. It must have taken clever spellwork, too, since I'll wager you had to get around a deathbinding curse."

Jinx clenched his fists. "I would never hurt Simon. He's one of my favorite people."

"You can't have met many people, then," said Angstwurm. "And now you're trying to set up your own empire, at the age of what—twelve?"

"Fourteen and a half," said Jinx, and immediately wished he'd left off the half. It smacked of trying too hard. "I'm not setting up an empire. I'm trying to actually help people! Because I'm not the kind of magician that goes around putting up flimsy wards and then charging people money for my 'protection.'"

That angered the wizard—a little red flash, which didn't show on his face. "But I see you are the kind of boy who sits around daydreaming, off the path, without a thought of what might come along and harm him. Are you sure you wouldn't care to step back *on* the path?"

Jinx took the wizard's meaning. On the path, the Truce would apply, and Angstwurm couldn't hurt him.

"No, thanks. I'm fine where I am," said Jinx.

He felt for the Urwald's lifeforce. What a time to find out it wasn't behaving as it should.

The wizard certainly knew more magic than Jinx did.

Jinx braced himself and waited to see what Angstwurm was going to do, and how much it was going to hurt.

"And now I'm hearing that you want my iron," said Angstwurm. "To make weapons to arm your minions."

"I don't have any min—"

"And you're offering more money than the Wanderers pay."

"The Wanderers aren't coming," said Jinx. Summoning patience was harder than summoning the Urwald's power. "They don't trade with nations at war, and we're at war. And I don't see how—"

He stopped himself. Wendell would probably say that now wasn't a good time to tell Angstwurm the iron belonged to the people who mined and smelted it, not to Angstwurm.

Angstwurm's thoughts flashed amusement. Jinx struggled valiantly against losing his temper. He explained to Angstwurm about the need for the Urwald to unite against threats from without and within—Reven, King Rufus the Ruthless, and, of course, the Bonemaster.

"Ah, the Bonemaster," said Angstwurm. "He went bad, that wizard."

"You think?" said Jinx.

"You'll want to be careful that you don't do the same," said Angstwurm. "I don't think even the Bonemaster started so young."

Just then Jinx became aware of a cold, heavy sensation. He looked down. His feet weren't there. No, that wasn't it—they'd sunk into the earth.

He tried to pull them out. His legs strained and ached with the effort. It was as if his feet weighed a ton. He couldn't move them.

Angstwurm was more amused than ever.

Jinx felt his way into the spell. He saw how it worked. He started to summon the Urwald's power, to throw the same spell back at Angstwurm.

Wait. Not a good idea. Angstwurm would retaliate with a different spell, probably something Jinx had never seen before and wouldn't have time to figure out. Jinx could set Angstwurm on fire, but the wizard would easily put that out, and the battle would escalate.

And that wouldn't help Jinx get the iron that the blacksmiths needed to make axes so the Urwalders could defend their country.

It occurred to Jinx with a sudden, horrible certainty that diplomacy meant he had to lose this fight.

He took a deep breath.

"And then there's the Blacksmiths' Clearing," he said. "They need the iron because—"

He went on explaining, and sinking. He was calf-deep in the ground now. He told Angstwurm about Witch Seymour's cottage—an attack on a fellow magician might seem more heinous to Angstwurm than attacks on mere clearings. He talked about Reven's army. The ground was up past his knees.

And that was really quite far enough. Jinx felt his way into the spell, and reached for the Urwald's power. The power was there, slippery and hard to tug at. Jinx was able to grab just enough to drag into the spell. He stopped himself from sinking.

He thought about pushing back, making himself rise again. No—he had to keep Angstwurm listening.

"We need magic to fight back," said Jinx. "It's the one thing we've got that those kings don't."

"So you're trying to bring the magicians into your empire as well?" said Angstwurm. He frowned, and sent more power into the spell.

Jinx used more power, and was able to keep from sinking further. "It's not an empire. It's just us Urwalders, fighting to protect our country. That's all."

"You say we have magic, and the kings don't. But what about the Bonemaster?" The wizard sent yet more power into the spell. Jinx would have sagged to his knees from the force of it, if his knees hadn't been underground.

Jinx summoned more strength from the Urwald. "Well, yeah, the Bonemaster's got magic. But not more than all of us magicians put together."

There was a pink bubble of concern—Angstwurm didn't know why his spell wasn't working. The Urwald's power had stopped slipping away, and Jinx saw how he could reverse the spell and get himself out of the ground. But he needed to keep Angstwurm talking to him.

"I know you don't approve of the Bonemaster." Jinx could see that quite clearly.

"The Bonemaster is a terrible man," said Angstwurm.

"He's wiped out three clearings," said Jinx.

"Yes, I know."

"It's our responsibility to stop him," said Jinx. Angstwurm's thoughts gave an unpleasant twitch at the word *responsibility*, but Jinx soldiered on. "There're plenty of people that're willing to fight him"—well, at least fifty or so—"but they don't really stand a chance without help from magicians.

"We *are* being invaded. Go ahead and find out for yourself. I'm sure a"—he took a deep breath, steeled himself, and went on—"powerful wizard like you has all kinds of ways to find stuff out."

There was a sound of voices coming along the path. Jinx recognized Wendell's voice, then Hilda's, then Griselda of the hoe.

Well, enough was enough. Jinx wasn't going to have everyone see him stuck in the ground, losing a magical battle. He summoned the Urwald's power, reversed the spell, rose up, kicked dirt off his feet, and jumped quickly onto the path.

Angstwurm looked at him thoughtfully. "Interesting."

Wendell, Hilda, and Nick had explained the doorpaths. The Deadfallers agreed to let Jinx use their knowledge.

Jinx made two doorpaths, one to the Doorway Oak, and one to the Doorway just outside Blacksmiths' Clearing. He told the ward around Blacksmiths' Clearing to let in the Deadfallers. But not Angstwurm. He didn't trust that wizard.

They spent the rest of the day moving iron to Blacksmiths' Clearing. When it was time to go home, Nick and Hilda announced they weren't going.

"There must be more clearings in the west we can contact," said Nick. "We'll follow the path and find them."

"But you won't be able to make doorpaths and wards," said Jinx.

"You can come do that later, sir," said Hilda. "After we've explained everything to them, you can doorpath through to Deadfall Clearing and we'll take you to the clearings we find."

"What about small Silas, though?" said Jinx.

"Other people will look after him," said Hilda. "Besides, it's really you he'll want to see, sir."

"He thinks the world of you," said Nick.

Jinx was surprised by this view of things. He thought small Silas was a small nuisance.

"What you really think," he said, "is that I don't have

enough tact or diplomacy or whatever to talk to people."

"It's not that, sir," said Hilda. "It's that most people are a little nervous around magicians."

Jinx hmphed. He could tell she was using tact on him.

"It's just that you're very, um, Urwish," said Nick.

"So are you Urwish! So is everyone Urwish! Except Wendell," Jinx added.

"Don't mind me," said Wendell. "It's just that you're a little—"

"Don't be tactful at me!" Jinx snapped.

Wendell stopped, and looked thoughtful. "I'm not sure of the Urwish word. Overbearing?"

Nick and Hilda nodded.

"But not in a bad way," Wendell added.

Jinx's hands were sore from carrying the rough iron blooms. And he hadn't had a bath since he'd left home. And he was hungry. So was Wendell. So they went first to the kitchen to see what there was to eat (cold baked sweet potatoes and some inhospitable bread), and then into the south wing.

Sophie was in the workroom. And so was Elfwyn.

Jinx had been afraid he'd never see Elfwyn again. He had imagined a thousand things the Bonemaster might do to her, all of them awful. He was delighted to see her.

He felt a bit awkward.

And so did she, Jinx saw. She didn't run up and hug him, like she used to. There was that familiar green glow, which meant she was glad to see him, but there was something different about her as well. Something sort of—sore, Jinx thought. Raw and red, like his hands from handling the iron blooms. She'd seen bad things.

"Hi," he said.

"Hi," said Elfwyn.

"Wendell, you remember Elfwyn," said Sophie.

"Sure," said Wendell. He smiled, and Elfwyn smiled at him, more warmly than Jinx thought was necessary.

"You've left the Bonemaster then," said Jinx. "Permanently, I mean. Like not going back to him. Like, ever. Right?"

Elfwyn nodded.

"Good," said Jinx.

"I . . . figured stuff out," said Elfwyn. "And then I had to leave, because he might ask me. And if he knew that I knew, he would probably . . ."

She trailed off. There was a kind of sad blue cloud that was most un-Elfwyn-like, and Jinx wished he could think of something to say to make it go away.

"What did you—" Jinx stopped himself.

"He's been spending time in Samara," said Elfwyn.

"What!" said Jinx. "But he can't!"

"He's away a lot," said Elfwyn. "And when he comes

back he brings books in another language, and I think it's Samaran. I kind of worked out a little of it." She turned to Wendell. "Door, onion, aquifer," she said in Samaran.

"That's very good," said Wendell.

"But there's no way to get to Samara except through this house," said Jinx. "All the ancient portals were closed."

"There is the portal you made last year," said Sophie.

"Yeah, but . . ." Jinx thought. The KnIP portal was the biggest spell he had ever done. It had taken much more knowledge than the doorpaths, because it breached a dimension. It went from the prison in Samara to the Urwald.

He'd put up a ward to protect it. And he'd gone back to check on it frequently. Well, as often as he could, anyway. Maybe not so much lately. He'd been busy.

"The ward should have stopped him," said Jinx.

"As I understand wards," said Sophie, frowning, "they require very specific instructions."

"I told it to stop the preceptors," said Jinx, with a sinking feeling.

"So the Bonemaster could have gotten through," said Sophie.

"If he did, he'd just find himself in the prison," said Jinx.

"I'd bet the prison guards had orders to summon the

preceptors if anyone just appeared out of nowhere," said Sophie. "Anyway, couldn't the preceptors have made a new portal?"

"I think not," said Jinx. "Because they don't really *know* the Urwald. They know how much money it's worth, but they don't know that it's all one"—he put his hands together, intertwining his fingers—"thing. They think it's just a bunch of trees."

"Er . . . it isn't?" said Sophie. "I mean I know it's the people, too, but—"

"No, there's this whole . . . thing," said Jinx. "Like, there's this, well, lifeforce, and that's the Urwald. The trees and the people and the werewolves and stuff are all part of it but you can't look at them and *know* the Urwald if you don't know that it's all . . ." He hooked his fingers together again. It was too hard to explain.

"Hm." Sophie leaned back on the workbench. "Nonetheless, Elfwyn's pretty sure he's gotten through somehow."

"Excuse me," said Wendell. "But doesn't that mean that he's—well, out of the Urwald, and that's a good thing?"

"No," said everyone at once.

"If he learns KnIP, that's going to make him even more dangerous," said Jinx. "And if he finds a way to bring the preceptors into the Urwald . . ." The only hope there, Jinx thought, was that the Bonemaster wouldn't necessarily *want* the preceptors in the Urwald.

And the only hope of him not learning KnIP was that the preceptors didn't exactly volunteer the information that KnIP existed.

Other than that, not much hope.

~ ~ ~

Wendell went home to Samara. Jinx and Elfwyn stayed up late talking. Jinx wanted to know about Simon.

"He's still the same," said Elfwyn sadly. "Frozen inside that slab of ice, looking like he's about to cast a spell."

"And you don't—" He stopped himself.

"No," said Elfwyn. "I don't know what the Bonemaster did to him. I looked in his new books, because I thought it might be in there. But I couldn't understand them."

"We *have* to get Simon back," said Jinx.

They both looked at the bottle on the workbench.

"Sophie said she might find the answer in the Eldritch Tome," said Elfwyn.

"She's been trying to find an answer there for over a year," said Jinx. "She needs to show it to Malthus. I bet between them they can figure it out. But she won't let him—"

"I think maybe she's already figured something out and doesn't like it," said Elfwyn. "Who's Malthus?"

Jinx told her. Then he told her everything that had been going on with the clearings and the war.

"You know what I think?" said Elfwyn. "I think

Reven might be trying to conquer the Urwald *first*, and then Keyland."

Jinx hadn't thought of that. "Wh—I don't see why."

"Because conquering the Urwald might be easier."

"That's what he thinks," said Jinx.

"Tell me what it's like in Samara," said Elfwyn.

So Jinx told her about his adventures in the Temple, and about Crocodile Bottom, and how he'd taught himself KnIP and broken Sophie out of prison. It had been a pretty exciting time; he hardly had to exaggerate at all.

Unfortunately the result was that Elfwyn decided she wanted to go to Samara.

"But I just told you how dangerous it is!" said Jinx. "And you don't speak Samaran."

"I'm learning," said Elfwyn, hurt.

"'Aquifer' isn't going to help you much if you get attacked by thugs or kidnapped by the preceptors."

"I don't see why that would happen. They're looking for you, not for me."

Jinx tried to think of something to distract her from this crazy idea. "We're going to have to go and strengthen the ward around the portal," he said. "We'd better do that tomorrow."

To anybody who didn't know the portal was there, it looked like just another bit of Urwald—tall trees rising from a tangle of undergrowth and fallen branches. But to Jinx, who had made the portal a year ago, the stark stone hall of the Samaran prison was clearly visible among the trees. A Samaran guard stood staring blankly out at the Urwald. What the guard actually saw, Jinx was almost certain, was the gray prison wall.

A wolf was curled up on the forest floor, right inside the ward. Its paw rested on a pair of gold-rimmed spectacles.

"Hi Malthus," said Jinx. "Um, this is Elfwyn."

The wolf and the red-caped girl looked at each other.

Malthus stood up, stretched, and kept stretching, sliding into a shape that stood on its hind legs. He put on his spectacles.

"Malthus is the werewolf I've told you about," said Jinx.

"Nothing bad, I hope," said Malthus. "And you must be the girl that I have been told a great deal about. I'll ask you no questions."

"Um, thank you," said Elfwyn.

"What are you doing here?" said Jinx. "Have you been guarding the portal?"

"Somebody ought to," said Malthus. "Unfortunately I've been unable to awaken much interest in the task among the werewolves. They don't understand the seriousness of the situation. Nor, I fear, do you."

"Elfwyn thinks the Bonemaster has gotten through to Samara."

"Correct," said Malthus.

Jinx felt a sinking sensation in his stomach. "Is he there now?"

"That I do not know," said Malthus. "I'm not able to get here as often as I like, nor stay as long as I'd wish. Other responsibilities intervene. There are new cubs."

"Um, yours?" said Jinx.

"Yes. Six of them. I have a picture." Malthus flipped open his ever-present notebook and held up a pencil sketch of what looked to Jinx like a heap of bald puppies.

"Congratulations," said Elfwyn. "They're, um, adorable."

"Um, yeah. That's great," said Jinx. "Why didn't you try to stop the Bonemaster?"

"You're aware that he's an extremely powerful wizard?" said Malthus. "Quite aside from being the other wick, of course."

"Yes, but—" said Jinx.

"I had no desire to be burnt to a crisp, or turned into a toad," said Malthus. "So I took cover behind that tree over there, and lurked."

Some help you are, Jinx didn't say. "How long ago was this?"

"About six days," said Malthus. "I tried to come and

tell you, but it's difficult to get near your lair with all those people running around. People so often misunderstand werewolves."

"And we so often don't. I was away anyway," said Jinx.

"Six days ago?" said Elfwyn. "That's before I left Bonesocket. I think he'd been back and forth through the portal a lot of times before then."

"It's quite possible," said Malthus. "As I said, I haven't been around much. What I don't understand, though, is how he knew the portal was here."

Blue-green guilt from Elfwyn.

She told him something, Jinx thought. But they didn't need to talk about this in front of Malthus.

"I must say I envy him," said the werewolf, gazing at the portal. "The libraries of Samara!" He gave a hungry sigh, then turned to Jinx. "Was it there that you saw the Eldritch Tome?"

"Yes," said Jinx, not adding that he'd brought it home with him. He wondered if Malthus would be able to help Sophie decipher the Tome. Preferably without eating Sophie. He'd have to talk to Sophie about it. Meanwhile— "We have to work on this ward spell."

Malthus gave Jinx a thoughtful look. "Then I'll just be slinking off."

He did so.

"He doesn't like to hang around when I'm doing magic,"

said Jinx. "In case he accidentally eats me while I'm concentrating. Did you—" He stopped himself. "I guess you must have told the Bonemaster that the portal was here. But how—I mean, I don't know how you knew."

"Well, I knew *something* was here," said Elfwyn. "Because when I came to my grandmother's cottage to visit you last year, she told me where the Wanderers had found you. And I went to look for the place. And there was the ward spell, of course, I noticed that. And—well, the Bonemaster asked me a lot of questions. I'm sorry."

"It's not your fault," said Jinx. Except that you insisted on being at the Bonemaster's house to begin with, he didn't add. "The Bonemaster's really good at asking questions. He's gotten stuff out of me whenever I've talked to him, and I don't even have a curse on me. He makes me tell him things I didn't even know I knew."

Jinx said this to make her feel better, but he could see it wasn't working. The fact was, the Bonemaster finding the portal was a disaster. And Elfwyn knew it.

"Are you good at—I mean, I wonder if ward spells are something you're good at," said Jinx.

"So-so," said Elfwyn. "He didn't really want me to learn them, so I had to work it out on my own. I can see what you've done here. It's really strong, but it doesn't have enough exclusions."

"Yeah," said Jinx. "I know."

They worked on the ward together. They told it to keep anybody, anybody at all, from passing through.

Once again Jinx found that the Urwald's lifeforce wasn't all there. When he tried to pull power into the spell, something pulled back.

He didn't tell Elfwyn this.

Instead he explained how the KnIP portal worked, and he was rather put out that within a few minutes she was able to see the Samaran prison corridor.

"That's amazing," said Elfwyn. "You did that?"

"Yeah," said Jinx.

"And you used the preceptors' knowledge as power for the spell?"

"Yup."

"So, do I have a golden ball of knowledge too?" she asked.

"Yeah. Everyone does."

"Can you see my knowledge-ball?"

"Of course," said Jinx.

She looked vaguely uncomfortable at the notion.

"It's nice, it's all sparkly," Jinx assured her.

"And you could use it to do a KnIP spell?"

"If you were standing close enough to me, yeah," said Jinx.

"Well, don't!"

"I won't without asking you first," said Jinx.

Elfwyn pressed her hand against the ward. "The space between the portal and the ward is a problem," she said. "I wonder if someone from Samara stood in that space and showed the Bonemaster how to get through the portal."

"One of the preceptors," said Jinx. "Yeah, I guess they could have. If they noticed him sniffing around the portal site."

"Can we push the ward further in?" said Elfwyn. "So there's no space?"

"The ward can't touch the portal," said Jinx.

"Why not?"

"Because KnIP spells and wizard's spells can't touch," said Jinx.

"Well, we can put them closer together, anyway," said Elfwyn.

And that was when Jinx discovered the Urwald's life-force wasn't there at all. Or not in a way he could draw on—any more than, say, Elfwyn could. All he had was the power of the fire inside him, which wasn't enough to shift a ward this strong. Neither was Elfwyn's power.

"Why can't we move it?" she asked.

"Because something's happening to the Urwald's life-force," said Jinx, fighting panic. "I can't reach it. It's like it's being pulled away from me."

"You use the Urwald's lifeforce for power?"

Elfwyn listened as he explained what had happened.

"Cripes," she said. "Do you think it has something to do with the Bonemaster getting through to Samara?"

"I don't know." Jinx thought of what Malthus had said. Once the Bonemaster understood that he and Jinx were both wicks, he would act against Jinx.

"You do think that," said Elfwyn. "You just don't want me to feel bad about helping him get through."

Jinx shrugged.

"But what could he do to take over the Urwald's life-force?" said Elfwyn. "He thinks it's impossible to draw power from the Urwald. He told me so."

"I don't know how he's doing it," said Jinx. "But it's making it easier for Reven to invade the Urwald, and harder for us to fight back. And I've got to stop him."

"How?" said Elfwyn.

"I don't know. I have to find out," said Jinx. "I need to get Sophie to let Malthus look at the Eldritch Tome."

Peas and Beans

Summer blazed out into autumn, the leaves turning the many colors of fire. It quickly became the coldest autumn Jinx could remember. He yearned to go and find out what had become of Simon. But he couldn't. He had to get all the clearings armed and protected by wards.

The drain on the Urwald's lifeforce went on. It wasn't constant. Sometimes the lifeforce was there and Jinx could use it. Other times it was gone.

As soon as Jinx had a chance, he went and asked the trees about this.

The lifeforce goes deep, said the trees.

Well, it doesn't seem to be there at all sometimes, said Jinx.

What's happening to it? Where's it going?

We do not know.

How can you not know? Sometimes Jinx found it hard to be patient with the trees. *The power comes from you.*

The trees were confused by this. *The lifeforce power? From us? No. The power does not come from us.*

Now Jinx was confused. *It's your power! How can it not come from you?*

The lifeforce runs through us. It runs much deeper than the roots of trees, they said. *It doesn't come from us. We come from it.*

Your roots go deeper than ours, the trees added.

There was no getting any sense out of them. They were worse than the Eldritch Tome.

~ ✈ ✈

Blacksmiths' Clearing was under siege. Reven's soldiers surrounded it, attacking anyone who came out.

When a party from Deadfall Clearing came through the doorpath to deliver iron blooms, Reven's soldiers were momentarily too surprised to do anything. They just weren't used to people appearing out of thin air. But then the soldiers closed in. One of the Deadfallers was killed. A few managed to flee into the safety of the Blacksmiths' Clearing ward. The rest ducked back into the Doorway— or, from the invaders' point of view, simply vanished.

"What about the iron?" Jinx asked, at a crowded meeting in Simon's kitchen when the angry Deadfallers showed up there the next day.

"Forget the iron," said Oswald. "They killed Gustaf!"

"We had to drop the iron," said Griselda. "It's sitting on the ground twenty paces outside Blacksmiths' Clearing. The smiths owe us for it."

"It won't be there anymore," said Elfwyn. "Reven will have taken it, because he knows we need it."

"Well, that explains why we haven't received those axes we expected. The blacksmiths can't get out," said Sophie. "And we can't get in. Oh dear, and the blacksmiths don't grow their own food. Jinx, you're going to have to make them a new doorpath. One that ends inside their clearing."

"I can't," said Jinx. "KnIP won't work against Urwish magic."

"But you *made* their ward spell," said Elfwyn. "It wouldn't stop you anyway."

"It'll stop KnIP, though," said Jinx. "No one can KnIP their way through a ward spell."

"What if you take their ward down, make a new doorpath that ends inside Blacksmiths' Clearing, and then put the ward up again?" said Elfwyn.

The crowd shifted uncomfortably. They weren't used to hearing magicians talk about magic, and Jinx could see that they felt there was something vaguely dirty about it.

"Making a doorpath right into Blacksmiths' Clearing would make them too easy to attack," said Jinx.

"They're already being attacked!" said Griselda angrily.

There was grumbling in the crowd. The residents of Simon's clearing didn't approve of a westerner speaking rudely to Jinx.

"They're not being attacked. They're under siege," said Elfwyn.

"How about another ward?" said Sophie. "One that protects a path from the Doorway to Blacksmiths' Clearing? A sort of ward tunnel?"

"I could do that," said Jinx. "But—"

He stopped. He didn't want to tell everyone how much trouble he was having accessing the Urwald's lifeforce. It was worst on the coldest days—the lifeforce seemed to struggle and slip away from him. It was like trying to catch eels with your hands.

What was the Bonemaster *doing*?

"I'd have to concentrate for a long time," he said. "And while I was doing that, the soldiers would kill me."

Cottawilda, Jinx's ex-stepmother, spoke up. "We have to attack. We have to drive those soldiers away."

"There aren't enough of you to drive them away," said Oswald.

"There are at least a hundred soldiers there," said Griselda.

"We just have to hold them off for long enough for Jinx to make that fancy ward-tunnel thing the scholar-lady's talking about," said Cottawilda.

There was near silence as everyone considered this.

"I suppose," said Sophie. "With all of us here, we may have enough people to—"

"I hope you're not counting us Deadfall folk," said Oswald. "Because we don't want to risk our lives any more against those soldiers from Keyland. We've got our own problems with our war in the west."

Patience. "It's the same war," said Jinx. "Rufus and Reven are planning to divide the Urwald between them. The axes the blacksmiths make defend your clearing."

"If it's a war, then why aren't you people fighting?" Oswald demanded. "Why haven't you dealt with those soldiers around Blacksmiths' Clearing?"

"We're trying to!" Cottawilda shot back. "We're willing to fight, but you Deadfallers just want to run back home and—"

Cottawilda's husband, Jotun, who seldom spoke, gave a low preliminary rumble. "I never said *I* was willing—"

And then everyone started talking at once. Some people wanted to go to the aid of Blacksmiths' Clearing and fight Reven; others wanted to leave the blacksmiths to their fate. They went from talking to yelling, and soon there were a couple of fistfights. Jinx and Elfwyn broke them up by freezing the combatants' clothes.

"Let's put it to a vote," said Sophie, when relative calm was restored.

"A what?" Cottawilda demanded. "Is that some kind of spell?"

Sophie explained.

The Urwalders eyed each other suspiciously. They all liked the idea that *they* got to vote, but some of them, Jinx could tell, weren't too thrilled about the idea of *other* people voting.

Sophie went to the cupboard and rummaged around. She dumped a handful of dried beans and a handful of peas on the table. "Pick up a bean if you think we should fight, and a pea if you think we shouldn't, and put it"—she clunked a bucket onto the table—"in here."

Everyone crowded around and grabbed at the two piles. Jinx listened to the plink and rattle of beans for battle and peas for peace. Other than that the kitchen was tensely silent.

When it was his turn, he dropped a bean in the bucket.

"Now we'll count," said Sophie. "Oh dear."

Jinx peered into the bucket. There were far more beans and peas in the bucket than there were people in the kitchen.

"We'll have to try again," said Sophie. "And—"

"We need people to watch the bucket," said Cottawilda. "I'll watch."

"You?" said Oswald. "You think we trust you? You're—"

"If you could both watch," said Sophie, "that would be wonderful."

Everyone voted again.

"Now we'll count—" Sophie began.

"The Truthspeaker," someone said. "Let the Truth-speaker count."

So Elfwyn counted. There were twenty-seven peas in the pot. And thirty-seven beans.

Jinx felt simultaneously relieved and somewhat ill. He'd been terrified that they wouldn't fight, that they intended to let the blacksmiths starve and the Urwalders' source of axes vanish. But it hit him that if they fought Reven's soldiers, some of the people in the kitchen were probably not going to survive. And one of them might be him. And one of them might be Elfwyn.

"I don't think girls should be allowed to fight," he said.

Sophie frowned at him. "I don't think anyone under eighteen should fight."

"*I* intend to fight," said Cottawilda.

"Well, I don't," said Oswald. "So we'll just be on our way."

"Wait a minute!" said Jinx. "You have to! We voted! It's what was decided!"

"*I* voted no," said Oswald. "So good-bye."

Everyone started yelling again.

When the shouting was over and the fistfights had been stopped, Sophie announced there would be another meeting that evening to plan the battle. "And anybody can come to it who thinks they should," she added.

The Deadfall Clearing people began to shout and argue with each other. Jinx was surprised that in the end, they all decided to join the attack. Including Oswald.

The battle plan meeting began with shouting, and ended with calm, tense talk, long after midnight. There was a plan. Everyone more or less agreed on it. Jinx wasn't crazy about it, but he didn't want to hear any more shouting, so he didn't say so.

People wandered off to their various sleeping places. Sophie, Jinx, and Elfwyn headed back to the south wing.

Sophie went upstairs. Elfwyn started to go, too, then stopped, sat down on the bottom step, and sunk her chin on her hands.

"I don't think I can do it," she said.

"We have to," said Jinx. "Everyone's counting on us."

"Do *you* think you can?" said Elfwyn.

"Well, I—" Jinx had been having exactly the same thoughts, but there was no way he would admit it. "Yeah, of course."

"Without giving those soldiers any warning or anything?"

"If we give them a warning, they'll kill us. They outnumber us. Besides," said Jinx, "I've set people on fire before. Well, one person. And some trolls."

"When they didn't even know you were there?"

"Well, no," Jinx admitted. "When they were attack-ing me."

"That's different."

"But—"

"I don't think you can do it either," said Elfwyn.

"I have to. Magic's the only advantage we've got. And you and me are the only magicians in the clearing."

Elfwyn looked up suddenly. "No, we're not."

"You're right! We forgot—"

"He likes to be forgotten," said Elfwyn. "It's a witch thing. Let me get my coat." She hurried upstairs.

They picked their way through the kitchen full of sleeping people, and went out into the dark clearing. It was so cold that Jinx's knuckles stung as he rapped on the door of the shed. He had to knock for a long time. "Witch Seymour! Open up!"

At last the door creaked open and the witch blinked blearily at them. "What do you mean by pounding on one's door at this hour? Something had better be on fire."

"It is," said Jinx. "Let us in, please."

The witch grumbled and muttered and stepped aside. The doorway was only four feet high. Jinx and Elfwyn ducked through it.

The witch was stirring up the fire. "Since one isn't to be allowed one's beauty sleep, we might as well have some brew. Sit down."

Jinx and Elfwyn sat down on a log, displacing several chickens, which flapped and squawked before settling down again—one on Jinx's knee, two on his shoulders, and one on Elfwyn's head. Jinx explained what had happened at Blacksmiths' Clearing, and at the meetings.

"And you intend to go marching off like heroes in a story, outnumbered five to one, and give your lives for Blacksmiths' Clearing?"

"It's more like two and a half to one, I think," said Elfwyn.

"And we're kind of hoping not to," said Jinx. "Give our lives, that is."

"So are the heroes, generally," said Witch Seymour. He handed them each a cup of brew. "Well, it will make a good tale, I suppose. Pity you won't be around to hear it told. With luck, there may even be a song."

Elfwyn took the chicken off her head and set it on the floor. "We were hoping you could help."

"I don't think so," said Witch Seymour. "I'm not much good at writing songs."

Whitlock the goat butted Jinx's arm, making him slosh his brew on the dirt floor. Jinx shoved the goat away. "You know what we mean. Magical help."

"In a war?" said Witch Seymour. "One scarcely approves of war."

"Does one approve of having one's cottage overrun by soldiers?" said Jinx. "Wouldn't you rather have it back

than—" He shoved another goat away, jostling the chickens on his shoulders. For a moment the world was full of
wings. When they settled down, one of the hens gave Jinx
an admonitory peck on the ear.

"Well, it's cozy in here," said Witch Seymour. "But
it's not quite like home, I admit. And though one does try
to keep the place clean, there's a certain odor. But how is
this battle you're planning going to get my cottage back?"

"It's not," Jinx admitted. "But it's, um, a step."

"Hm." Witch Seymour's thoughts roiled purple and
blue . . . but there wasn't any struggle, Jinx realized. The
witch had already decided to help, and was merely spin-
ning things out because it amused him, and because he was
annoyed with them for waking him up.

Jinx turned to Elfwyn. "What can—"

"No questions," said Elfwyn irritably.

"I was *wondering*," said Jinx, "what kind of magic a
witch can do that might help us."

"Illusions," said Elfwyn promptly.

"Really?" Jinx was so surprised he forgot not to make
it a question.

"Yes," said Elfwyn.

"But how—" Jinx stopped himself in time. "I thought
witches' spells used the lifeforce power of whoever they
were bespelling."

"Quite," said Witch Seymour, amused.

"Right," said Elfwyn. "Witchcraft illusion uses a person's lifeforce power to make them think they're seeing something they're not really seeing."

"Gingerbread houses!" said Jinx.

"Yes," said Witch Seymour. "Though I myself have always found gingerbread-oriented witches fearsomely dull."

"Great!" Jinx turned to Elfwyn. "We might not have to set anybody on fire."

"Set people on fire?" said Witch Seymour. "One would certainly hope not."

"Why didn't you use illusions to drive the ruffians off when they attacked your cottage?" said Jinx.

"Illusions can only do so much," said Witch Seymour. "They're useless without axes to back them up."

The Battle of
Blacksmiths' Clearing

"Shall we go and look now?" said Elfwyn as they left Witch Seymour's house.

"I'll go," said Jinx.

"You're not the only one who can do a concealment spell," said Elfwyn.

Jinx shrugged. "Okay."

He shivered. It was bitterly cold. They went to the Doorway Oak and stepped inside. They looked through into the forest outside Blacksmiths' Clearing. All Jinx could see was the dark shapes of trees, black against blackness. Cautiously, he stepped through, and quickly drew a concealment spell around him.

He sensed Elfwyn beside him—she had also made a concealment spell, and hers was stronger than his. Jinx hadn't been able to find the Urwald's lifeforce at all. What was happening to it?

They stood, and looked around.

I could build that ward tunnel now, thought Jinx. But he couldn't reach the Urwald's power, and as soon as he moved an arm to do the spell, his concealment spell broke.

"Intruder!" barked a voice.

Then a sword flashed out of the darkness. Jinx grabbed Elfwyn and stumbled through the doorpath. They leaned against the safe, rotting walls of the Doorway Oak. Jinx could feel his heart racing.

"So now we know they're on guard all night," said Elfwyn.

"And they're guarding the Doorway," said Jinx.

"That means we'll have to get rid of two bunches of them," said Elfwyn. "The ones around the Doorway and the ones around Blacksmiths' Clearing. We'll need a second Doorway."

⟞⟦⟧

People were not pleased to learn that Jinx and Elfwyn had changed the plan without asking them. They grumbled. They said that you couldn't trust magicians. Elfwyn retorted that if they didn't trust magicians, then fine, they could attack without magical help.

"Well, of course we trust *you*, Truthspeaker," someone said, and there were murmurs of agreement.

The night of the battle was, Jinx was relieved to find, slightly warmer, no colder than an ordinary autumn night. The moon was full. The Urwalders gathered around the Doorway Oak, dividing into attack groups, each one headed by someone who was able to work the doorpath and could draw the others through.

Suddenly a butter churn appeared in the air in mid-swoop. It thumped to the ground, sending the Urwalders stumbling and scattering out of its way.

Dame Glammer cackled as people picked themselves up off the ground. "Am I late, dearies?"

"What are you doing here?" said Jinx.

"One invited her," said Witch Seymour. "Well, to be perfectly honest, one pleaded."

"Need a few illusions, do you, chipmunk? Need dragons?"

"Yes, please," said Jinx.

"Werewolves," someone suggested.

"Firebirds."

"Werechipmunks, werebears."

"Ogres and trolls."

"You see, I can only do about half of those," Witch Seymour said, only loudly enough for Jinx to hear. "And my ogres tend to fall apart."

"I'm just surprised you could get her," said Jinx. "I can never tell whose side she's on."

A little puff of surprise from Witch Seymour. "Her own, of course. The same as any other witch."

"We'll put you on the second door, Dame Glammer," said Sophie. "All right, first-door attackers—line up behind Witch Seymour."

Jinx had to imagine what the next few seconds looked like to Reven's soldiers. A pile of monsters—ogres, trolls, a burst of firebirds, perhaps a dragon or two—rolled out of nowhere and lunged at them. As the soldiers stumbled back, Urwalders swinging axes leapt into existence.

As soon as the first party was through, Jinx drew on the knowledge of those behind him and *knew* a doorpath to a place just outside the Blacksmiths' Clearing ward. When he looked through the new Doorway, there were soldiers all over the place, running and shouting.

Beside him, Dame Glammer grinned, and Jinx saw a flash of fire as an enormous dragon appeared high in the air and swooped down toward the soldiers. Then, to Jinx's surprise, she hopped through the Doorway in her butter churn.

"Right," said Jinx to the people around him. "Come on. And remember the monsters aren't real."

Jinx stepped through with Elfwyn beside him.

Dark figures struggled in the moonlight. Axes swung.

Swords flashed. There were screams and grunts.

"They're not real!" a man yelled, in a Keylish accent. "The monsters ain't real!"

Jinx set his clothes on fire.

He stood back to back with Elfwyn. Neither of them had an ax. They just had fire, and it took time, and concentration. They were supposed to be watching the other Doorway, waiting for it to be clear so they could move in and build the ward tunnel. But in the confusion, Jinx couldn't even be sure where the other Doorway was.

"Let's get closer to the—"

"Why aren't the blacksmiths fighting?" said Elfwyn.

"I don't know." Jinx ran toward the battle. It was hard to tell who was who. But he knew his people didn't have swords, so every time he saw a sword swing, he set its owner's clothes on fire.

He tripped over something, and fell to the ground. A man towered over him, raising a sword. Jinx dodged as the sword point came down. The sword swung around, fast, and Jinx rolled to escape it. He bumped into the thing he'd tripped over and realized it was a body.

Then suddenly a glowing green dragon's head surged up out of the ground. The soldier raised his arm to shield his face from its nonexistent flame, and a butter churn landed on top of him.

Dame Glammer reached down and grabbed the sword

from the stunned soldier's hand. "Isn't there something you're supposed to be doing, chipmunk?"

Oh. Right. Him and Elfwyn. "Where's—"

"No time for 'where's.' Take this, and don't cut yourself. Run!"

Jinx grabbed the sword—though he had no idea how to use it—and ran toward the first Doorway. It was supposed to be Elfwyn and him together making the ward tunnel, but he didn't know where Elfwyn was and there wasn't time to find her.

Jinx reached the other Doorway. Now . . . concentrate. Jinx struggled for the trees' power, then gave up and used his own. He formed the ward spell into an arch overhead, and began walking slowly toward the Blacksmiths' Clearing, drawing the spell after him. He wished that he had Elfwyn to help him, or that the witches could have helped. But ward spells weren't a part of witches' magic.

So far no one had seen him. He had to turn aside, once, to avoid a fierce struggle. He couldn't interfere because he needed to do *this*; this was the whole point of the attack.

He had to make the ward spell go right over another dead body. Jinx didn't break concentration to look at it.

Once a sword swung at him, and skittered off the ward. Jinx ignored it, and kept working on the spell.

At last he reached the Blacksmith's Clearing ward. He passed through into it.

There was a crowd of people standing around, some holding axes, all looking uncertain.

"Why aren't you guys out there?" Jinx demanded. "We're doing this for you!"

"We didn't know that," said a blacksmith. "We just heard fighting, is all."

"They didn't believe me," Elfwyn yelled. She was standing outside the ward, unable to get through. "I tried to tell them, but they think I'm a spy or something!"

Jinx was enormously relieved to see her, even though she was furious. "Come on," he said. "You've got to help me strengthen the ward tunnel. And you guys"—he turned to the blacksmiths—"have got to go out and fight! There's not enough of us Urwalders!"

"And how are we supposed to know the Urwalders from the Keylanders?"

"We're the ones with axes!" Jinx yelled.

"You have a sword," said a woman "And some of the Keylanders have axes."

Jinx threw his sword down and cursed. "Just go! And when you see a green flash in the sky, retreat."

Elfwyn and Jinx worked feverishly on the ward tunnel. They strengthened it as much as they could. And then they hurriedly told it all the people it had to let pass through.

"I think that's as good as we're going to get it," said Elfwyn, and she sent up the green flash.

Under a cover of dragons and firebirds, the Urwalders

fled to the Doorways, Reven's soldiers in pursuit. Jinx and Elfwyn stood by to hand people through. Jinx was looking around desperately for Sophie, and was relieved when he finally saw her staggering toward the Doorway, carrying someone over her shoulder.

He hurried to help her. The someone was his exstepmother, Cottawilda, and she was still alive.

"Jinx, what happened to you?" Sophie asked, as everyone stumbled into the kitchen.

"Nothing," said Jinx, looking down at himself. He was covered in blood. "It must have come from—"

Then he noticed he was bleeding from several cuts on his legs and one on his arm.

In stories, when a young man is handed a sword for the first time he instantly knows how to use it. In real life, when you run around in the dark carrying a long, doubleedged knife, you generally end up cutting yourself. And that was what Jinx had done.

"It's no big deal," he said.

❧ ❧ ❧

The battle had changed them.

Three Urwalders had died. One of them had been Oswald, who hadn't wanted to fight in the first place. Jinx felt awful about this.

He expected people to be angry. But they weren't. Instead, they pulled closer together. The divide between westerners and the people of Simon's clearing seemed to have slipped somewhat. They were all Urwalders.

Cottawilda lay on the huge stone stove, with her bandaged arms and legs elevated. She was very pale and rather pleased with herself.

"We need a battle cry," she said. "So that next time, the people we're trying to rescue will know who we are."

"The Urwald," said Jinx promptly.

"The Urwald!" cried small Silas. He jumped down from the high stone stove, and Jinx caught him.

Jinx was glad to see that people weren't discouraged. *He* was discouraged. They'd only fought a small portion of Reven's forces. They'd used the best magic they could manage. And though they had done what they'd set out to do—built the ward tunnel—their utmost efforts had succeeded in driving off Reven's soldiers for about five minutes.

In fact, the only thing the Urwalders could do in this war was lose it. Jinx kept that thought to himself.

❧

It was only in the south wing, to Sophie and Elfwyn, that Jinx said what he really thought.

"We can't fight them without more magic. There's just too many of them."

He was lying on his pallet, staring up at the vaulted ceiling of Simon's workroom. Sophie was sitting on the stool, and Elfwyn on the workbench.

"You need to learn to use something else for power," said Elfwyn.

Jinx wondered what. There was Simon's bottled life-force, but he could no longer sense any power coming from it at all. He looked over at the bottle in Sophie's hands. The Simon in the bottle breathed so shallowly that sometimes you had to stare for a long time to see that the tiny chest was moving at all.

Besides, he didn't want Simon's lifeforce for power. He wanted it back in *Simon*.

There was Calvin, of course, but Jinx absolutely was not in any way ever going to use the skull for power. Calvin was a deathforce power source.

Jinx had tried to learn the chants and chalk drawings and stuff that Elfwyn knew, but he wasn't very good at it. Chanting just made him feel silly. And it wouldn't be anything close to the amount of power he was used to having—and needed, if he was going to defend the Urwald.

He needed to get the Urwald's power back. And he needed Simon.

But there was no way to get him. No possible way.

"I don't understand what's happened to the Urwald's lifeforce," said Sophie. "Is it because it's nearly winter?"

"No," said Jinx. "The power's always been there in the winter before." He put his feet up in the air and thought. "It's not the cold weather that's making the power go away. It's almost like it's the other way round."

A blue tangle of confusion from Sophie. "The power going away makes the weather cold?"

"Right." Jinx knew this sounded ridiculous. He sat up.

"What could be making the weather cold?" said Sophie.

Jinx shrugged. He felt sure it was the Bonemaster, but he felt stupid saying it.

"The Bonemaster," said Elfwyn. "There was that ice he put Simon in."

Jinx put his hands flat on the pallet and walked his feet up the wall. "The Paths of Fire and Ice," he said.

"But they've always been there," said Sophie.

"This has something to do with—" Jinx found it rather hard to breathe in this position. "What he's done to Simon."

Gingerly he moved his feet off of the wall so that he was standing on his hands. Dust fell off his socks into his face.

Tumbling blue-gray thoughts from Sophie. Jinx remembered what Elfwyn had said. Sophie thinks she knows what's happened, Jinx thought. But she doesn't want to know.

"That's just a theory I had," said Sophie. "There's no reason to think—"

"Malthus thinks so," said Jinx. "He said the Bonemaster might use the paths to get at me in some way. And now I can't use the Urwald's power."

"But that seems so . . ." Sophie trailed off. She looked at bottled Simon.

"Abstruse," said Jinx, upside down.

"I think that's what the elves said," said Elfwyn.

Jinx fell over in surprise. "You talked to elves?"

"No. The Bonemaster did," said Elfwyn. "They didn't know I was listening."

"When? Why didn't you tell us?" Jinx demanded.

"About six months ago! I forgot! Stop asking questions!"

"Sorry," said Jinx.

"I'm sure we would both like to hear what they said," said Sophie.

Elfwyn swung her feet. "They told him—" She frowned. "I think they told him he could draw fire through the seal, and then they sort of warned him."

Bright clouds of horror from Sophie.

"What kind—" Jinx began. "Er, I wonder how they warned him."

"They said without balance, he'd—" Elfwyn sighed. "He'd . . . something. I don't remember. It went all dazzly."

"Blue sparks," said Jinx. "They do some kind of memory spell."

"I think they just did it on me, though. Not him."

"They want him to know what he is." Jinx thought of what Malthus had said. "That he's the other wick. Sophie, you've got to let Malthus see the Eldritch Tome."

"Really, dear—" said Sophie doubtfully.

"He knows about this stuff," said Jinx. "And you're kind of stuck, aren't you?"

A red wave of hurt from Sophie. Ouch. Jinx tried another tactic. "Malthus is really interested in Samaran scholarship. He wishes he could go to Samara. But he can't, because they'd be sure to notice he's a werewolf, and—"

"Oh, the poor creature," said Sophie. "But I don't know, the Eldritch Tome . . ."

"He might be able to figure out what's happened to Simon," said Jinx.

That seemed to be the wrong thing to say. Sophie's thoughts clenched up in a tight blue ball.

"Or anyway, he could figure out what the Bonemaster's doing," said Jinx.

Sophie looked uncertain.

"I'm sure he'd be careful with it," said Jinx, willing her to agree.

Sophie's thoughts wobbled. It wasn't that she was afraid of the Tome being damaged, Jinx thought. She was afraid of finding out there was nothing that could be done to save Simon.

"Well, I suppose I could talk to him about it," she said at last.

The Winter of Exploding Trees

Elfwyn went a few times to the market in Samara with Wendell. It infuriated Jinx that he couldn't go with her. He wanted to. But Sophie told him that it would be a disaster for everyone if Jinx got arrested in Samara and boiled in oil. And Jinx had to admit that it would certainly be a disaster for him.

Jinx made several trips to the west, to build wards and doorpaths for the newfound clearings. The Urwald's life-force was usually out of reach now, especially on the coldest days. Elfwyn, when she wasn't in Samara, joined Jinx on his journeys, and together they put up the best wards they could manage.

To prevent another siege like Blacksmiths' Clearing, Jinx made the Doorways first, inside the clearings, and the wards afterward. That way an enemy couldn't get between the Urwalders and their means of escape. He and Elfwyn put separate, small wards around the Doorways, just in case an enemy figured out how to use the doorpaths.

"I just hope the wards are strong enough," said Elfwyn.

"Even if they are, it's no good," said Jinx. The realization had been weighing down on him more and more as they walked.

"You mean it won't stop King Rufus the Ruthless from invading the Urwald," said Elfwyn.

"Yeah. Exactly."

"But it'll at least protect the people in the clearings," said Elfwyn. "And they'll be able to escape if they need to."

"And then they'll all come to Simon's house!"

"At least it gives us time," said Elfwyn. "To find out how the Bonemaster is draining the Urwald's power, and stop him."

Jinx heard a crunch and looked up. Werewolves were moving through the trees, keeping parallel to Jinx and Elfwyn as they walked.

Jinx stopped. The werewolves stopped too.

"Hi," said Jinx.

The werewolves gazed at him.

"We need to talk to Malthus," said Jinx.

The werewolves grinned. Jinx could almost taste their hunger.

"Could you ask him to meet me at, um, at the edge of Bone Canyon tomorrow—"

"We won't be home by tomorrow," said Elfwyn.

"Thursday, then," said Jinx.

The werewolves stood watching Jinx and Elfwyn with golden eyes. Jinx was sure they had understood him.

"And tell him we'll lend him the Eldritch Tome."

The werewolves still didn't respond.

"Please," Jinx added.

One of the werewolves peeled away from the pack and trotted off into the forest.

"Thanks," said Jinx uncertainly. He and Elfwyn walked on, and the werewolves kept pace.

"You're sure they're on our side?" said Elfwyn, very quietly.

"Yeah. Well, the Urwald's side, and they understand that's the same thing."

"For now," said Elfwyn.

"Yeah."

"They still make me nervous."

"Yeah," said Jinx. "Me too."

They both tried hard not to show it.

Jinx and Sophie stepped through the Doorway at the edge of Bone Canyon. Malthus was waiting for them in wolf-form, but slid up into a more human shape when he saw them.

Jinx could see the roiling clouds of terror enveloping Sophie, although they didn't show on her face.

"Malthus is all right," Jinx told her. "Or, well, he kind of leaves suddenly so he doesn't eat you. Malthus, this is Sophie."

Malthus's golden eyes gleamed. "Ah, Sophie the Scholar! This is an honor."

Jinx was impressed by how calmly Sophie managed her first hand-and-clawshake with a werewolf.

"I have great respect for Samaran scholarship," said Malthus. "It's been years since I've really had a chance to sink my teeth into—"

"Sophie has some questions she wanted to ask you. About"—Jinx watched closely, in case Malthus suddenly attacked—"the Eldritch Tome."

"You have it with you?" The werewolf gleamed hungrily. Jinx braced himself in case he had to make a ward spell in a hurry.

"Yes." Sophie drew the slim blue book from her coat, pulled off her woolen mittens, and paged through it. "I was wondering about the balance of lifeforce and deathforce. If you'll look here—"

Malthus leaned over the book eagerly. "Ah, yes, I see. The Paths of Fire and Ice?"

"Are they real paths?" said Sophie.

"You see this word here—" The werewolf pointed and made a grating, snarly sound. "Means 'paths.' They are real. The infixes mean 'ice' and 'fire.'"

"I know that," said Sophie. "You told Jinx that when the two paths meet there are explosions."

"At the upper levels," said Malthus. "In the visible world. Where the metaphysical manifests itself in the physical realm. You're familiar with Sort's Taxonomy of Pseudophenomena?"

"Of course," said Sophie. "But—no offense—I'm a little surprised that you are."

"I have his book," said Malthus. "Something to chew over in the winter evenings. I've often thought that if he'd actually visited the Urwald, he might have reassessed his stipulation that—"

"But haven't you read Luzani's commentaries?" Sophie asked. "They refute the whole basis of his classification of—"

"'Scuse me," said Jinx. "Malthus doesn't stay long. He always has to run off somewhere. So could we kind of—"

Malthus frowned at him, which was the most uncomfortable thing Jinx had had happen to him all day.

"What happens if the paths meet at the bottom, instead of the top?" said Sophie.

"I'm not certain that could happen," said Malthus. "Not without considerable magical intervention."

"What if there *was* magical intervention?" said Jinx. "Like from the Bonemaster?"

"Then I suppose that they could meet. Whether there would be explosions or not, I don't know," said the werewolf. "Sort's Taxonomy suggests not. But what did he know, really?"

Sophie flipped over several pages, and pointed to another passage.

"'Where the paths meet, the paths part. Let ice touch fire, let fire breach ice,'" Malthus translated. "Hm. It does sound like they cross, or meet, somewhere. And yet that's against their very nature."

"If someone—the Bonemaster, for instance—forced the paths to meet in some way . . ." There was a catch in Sophie's voice.

"Up here, it would cause an explosion. Down there . . . I don't know. I have always assumed the rules are different down there." Malthus tapped a fang thoughtfully.

"There's this, too," said Sophie, reaching past the werewolf's claws to flip the pages again.

"'Let life equal death, and let living leaf equal cold stone. Take leaf to life, and dearth to death, and seal the whole at the nadir of all things.' Hm. I see your point."

Jinx remembered the note Sophie had made: *Seal = Simon?*

"So you think the paths meet at the nadir," said Mal-thus.

"I think they've been joined," said Sophie. "And that the Bonemaster is somehow using"—her voice shook, pos-sibly with the cold—"that is, I think the Bonemaster may have found a Qunthk spell for joining the paths."

"I believe this may *be* the spell." Malthus touched the open book with a claw. "He doesn't have the Eldritch Tome, does he?"

"I don't know," said Sophie. "I've never heard of there being another copy, but—"

"The elves could have taught him the spell, I suppose." Malthus jotted a note in his notebook.

"So if he's joined the paths," said Jinx, "that's how he's draining my—the Urwald's—power, right?" He remembered what Elfwyn had said. The elves had told the Bonemaster he could draw fire through the seal. "And Sophie thinks he's using Simon to connect the paths—"

A blue-brown wave of horror from Sophie. Jinx decided not to say any more about that.

"Of course, I'm not sure if I'm interpreting it correctly," said Sophie.

The werewolf looked at her with sudden sympathy. "I see. May I— If it's not too much to ask, may I borrow the tome?"

"Please do," said Sophie.

Malthus flashed that red-gold delight that was

uncomfortably like hunger.

"Perhaps I could come with you to study it," Sophie suggested.

"Don't!" said Jinx.

"I think it would be best not to," said Malthus regretfully. "Although I'd be delighted to have your company, I'm afraid the other werewolves in my pack would . . . also be delighted." He took the book in his claws. "The Eldritch Tome! I can hardly believe it."

More red-gold hunger. Jinx could tell that Malthus was now having a lot of trouble not eating them.

"We'd better go," said Jinx, grabbing Sophie's arm and pulling her away.

It grew colder and colder. On their journeys between the clearings that Hilda and Nick had contacted, Jinx and his companions got frostbite on their fingers and toes. One night, in a crowded, drafty hut in Churnbottom Clearing, they were awakened by a loud explosion.

"What's that?" cried Hilda. Most of the people in the hut huddled, terrified, but she went to the door and opened it.

Jinx followed her out into air so cold it hurt to breathe. Nick joined them, his feet squeaking in the snow. Jinx could see tiny ice crystals floating in the moonlight. He listened to the forest.

Two more explosions, one right after another.

"Exploding trees," said Jinx.

"Is the Bonemaster doing it?" said Hilda.

"No," said Jinx. Several more trees exploded, and he heard the forest murmur and moan.

"When it gets really cold, their sap freezes, and it expands, and—bang," Jinx explained. "It hasn't happened in like a hundred years, but—"

"Not the Bonemaster, then?" Hilda rippled cold silver doubt, and shivered.

"How could it be?" said Jinx.

"I think you think it is, sir," said Hilda. "We're just getting everything organized, getting people ready to fight, so that we can hold out while you go after him. Right?"

"But we'll go with you, of course," said Nick. "I mean, not that we can do much against a wizard, but—"

"No. You're good with people," said Jinx, shivering. "You'll have to help Sophie hold them all together while I go."

"Go where, sir?" Hilda was shivering, too. "Bone-socket?"

Jinx thought of Simon, and of the Paths of Fire and Ice. "I'm not really sure yet."

Out in the forest, another tree exploded.

❧ ❧ ❧

The cold autumn became a cold, cold winter. By now Jinx couldn't feel the Urwald's lifeforce anywhere.

Elfwyn and Sophie tried to make a pumpkin pie for

Jinx's birthday, as Simon always had. Jinx appreciated their effort.

Satya stopped showing up to work on the map. They'd found several new clearings, and Sophie added them in pencil, but she said she wasn't sure she'd gotten them right.

"Is it too cold for Satya here?" said Sophie. "Because we could take the map through to the Samaran house."

"She's busy right now," said Wendell. "You know. With her stuff."

There was an uncharacteristic red flash of resentment when he said it.

"Ah. Yes." Sophie asked no more questions. "Well, I think I'll go through to the Samaran house for a bit, any-way. My toes are turning blue."

She went through the KnIP door, which they usually left open now to heat the south wing. Even though Jinx knew that people who didn't know the door was there wouldn't be able to see it, having it open still made him nervous.

"So did you have a fight with Satya, or something?" he asked.

Wendell shrugged. "She's really into the stuff she's into. That's all."

"The Mistletoe Alliance, you mean," said Jinx.

"It's the only thing that matters to her," said Wendell.

"No, it's not," said Jinx, feeling very awkward and

uncomfortable. Satya didn't have pink fluffy thoughts about Wendell, oddly. But she had some purple twisty ones that as far as Jinx could tell were of a highly pro-Wendell nature.

He didn't really want to talk about it, though, and he hoped Wendell wouldn't want to either.

"It's fine, it's no problem," said Wendell. "If she cares about the Company—"

"The Mistletoe Alliance," said Jinx.

"—more than anything else, you know, that's her own business, obviously. But she shouldn't expect me to care about them."

"No," said Jinx. "I guess they do good work, though, don't they?"

He wasn't sure about this. The Mistletoe Alliance's avowed mission was to free the knowledge that the preceptors kept locked up in the Temple of Knowledge. But sometimes Jinx wondered—since the Alliance itself was so secret, how did they manage to free knowledge?

"The trouble with being in the Company," said Wendell, "is that you have to do what you're told. Rather than think for yourself."

"Oh," said Jinx. "You haven't joined it, have you?"

"No," said Wendell. "I like being alive."

"Oh," said Jinx.

"Which, actually, so does Satya," said Wendell. "But

she was born into the stupid Company, you know? She thinks it's what's true. Kind of like me before I realized my grandpa wasn't really a god."

"Right," said Jinx.

"So she thinks she's got to stay there in the Temple trying to free knowledge from it, until eventually she gets caught by the Preceptors doing something illegal, gets stuck in jail, and gets ex—" Wendell's voice caught, and he kicked the wall angrily.

"Executed?" Jinx offered.

"Grandpa's arse! She doesn't even think about the stuff they tell her to do, about whether it's right or wrong."

Jinx was surprised. "That doesn't sound like her."

"No, it's not her," said Wendell. "It's the Company. That's my whole point. Grandpa's arse, you don't know what it's like. No one ever told you what to believe, did they? I can tell they didn't."

Jinx thought about this. Simon had certainly told him what to *do*, but . . . "I guess not."

"If you hadn't come along and told me it was okay to leave the Temple and forget about what Grandpa wanted, I'd still be there. That's how it is."

"Well, can't you tell Satya that it's all right to leave—"

"I have! About a million times. She says she doesn't want to."

"Then maybe she doesn't want to," Jinx ventured.

There was a sudden orange wriggle in Wendell's thoughts, and for the first time ever, Jinx thought Wendell was hiding something from him.

"Did she ask you to join the Mistletoe Alliance?"

"No," said Wendell. "You know, I think she only hangs around with me for the Company's sake. So she can get away from the Temple by pretending she's coming down to meet me at the Twisted Branch."

Even someone who couldn't see thoughts would've been able to tell Wendell was lying, Jinx thought. "You don't think that. What did you really fight about?"

"I told you. The stupid Company."

The wriggle in his thoughts seemed to say this was the truth, but that Wendell, who was in his own way very honest, didn't consider it exactly the real truth.

"What did they ask her to do?" said Jinx.

"Doesn't matter," said Wendell. "The Mistletoe Alliance is what we had a fight about, since you ask, and that's all."

Wendell walked away quickly, into the kitchen, and out of range of Jinx's ability to see any colored clouds.

It was just as Jinx had feared. With the wards and the weapons, the clearings were able to defend themselves, but not to stop the invasion. And without the Wanderers, the situation was more desperate than Jinx would have expected. He'd never realized before just how much stuff the Wanderers moved. The clearings now had to feed themselves on what they'd grown, and none of them could do it. In the west, people couldn't go into the forest to for-age for food because they were afraid of being attacked by the invading army from Bragwood.

The werewolves harried the invaders, but there were far more invaders than werewolves. Some werewolves were killed, and after that the werewolves hung back, watching the situation but reluctant to interfere.

Jinx used the doorpaths to go to Keyland to buy food—and axes. Blacksmiths' Clearing wasn't making them fast enough to supply the growing free and independent nation of the Urwald.

Making a doorpath to the palace square in Keria was no trouble; the power that Jinx got from knowledge hadn't faded like the Urwald's power. Market days were Mondays. These were also the days that the Keylish troops drilled in the palace square.

There were a couple of thousand of them, Jinx guessed. All in green uniforms, all with glistening, sharp swords. They moved in unison, swung in unison, stabbed in unison.

Jinx turned his back on them, and bargained with a woman for a large wheel of cheese. He offered ten pen-nies. She accused him of trying to rob her and asked for eighteen. He offered twelve.

"What do you need all this cheese for?" said the woman, when they had agreed on a price of sixteen pennies. "Feeding an army yourself?"

Jinx laughed as if that was a joke.

"Urwish, aren't you?" said the woman. "You've got that accent."

"Yup." Jinx counted out the pennies. "I'm a woodrat."

"Don't use that word. It's not nice," said the woman, counting the pennies over again.

"What?" Jinx was more offended by her recounting his pennies than by the word *woodrat*. "I don't mind."

"But I do," said the woman. "They're people too, those Urwalders. If you want to know what I think, I think it's not right, those men"—she nodded at the soldiers in the square—"going into the Urwald after King Rufus of Bragwood and—and the other one. Innocent people could get hurt."

Jinx looked at the soldiers in alarm. "They're going to invade the Urwald?"

"Working in the market, you hear all kinds of things," said the woman. She flipped the cheese on its side and rolled it across the counter.

"Er, what kinds of things?" said Jinx, catching the cheese. "Like, what else?"

"Well, you might hear that some Urwalders attacked those rebel soldiers in the woods—"

Hearing Reven's soldiers described as rebels was odd, but Jinx supposed that was what they were.

"—and you might hear that some boy magician led the attack." She looked him over. "A tan-colored boy, not very tall . . . but that could describe a lot of people. And you might hear that the rebels were planning to attack the boy wizard's castle in revenge."

"What? When?"

The woman shrugged. "Don't know. You didn't hear it from me." She turned away quickly and put Jinx's money into her cashbox.

Jinx looked back at the soldiers. Their vicious sword strokes suddenly looked extremely personal. That made *three* armies invading the new free and independent nation of the Urwald—Reven's, Keyland's, and Bragwood's. And Reven was planning to attack Simon's house.

❧ ❧ ❧

Elfwyn was getting better at the Samaran language. She insisted on practicing it with Jinx and Sophie.

"You've got your *V*'s wrong," Jinx said.

"I know. That was Wendell's idea," said Elfwyn. "It's to make people think I'm from Benicia. He said I'm going to have an accent anyway, so people should think they know where it's from. I looked for axes in the markets, but they don't sell many in Samara. There are plenty of black-smiths, though. I could ask to have axes made."

"Absolutely not," said Sophie. "That would draw the attention of the preceptors. Elfwyn, you have no idea how closely people in Samara are watched."

A little green cloud of annoyance from Elfwyn. "I'm not stupid, you know."

"Nobody thinks you are, dear," said Sophie.

⁓ ⤳ ⤳

Simon was fading.

He had lost color, like an evergreen black against the snow. You could hardly see him breathe. In fact, you could hardly see him at all.

Sophie held the bottle up to the window, and she, Jinx, and Wendell peered anxiously at the tiny shadow of Simon in the depths of the bottle.

"As long as he's not transparent, he's not dead," said Jinx. "Well, not supposed to be."

"There's nothing about this in the Crimson Grimoire," said Sophie. "And as for the Eldritch Tome—"

There was suddenly the sound of shouting from the far end of the corridor . . . from Samara.

"Get your hands off me! Let go!" It was Satya's voice.

"Just—just—just you tell them!" Elfwyn's voice, out of breath. "You—tell them!"

Sophie hurriedly shoved Simon onto a shelf, and she, Jinx, and Wendell ran through the KnIP doorway and into the Samaran house.

Elfwyn had seized Satya, who was struggling and kicking furiously.

"Stop that at once!" Sophie grabbed Elfwyn. Satya broke away and made a dash for the Samaran door.

Jinx charged after her and grabbed her arm. Satya kicked him.

"Jinx! Let go of Satya!" said Sophie. "I'm ashamed of you."

"Hey, yeah, let go of her," said Wendell, coming over and looming largely. He grabbed Jinx's shoulder and gave him an experimental shake.

Jinx shrugged away from Wendell. "Block the door so she can't run away, and I will."

Wendell grabbed both of Jinx's arms, and Satya simultaneously bit Jinx and shoved him away. Satya made it only a couple of steps before she suddenly stopped, teetered, and fell over. Elfwyn had done a clothes-freezing spell on her.

Wendell let go of Jinx and went to tilt Satya upright.

"Take this spell off me!" said Satya.

"Jinx, really!" said Sophie. "I'm very disappointed in you."

She couldn't tell it was Elfwyn's spell.

"I just want to find out what this is about," said Jinx. "Because Elfwyn doesn't usually grab people and—"

"Oh, doesn't she?" said Satya. "I have a right to leave if I want to." She struggled against her immovable clothes, swaying and nearly toppling over again.

Sophie looked at Satya thoughtfully. "You will stay here and discuss this, Satya. I . . . that's an order."

Satya stopped struggling.

"Take the spell off her, Jinx," said Sophie.

"It's my spell," said Elfwyn.

"Take it off her, please," said Sophie.

Elfwyn did. Jinx was ready to grab Satya, but she didn't try to get away. Some kind of Mistletoe Alliance thing, Jinx guessed. He didn't know anything about the inner workings of the Mistletoe Alliance, but he supposed Sophie must be higher in rank than Satya.

"Now," said Sophie. "We'll hear Elfwyn's side first, and then Satya's."

"She's feeding information to the Bonemaster!" said Elfwyn.

"What?" Jinx rounded on Satya. "Are you insane? The Bone—"

"Jinx!" said Sophie sharply. "We're hearing Elfwyn's side. Not yours." She turned to Elfwyn. "Tell it from the beginning."

"Well, I knew the Bonemaster had been going to Samara," said Elfwyn. She was still out of breath. "Back when I was still at Bonesocket, he'd be gone for weeks sometimes. I think they admitted him to the Temple. And then I think once he was in there, he somehow contacted the Mistletoe Alliance and joined them. And then—"

"Where's your evidence?" said Wendell.

"Wendell," said Sophie warningly. "Go on, Elfwyn."

"My evidence," said Elfwyn, "is that the map I saw in the Bonemaster's house was an exact copy of the map that Satya drew. Remember, Sophie was surprised when I said the Bonemaster had a map. Because there aren't any maps of the Urwald, Sophie said. And Sophie would know, because I bet she's studied everything that's ever been written about the Urwald. Isn't that so?"

"I've only studied everything the Temple has, and everything Simon has," said Sophie. "I wouldn't know what the Bonemaster has."

"He only got this map a few months ago!" said Elfwyn. "It's an exact copy of Satya's map, and he didn't have it before!"

"There could be other explanations," said Wendell.

"Name one," said Elfwyn.

Everyone looked at Satya.

"Very well," said Sophie. "And your side, Satya?"

"I don't know who you're talking about," said Satya. "If somebody was being helped by the Company"—she looked at Sophie—"it would be wrong for me to say who they were. I can tell you we're not helping anyone named 'Bonemaster,' though."

"Are you helping anyone with a long, white beard and

kind of flashing blue *eyes?*" said Jinx.

"No," said Satya scornfully.

"Illusion," said Jinx.

"Satya," said Sophie. "We're going to need you to tell us the truth."

"You know I can't—"

"Really—" Wendell shifted uncomfortably. "I think you should tell them."

Sometimes Jinx could see the iron that underlay Sophie's niceness. This was one of those times. "Satya, I'm *ordering* you to tell us," she said.

There was a long pause. Jinx watched Satya's thoughts wrestle with each other.

"He said knowledge should be free to everyone," said Satya defiantly. "That's what *we* believe."

"Just because someone believes the same thing you do doesn't mean they're a good person," said Elfwyn. "Besides, he doesn't believe that. He thinks it should be free to *him*."

"Satya, I think I need to discuss this with the council," said Sophie.

"You can't talk to the council," said Satya. "You're not even supposed to come into Samara."

"Then they'll have to come here." Sophie went to a desk in the corner. "I'm going to write a message to the council, and I would like you to deliver it, please."

"You trust her?" Jinx demanded. "You trust her to go deliver some message?"

"Jinx, please," said Sophie.

Satya sat down on the Samaran couch and folded her arms. "Fine. I'll deliver the message."

Sophie wrote. Jinx glared. Wendell rocked back and forth from his heels to his toes, looking anywhere but at Satya.

Sophie folded the note and sealed it. Satya took it and left.

"I've asked them to come here at midnight tonight," said Sophie. "I'm afraid none of you will be allowed to be present."

"I thought Satya was on our side!" said Jinx angrily.

"She, um." Wendell looked at the door, and then at the ceiling, and then at the floor. "She asked me to take a book and hide it in a treehouse off the path. She said it was Company business."

"And you said no?" said Elfwyn.

"Yeah. Well, obviously. I mean, yeah. I mean, I didn't know who in the Urwald she would want to pass along a book to, without telling you guys, you know?"

"What was the book?" said Jinx.

Wendell looked at the ceiling again. Then he looked at Sophie. Then back at the floor. "You shouldn't blame her for keeping secrets. She's been keeping secrets since she was four. She's *good* at it."

"Wendell, she chose to work for the Mistletoe Alliance," said Sophie. "She—"

"Well, I mean. Maybe people aren't real good at choosing when they're four, you know," said Wendell. "Which is when she started training. Same as you—"

"She can stop whenever she wants," said Sophie. "No one has to stay in the Company."

"*What was the book?*" said Elfwyn.

Wendell looked at his feet. "The Eldritch Tome."

"What?" said Jinx.

"But I didn't bring it!" Wendell added hastily. "And we, um, disagreed, and she hasn't come back to the Urwald since then."

"Ah," said Sophie. "Then there's no harm—"

"But he's already got the Crimson Grimoire," said Wendell.

Jinx woke up late the next morning. Sophie was sitting on the stairs, staring into the bottle of shadow-Simon. She was almost hidden in a deep gray cloud of gloom.

"What'd the council say?" he asked her.

"Oh." She looked up, rather vaguely. "They agreed not to help the Bonemaster anymore."

"But that's good!" What was the gray gloom about, then?

"Yes." Sophie set the bottle down.

"So what's the matter?"

"They've already taught him KnIP," said Sophie.

"What? How can they have taught him KnIP? I thought they didn't even know KnIP!"

"Some of them do," said Sophie.

"Including Satya, because I taught her." Jinx was catching Sophie's gloom in a hurry.

"I wanted them to tell me what the Bonemaster's been doing in Samara," said Sophie. "And they did. The preceptors admitted him to the Temple. They were thrilled to have an Urwalder, and even more thrilled that it was a magician. They tried to get the Bonemaster to take them through your ward, but he couldn't or wouldn't—"

"Probably couldn't," said Jinx. "You can't lead someone through a specific exclusion, I don't think."

He hoped not, anyway.

"The preceptors want him to find the old portals," said Sophie.

"What old portals?" said Jinx. Then he remembered. "You mean the ones that connected the Urwald and Samara? They were closed a century ago."

"They couldn't really have been closed," said Sophie. "Not completely. It's impossible to undo a KnIP spell, because—"

"Once someone *knows* the spell's been done, it's

impossible to unknow it," said Jinx.

"Right. But in the case of the portals, since hardly any-one remembers they exist, they're effectively closed," said Sophie. "Knowledge can die out."

"Especially in the Urwald. Anyway, he won't be able to find the portals." Jinx hoped this was true.

"The Mistletoe Alliance hasn't seen him since before you and Elfwyn reset the ward around the portal."

"We trapped him in the Urwald," said Jinx. That was something anyway. "But if he's got the Crimson Grimoire, that means he can bottle lives again."

"And deaths," said Sophie.

Rattling Bones

They didn't see the Bonemaster, but they had news of him. It came about a week after they took the Eldritch Tome to Malthus.

More refugees kept dribbling into Simon's clearing. Most of them came from the west, where they reported attacks by King Rufus's army. They also reported that the paths were overgrown—completely gone, in some places.

One man arrived from the south. His skin was pale gray and his eyes stared at nothing, and when Jinx spoke to him all the man said was *"Rattling bones, rattling bones."*

Loud noises, voices, children, and nearly everything else upset the new arrival, so Witch Seymour took him off to the shed and gave him brews to calm him down.

The witch came into the kitchen a few hours later to report. A crowd gathered round him as he leaned back in his chair and prepared to tell the tale.

"He says his name is Mortimer," said the witch. "Or anyway, somebody's name is Mortimer. One's not altogether sure it's his . . . and neither, one gathers, is he. He says he was out hunting with a companion—perhaps the companion was named Mortimer—and a wizard appeared out of nowhere and threw purple potion at them."

"The Bonemaster," said Jinx.

"One suggested that," said Witch Seymour. "After which one got nothing but *Rattling bones, rattling bones!* for the next hour. So—"

"So the Bonemaster turned the companion into bones," said Jinx.

"Young man, you're interrupting a perfectly good story." The witch frowned until Jinx muttered, "Sorry."

"The purple potion splattered the victim," the witch went on. "It narrowly missed our friend. There was a sizzling sound, and then a bright purple flash, and then—"

The witch looked around and smiled in satisfaction at the rapt expressions of his audience.

"Bones," said Jinx.

The witch looked annoyed. "A skeleton. A skeleton which took a step toward our friend, and then another.

Our friend very naturally turned and fled. He thinks he ran for hours along the path. Maybe days, he doesn't know. And all the time he heard the bones behind him, rattling, rattling, rattling as they ran."

Silence greeted this. Jinx pictured the skeleton chasing the man down the path, and then very much wished he hadn't.

"And then what happened?" said small Silas.

"The skeleton began to lose bits of itself," said the witch. "A fibula here, a scapula there. Finally it was just a thigh bone and a rib or two in the lead, with a skull and a few phalanges scurrying along behind. After that our friend found a treehouse and stayed in it until the remaining bones lost interest and wandered away."

"Do you think he's telling the truth?" said Jinx.

"*He* certainly thinks he is."

Jinx nodded, digesting this. It sounded like the Bonemaster was learning some new tricks. Including—

"'Appeared out of nowhere,'" said Sophie. "Is he sure about that?"

"Madame, he's not even sure of his own name," said the witch.

Jinx knew what Sophie meant. "Where did this happen?"

"For all I know, only in our friend's imagination," said Witch Seymour.

"I don't think so," said Jinx.

"So the Bonemaster's learned to use the doorpaths," said Elfwyn.

Jinx had been hoping no one would actually say it. It caused flaming billows of red horror in everyone who hadn't already figured it out, and then a hubbub of panicked cries.

"He can't get in . . . shut up!" Jinx shouted. Most people did. "He can't get in here. The ward around this clearing is really strong. But some of the wards are weak, especially in the west. We're going to need to evacuate everyone from those clearings into the clearings with stronger wards."

Blast. And a selection of Jinx's favorite swear words. They were going to have to abandon the west.

❧

Jinx sprawled among the crawling roots of a large willow and leaned his head against its cold trunk.

Trees are dying, said the forest. *The Restless are cutting trees. And we cannot take revenge, because the power slips away.*

Where are they cutting? Jinx asked.

Toward the evening sun. That was what the trees called the west. *The Terror.*

It's King Rufus of Bragwood, said Jinx. *His soldiers must be making camp. Where are they?*

The trees gave him some idea of where, but they weren't interested in who King Rufus was. King Rufus might as well have been a porcupine or a raccoon as far as they were concerned: He was one of the Restless. If he harmed trees, he was the Terror.

King Rufus isn't even an Urwalder, Jinx explained, irritated.

Something warm and rather nasty dripped on his hand. With it came a strong canine smell of dirty fur.

A werewolf's face was inches from Jinx's own, all fangs and drool. This werewolf was not Malthus. Its thoughts were full of fresh-caught meat.

"I see what they mean about you," said the werewolf. "You *are* easy pickings, aren't you? You just sit off the path dreaming away. I'm surprised no one's eaten you yet."

Jinx scrambled to his feet and pressed back against the tree. "I'm the Listener! Malthus knows me."

"Yes, yes, I know." The werewolf made an impatient gesture. "Ever-so-civilized Malthus. We're not all like Malthus, you might as well get that straight."

"I know that," said Jinx. "Werewolves killed my father." He clenched his hand around his knife, and reached for the fire inside him.

"Let's skip the sob stories, shall we?" said the werewolf. "Humans killed my mother." It stuck out a clawed hand. "I'm Leisha."

"Leisha?" Jinx let go of his knife to shake the hand, which was matted and dirty. He somehow had always thought of werewolves as *he.*

"Yes, and you're Jinx. I've been sent to take you to Salt City. You and that other slab of meat. The one with all the book-learning."

"Sophie is not a slab of meat," said Jinx. "Salt City? Who sent you?"

"Malthus."

Jinx wasn't sure if he believed Leisha or not. She was nothing like Malthus. She was much more like people's idea of a werewolf, which was a hairy clawy fanged thing that would sooner eat you than talk to you. Jinx could see she was thinking about eating him, right now. "Why didn't Malthus come himself?"

"How should I know? Busy, I suppose. Said it's about the—what was it, some kind of gnome?" Leisha twitched an ear. "No, dome. That was it. The Elvish Dome."

This did not sound very convincing. "Are you talking about a book?"

"Probably. Malthus likes books. I don't know why. Can't eat 'em."

"And where's this Salt City?"

"Can't tell you. Have to just take you there."

"Don't you think that's an awful lot of me trusting you for no reason?" said Jinx.

"Sure. But Malthus said you were kind of crazy," said Leisha. "Are you going to go get the meat?"

"I'll *ask* Sophie what she thinks," said Jinx. "Wait here."

Sophie, Jinx, Elfwyn, and Wendell all went, in case there was safety in numbers.

Salt City was underground, and full of werewolves. It was not the kind of place you could go into with a calm mind, because every Urwish human instinct screamed at you not to go in there at all. It was down a wide staircase carved of salt, which ended in an underground street carved of salt, lined with buildings carved of salt.

The humans had never seen anything like it before. They stared around in wonder.

"Werewolves built this?" said Sophie.

"I believe not," said Malthus, and tactfully left it at that.

"It's probably the entrance to an old salt mine," said Wendell.

"Werewolves mine salt?" Sophie was being unusually slow on the uptake.

"No, humans mined salt, I'm sure," said Jinx. "And werewolves came along and ate them. They probably had a nice salty flavor."

"Perhaps." Malthus gave a sigh, apparently at having missed the treat. "But it was long ago, and the story is lost in the ancient mists of the dawn of time."

"Uh-huh," said Jinx skeptically. Salt City didn't look all *that* old. He'd never heard of it before, but that wasn't too surprising. The Urwald didn't really have much of a history. People didn't generally live long enough to pass any along.

The other werewolves were moving through the street and in and out of the buildings with a studied air of not noticing the visitors. But Jinx could see that every single one of them was aware of every move the humans made. And that most of them were feeling rather hungry.

Malthus gave a long, low growl that ended in a sharp, snapping bark.

The other werewolves moved further away, with an air of doing it because they felt like it and not because of anything Malthus had said. Malthus nodded satisfaction and turned to Sophie.

"If you'll step into my study, we can discuss our thoughts and ideas. And perhaps avoid causing any disturbance in the streets."

They went into the nearest salt building. Jinx thought it would be Malthus's house, but instead it appeared to be a library. Bookshelves lined the walls. It almost reminded Jinx of the Temple of Knowledge. But many of the shelves were empty.

Jinx went over and looked—the books were in several different languages, but all looked very, very old.

Malthus sprawled on a heap of bearskins on the floor, in the midst of which the Eldritch Tome lay open.

"Do lie down," he said.

Feeling rather nervous, and with a lot of glances at the door, they sat.

Malthus had the book open to the line that had always bothered Jinx the most. He ran a claw along it.

"Nadir of all things," he said. "I think yes, we can assume that refers to the bottommost reaches of the two paths."

"And that's underground?" said Sophie. "Literally underground, not figuratively?"

"Oh yes," said Malthus. "I'm sure you've noticed the essential schema of the Tome—things are stated abstrusely, but never figuratively."

"And do you agree that the seal is likely to be my husband?" said Sophie.

"From what Jinx describes of him, yes. He's dabbled in all sorts of magic, hasn't he? Lifeforce and deathforce. Such a magician could touch both paths, and would form an adequate seal if properly applied." Malthus tapped a fang thoughtfully with his pencil.

"That's why Jinx can't use the Urwald's lifeforce power," said Elfwyn. "The Bonemaster's drawing it away. He's pulling it through the seal."

Jinx remembered what Simon had said to him in a vision he'd had. *The Bonemaster can strike at you through me.* By taking Jinx's power, of course; drawing the Urwald's power right through Simon and up the Path of Ice to himself.

"If the Bonemaster's doing that," said Jinx, "then he

must be hugely powerful by now. Why hasn't he attacked us yet?"

"I don't know," said Sophie.

She turned to Malthus. He shrugged his furry shoulders.

"I wonder," said Wendell, "if this has anything to do with the weather."

"Perhaps," said Malthus. "There is usually a thaw in January. Little creatures come out of hibernation for a few days." He licked his lips with a long, pink tongue. "But this winter has a strong grip."

"As though it's not just heat that's left the Urwald, but lifeforce," said Sophie musingly.

"So the winter could go on forever," said Wendell.

Jinx hadn't even thought of that as a danger. "That's not possible! Winter always ends!" He turned to the were-wolf. "It can't happen, can it?"

"I don't know," said Malthus.

"If we take the seal out," said Sophie, "then the Bone-master won't be able to draw on Jinx's power anymore."

"It's not my power, it's the Urwald's."

"*Can* we take the seal out?" said Sophie. "Or would—it—have to be . . ." She swallowed, then went on, ". . . destroyed?"

The Glass Ax

Malthus seemed to have been expecting this question. He looked at Sophie, his eyes glowing golden-green. "It would be necessary to walk the paths, and find out."

"How do I get there?" said Jinx and Sophie together.

They turned to each other. "I have to—" Jinx began.

"It should be me that—" said Sophie.

"Actually," said Malthus, "I doubt anyone but Jinx could do it."

Sophie's thoughts roiled blue-brown; she didn't like this at all. Jinx saw he would have to convince her. He sighed. It seemed unfair, given that he wasn't exactly thrilled with the idea himself. "I have to do it because I'm the other wick," he said. "You know that. I'm connected to the fire path."

"I'd better come with you," said Sophie.

"Really?" said Malthus. "Forgive me, Scholar, but what exactly do you imagine you could contribute to the operation?"

"*I* could contribute something," said Elfwyn. "I'm a magician."

"Magicians burn and freeze as easily as anyone else," said Malthus. "And I doubt anyone but Jinx or the Bonemaster would be able to locate the seal."

"What are the paths like?" said Jinx.

Malthus tapped the Eldritch Tome with his pencil. "No figurative language. Fire is fire. Ice is ice."

"Oh dear." Sophie looked as tense as Jinx had ever seen her. "I really ought to be the one to—"

"You can't go," said Jinx, "because you can't do magic."

"I'm going, anyway," said Wendell firmly. "At least as far as I can. It's not fire and ice the whole way, is it?"

"Nobody knows," said Malthus.

"How do I get there?" said Jinx.

"We. I'm going with you," said Elfwyn.

"So am I," said Wendell.

"You'll need this." Malthus reached into the pile of furs and drew out an iron rod, topped with a jagged piece of green glass, like a short pickax.

"We have axes," said Jinx.

"This is the Glass Ax," said Malthus. "Very ancient and precious." He handed it to Jinx. "Try not to lose it, please."

The ax was cold and heavy in Jinx's hand. The handle was a twisted shaft of wrought iron; the blade was a chunk of green glass, broken off to a point.

"It is our ancient truce symbol. It will show the trolls that you come in peace." The werewolf tapped a fang thoughtfully. "I hope."

"Trolls?" said Elfwyn.

"The paths can only be reached through the Glass Mountains," said the werewolf.

Which was where the trolls lived. The thought of trolls made Jinx's arm ache—the one that had been bitten nearly in half by the troll that used to be his stepfather.

"Like Elfland," said Elfwyn. "The Eldritch Depths. The entrance to that is through the Glass Mountains too. Witch Seymour told us that, when we were at his house with Reven."

Sophie roiled blue-brown worry, but didn't say any-thing.

Jinx thought of Simon. If the Bonemaster had really used Simon to seal the two paths together . . . "So if I go to the Glass Mountains, I'll find a way to get down there?"

"You would have to ask the trolls," said Malthus.

"*Ask* the trolls?" said Jinx. "It's really hard to ask trolls anything. I mean, I know they can talk, but they prefer to bite heads off."

"True," said Malthus. "Then again, some people might say the same of werewolves. With any luck, the trolls will show you the way onto the paths."

Or they might eat us? Jinx started to say this, but stopped himself. He didn't want Sophie to fuss.

It was a good thing the woman in the marketplace had warned Jinx that Reven was planning to attack. They'd had time to make what preparations were possible—to lay in as many supplies as they could get, and to build a weak ward tunnel to the Doorway Oak.

When they got home from Salt City, they found the clearing surrounded by Reven's soldiers. Several Urwalders were pacing around the inner edge of the ward, axes in hand.

"The Squawks showed up an hour ago," said Jotun, hefting his ax.

"Squawks?" said Jinx.

"It's the way they talk. Loud and fast. Like a hen yard," said Cottawilda.

"They're trying to scrape through the ward with their knives," said Nick.

"Can they do that, sir?" said Hilda.

"No. All they can do is dull their knives," said Jinx,

loudly enough for the nearby soldiers to hear.

He remembered the woman in the marketplace in Keria. "And don't call them Squawks," he added, dropping his voice. "They're people too."

Jotun stepped back and took an experimental swing with his ax. "If we have to remember they're people, how can we kill them?"

"I don't know," said Jinx, annoyed. You didn't normally get deep thoughts from Jotun. "You could just abandon them in the forest, I suppose, like you did my stepsister. Gertrude."

"*I* didn't," said Jotun.

"Really, Jinx," said Sophie. "Is this the time?"

"Yes you did," said Jinx, ignoring her. "And you're supposed to be looking for her."

"We always ask people if they've seen her," said Cottawilda. "I don't know what else you can expect of us."

"Jinx, we have to leave *now*," said Elfwyn, as Reven's soldiers began scraping knives all along both sides of the ward tunnel.

"I'm afraid that's true," said Sophie.

Jinx looked at the soldiers in dismay. The ward tunnel was not strong at all.

"Hey!" he called. "Is Reven here?"

One of the soldiers looked up. "His Majesty the King, you mean?"

"Whoever," said Jinx. "Is he here?"

"No," said the soldier, and went back to scraping.

"Before you go," said Sophie, "I want you to teach me the aviot spell, so that I can watch you."

Jinx opened his mouth to say that Sophie's magical skills were abysmal. Not tactful. "We haven't got a bespelled aviot to take with us."

"There's the one Reven gave back to you," said Elfwyn. "It's a good idea."

Teaching Sophie to use the Farseeing Window took nearly an hour. And meanwhile Reven's soldiers were scraping at the ward, and Simon was fading, and who knew what the Bonemaster was doing? But Sophie was determined to learn, and finally she was able to make the window show her Elfwyn, who was downstairs in the kitchen, holding the bespelled aviot.

This meant they had to take the aviot with them on their journey. Jinx wasn't thrilled about this, but he saw that Sophie was hugely relieved.

"And, Jinx," she said. "If you have to destroy . . . the seal—"

"I won't," said Jinx. "There's a way around most things in magic."

"Maybe not around this," said Sophie.

Jinx couldn't stand those gray clouds of despair. Why did she have to get like this? "I'm going to bring Simon back," he said.

"If you can't—" said Sophie.

"I can."

"Do whatever it takes," said Sophie. "Just break the seal between the paths."

Just as they got outside, there was a cry of triumph from one of Reven's soldiers. The Urwalders watched in dismay as the man squeezed his hand through the hole he'd made in the ward tunnel and waggled his fingers. Then he pulled his hand out, stood up, and grinned at the Urwalders.

It was lucky that Jinx had already made a doorpath to the Troll-way, which was the closest he'd been to the Glass Mountains. It meant that only he, Elfwyn, and Wendell had to run the gauntlet of the ward-tunnel.

"I'll go first," said Jinx.

"No, I'll go first," said Wendell. "I'm faster."

"Says who?" said Jinx.

"We should all go together," said Elfwyn.

"I'm going," said Jinx. And he started down the ward tunnel.

The soldiers rushed at the tunnel. It was weird, running through a tunnel of bodies, all pressed up against the invisible ward, all trying to get through it. Then an arm came through the hole and grabbed Jinx's ankle. He tripped and fell sprawling. He struggled, kicked, and got free. He scrambled to his feet and kept going.

When he reached the Doorway Oak he turned and watched Elfwyn run down the tunnel. To his horror, the hole where he'd been grabbed now had a sword stuck through it.

Elfwyn ran, jumped, and flew over the sword—almost. It slashed upward and caught the hem of her dress and she fell. Jinx ran toward her. She was struggling out of the way. The sword was poised to strike again. Elfwyn froze the sleeve of the arm that held the sword, and then Wendell came running down the tunnel, kicked the sword out of the soldier's hand, and they all ran through the Doorway that led to the Troll-way.

The last time Jinx and Elfwyn had accidentally found themselves on the Troll-way, their main concern had been getting off it again. Now they were there on purpose, and they started walking.

Late in the morning, when the path was just beginning to climb, they heard a troll approaching. They stopped, and Elfwyn and Jinx made a concealment spell.

The troll lumbered past, leaving a rotted-meat smell in its wake.

"We're going to have to talk to them sometime," said Elfwyn.

"Yes. Perhaps we should ask the next one we see to conduct us to their leader," said Wendell.

And that was how they ended up getting captured by trolls.

The Troll Trial

Jinx, Elfwyn, and Wendell were quick-marched up the Troll-way and onto a wide glass plateau surrounded by high glass cliffs. Their captors' names were Heg, Gak, and Blort. And soon they were completely surrounded by trolls. The smell of rotten meat was overpowering, and Jinx had to fight not to be ill. Wendell and Elfwyn looked quite green.

A troll who was bigger than the rest came forward and grunted at them. He was wearing a necklace of what appeared to be teeth.

"This is our leader," said Blort. "Great leader Sneep."

"Who're you?" Sneep asked.

"Jinx," said Jinx. "And—"

"That's him," said a voice from the crowd. "That's that no-good boy that cut off my arm."

Jinx fumbled in his coat for the Glass Ax. He held it up.

"Where you get that from? You kill a werewolf?"

"No," said Jinx, trying to be patient. "The werewolves lent it to us. It's to show we come in peace."

"In pieces?"

"We need to talk to you," said Jinx. "About threats to the Urwald. And we need to get to—"

Wendell laid a hand on Jinx's arm. "Er, maybe we should let Elfwyn tell it. That is, if she doesn't mind."

"Why—" Elfwyn began. "Oh. I see." She turned to Sneep. "Um, have you heard of, er, a person called the Truthspeaker?"

Mutters and grunts amongst the trolls. To Jinx's surprise, they nodded.

"Heard something about that person," said Sneep. "She always telling the truth. Like it or not."

"Oh good," said Elfwyn. "Well, um, that's me."

The trolls looked skeptical. "You the Truthspeaker?"

"Yes," said Elfwyn. "And that has to be the truth, because I can't lie."

The trolls frowned. They seemed to feel there was something wrong with this statement, logically, but they couldn't quite work out what it was.

"So now I'm going to tell you what we're doing here, and why we have the Glass Ax," said Elfwyn.

The trolls grunted.

She cleared her throat nervously. "Right. Well, you see, there are some soldiers from Keyland—"

She explained about the attacks on the Urwald, and about the three kings. Jinx thought she should have talked more about the Bonemaster, but the trolls seemed to be very incensed at the idea of the trees being cut down. They nodded and growled, and now and then let out an anguished roar which, as far as Jinx could tell, meant agreement.

"That's why we got no more Wanderers," said Heg. "'Cause of war."

"Yah, 'cause of war. We wondered why they stopped coming," said Blort. "We never ate any."

"But why you got to walk the Eldritch Ways?" said Sneep. "How that going to help?"

Two questions. Jinx winced. He knew how much Elfwyn hated being asked questions.

"It's Jinx who's got to walk them," said Elfwyn. "The Bonemaster's done something to the, um, Eldritch Ways that makes him able to drain the Urwald's lifeforce, and that's making it much harder for us to fight the invaders. But Jinx might be able to undo it."

Sneep frowned. "This some kind of wizard thing?"

"Yes," said Elfwyn.

"You all wizards?"

"Not yet," said Elfwyn.

"Don't like wizards," said Sneep.

"I'm sorry to hear that," said Elfwyn. "But the Bone-master's a wizard, and—"

"Heard about this Bonemaster. Would make a good troll." Sneep nodded at Jinx. "Supposing we let this wizard boy go down the hole. What good that do?"

"We think he can remove the seal that the Bonemaster's used to connect his power to the Urwald's power," said Elfwyn.

"You think that, huh. Maybe you not so smart for a wizard girl. Plenty people go down that hole. But nobody ever come back."

Ripples of dread from Elfwyn. Jinx was annoyed—what did she think was going to happen? Of course no one ever came back.

"Anyway," said Sneep, "we got other use for this wizard boy. Got to kill him."

"But we have the Glass Ax!" said Elfwyn. "That's supposed to mean you can't hurt us! Malthus said so."

"Don't mean we can't try a criminal. He a wanted boy. Cut off poor Bergthold's arm. *And* he set some trolls on fire."

"Now wait a minute," said Jinx. "That was self-defense."

"Don't know nothin' 'bout no fence," said Sneep. "Know the law, that's all. We have a trial. Kill you or eat your arm off, one."

Elfwyn, Jinx, and Wendell looked at each other in dismay.

"Can we have the trial after I get back from the Paths?" said Jinx.

"Huh. Think we stupid? Nobody don't never come back from there."

"Fine," said Jinx, frustrated. "Have a trial, then."

～ ♪ ～

The trial was very brief.

"That's him," said Bergthold. "Cut my arm off. With an ax."

Sneep turned to Jinx. "That true?"

"Yes," said Jinx. "But he—"

"Guilty," said Sneep. "Now we—"

"Wait a minute!" said Jinx. "He tried to bite my arm off last year. He broke it in two places! It still hurts on rainy days."

"So that the one we eat," said Sneep. "So's you still got one good arm. Fair enough?"

"No!" said Jinx.

"Also, he set many trolls on fire," said Bergthold. "Should be we set him on fire, after we eat his arm, right, chief?"

"But I put them out again," said Jinx.

"So maybe we put you out again, too," said Blort.

"Excuse me," said Wendell. He looked at Bergthold uncertainly. "Aren't you the stepfather who abandoned Jinx in the forest when he was six?"

"Huh. Gave him opportunities," said Bergthold. "Go out into world, seek his fortune. Boy does that, he always ends up rich and married to some kind of princess. What's wrong with that?"

"Well, it was sort of like killing him," said Wendell. "After all, the children who get left in the Urwald usually die, don't they? I mean, there was Jinx's stepsister, Gertrude—"

Bergthold let out a roar. "What?! What happen to Gertrude?"

"I don't know," said Wendell. "But the point is—"

Bergthold lunged at Jinx. "What happen to Gertrude?" he howled.

Jinx stumbled back from the smell of Bergthold's breath. "I don't know!"

"That lady abandon her? I know that lady abandon her! That lady a no-good lady!"

"You mean Cottawilda?" said Jinx. "Your wife? Well, I don't like her much either, but it's the same thing that you and her did to me."

"*NOT* the same!" Bergthold roared. "Gertrude *MINE!*"

Jinx turned to Elfwyn and Wendell. They looked as

perplexed by this development as he was.

"Going to get revenge for this!" said Bergthold. "Abandon *MY* baby! Huh."

"Instead of getting revenge, maybe you could look for her," Wendell suggested.

"*Going* to look for her, that no-good *lady!*"

"I meant look for Gertrude," said Wendell.

"Yeah," said Jinx. "That's what Cottawilda's doing, anyway." Well, what she was supposed to be doing.

"Jinx told her to," said Elfwyn, apparently thinking this might help. She turned to Sneep. "Anyway, Jinx has to walk the Paths. If he doesn't, we'll have no way to fight the invaders, and you want the invaders fought, don't you?"

Much discussion among the trolls. Shouting, howls, roars. Finally Sneep turned to Elfwyn, who he seemed to have decided was the leader of the human expedition. "All right. He go. You stay here. You and the big boy. Wizard boy doesn't come back, we eat you. Fair enough?"

"Not really," said Elfwyn.

"Yeah, you said nobody ever comes back," said Jinx.

"Nobody especially don't come back when we say we going to eat his arm off," said Sneep. "Take it or leave it."

Jinx looked around. There were at least a hundred trolls surrounding them. And Jinx wasn't even going to be able to find the entrance to the paths without their help. "I guess I take it," he said.

"Good. We show you the way to the Paths."

Jinx had heard tales about people who had to climb glass mountains to win a princess's hand, and presumably the rest of the princess as well. He had always wondered how it was done. Now he saw the answer. There was a stairway, carved into the mountainside. It wound around the mountain, glittering in the sun.

And it wasn't quite wide enough.

"Just don't look down, Jinx," said Elfwyn.

"I'm *fine*," Jinx snapped. He didn't appreciate being reminded that there even *was* a down.

They were escorted by several trolls. The company of trolls takes a lot of getting used to. It wasn't just the way they smelled. There was something very disconcerting about the sound of their gnarled, clawlike toenails on the glass steps.

When they finally reached the top of the stairs, there was a translucent platform, just a few feet square. Jinx backed up against the glass wall of the mountain and looked across, not down. The gray-white winter expanse of Urwald stretched on forever, broken here and there by evergreens.

"Do you mind not standing so close to the edge?" he said.

"We're not," said Wendell, surprised. "Er, I guess this is where we go in, then."

Jinx turned, not letting go of the wall, and saw a gap.

It was barely wider and higher than he was. "Not 'we,'" he said. "I'm going alone."

"Anyway, you our hostage," said Sneep, tapping Wendell on the shoulder with a gnarled fingernail. "Make sure magic-boy comes back so's we can eat his arm."

A breath of warmer air came from the gap. Whatever was in there, Jinx thought, at least he wouldn't have to go down the glass stairway.

He looked at Elfwyn and Wendell, and then at Elfwyn again. Seeing how worried they were didn't help.

"I think I could walk the paths," said Elfwyn. "Because I've—"

"No," said Jinx.

He handed her the Glass Ax.

She clutched it tightly. "Jinx, remember the stories."

"Which ones?" Stories were the last thing he needed to think about right now.

"You can't eat anything they offer you, or you'll be stuck down there."

"Who's going to offer me anything?" said Jinx. "Anyway I've got a loaf of bread in my pack."

"Elves, maybe," said Elfwyn. "And then, um, there's the thing about time."

Oh yes. The thing about time. In stories, when people came back from the land of elves they found a hundred years had passed in the Urwald. "Well, what am

I supposed to do about that?" he said.

Elfwyn looked miserable. "I don't know."

"Yeah. Me neither." He looked at Elfwyn and Wendell again. He had to come back, or the trolls would kill them.

"Don't worry about us," Wendell murmured in Samaran. "I've got a plan."

If anything, this made Jinx feel *more* worried. "Right. See you later then." He turned and ducked quickly into the gap.

And could see absolutely nothing. It was pitch dark.

He turned around and saw Elfwyn's and Wendell's heads silhouetted against the gray winter sky. "What's in there?" said Wendell.

"I can't see anything," said Jinx.

"Some magician, you," came Sneep's voice. "Can't even make fire?"

"Of course I can make fire," said Jinx irritably. "But I need something to burn."

A troll arm shoved through the gap. "Here. Burn this."

The arm came accompanied by a rancid smell, and Jinx was afraid "this" might be something foul. But no, it was Sneep's walking stick.

Jinx lit it. "Thanks."

The walls of a narrow chamber glinted glassily in the torchlight. Jinx looked around. Where was the—ah, there it was. A doorway. And black words printed over it, in Old

Urwish. The paint was peeling, and Jinx had to squint to read what it said:

entry not advisable

Well, duh, Jinx thought. "I'm going in," he called. "Bye."

There was a stairway, for a while. Then there was a path. The glassy walls were not quite as close as in Jinx's dreams of walking through ice.

Sometimes the path sloped steeply downward and Jinx sat down and slid, which would have been fun if he hadn't been worried about sudden drop-offs and things like that.

At the bottom of one long, steep slide, he found a heap of bones and a skull.

He stared down at it. Then he picked up the long-extinguished torch that lay beside the bones, stuck it in his belt for later, and walked on.

He could have taken a bone to burn, but he found he . . . couldn't. And anyway (the thought came unbidden) there would probably be others later.

It was some time after that that he heard the trees.

Listener. Where are you going, Listener?

He must be out of the mountains now, and under the forest. The walls were stone, and he could see no roots of trees, but he could hear them.

Listener, no, stop.

He has to go on. The roots of the Listener go deeper than the roots of trees.

I have to break . . . to remove the seal, he told the trees. *Before it kills all of us.*

The trees seemed to accept that, murmuring and mumbling their regret.

You don't happen to know how I do that, do you? Jinx asked.

Wizard's magic, said the trees.

Jinx sighed, and went on walking downward. Soon he couldn't hear the trees anymore. He was completely alone. The earth had ceased to be made of the remains of living things. It was all cold stone.

The stone, he felt, had once been fire. It had belched up, burning, out of the earth. He could not have said how he knew this, but he was sure that it was true.

The torch was now just a tiny stub in his hand. It spluttered and went out. The darkness was total, devoid of even the possibility of light. This was the dark that darkness came from, the place where night was born. He heard a faraway sound like whispers in distant rooms. He fumbled for the skeleton's torch and lit it. It flared, and Jinx knew the old dry wood would burn quickly. And then what would he do?

Send the fire into the walls.

Jinx wasn't sure where the thought had come from. It

almost but didn't quite feel like his own.

He tried it. He reached for the fire inside him and sent it into the walls.

The fire flared out from the walls, then leapt, much faster than burning, sending flames dancing down the walls of the tunnel and out of sight. The flames came leaping and spiraling back again. They raced along the walls behind him—he looked back, and saw them cavorting up the last slope he'd come down, and then they came dancing back. And then they went out.

But the walls glowed. Not orange like the embers of a fire, but a cool, pale yellow. They glowed into the distance as far as Jinx could see.

He extinguished the torch, and walked on, guided by the glow of the fire in the walls.

The floor under Jinx's feet was no longer stone—or at least, he didn't think it was. It looked like glass, or obsidian. It felt to his feet like ice. Jinx mentally dubbed it ice-glass. He walked on it as though it were ice, carefully at first. Then he skated along it. Then he ran and slid, ran and slid. Then he fell, hard, just as the path began to go down again.

The path was a spiral, and he was zooming around and around, faster and faster.

The Eldritch Depths

The slide ended abruptly and Jinx flew through the air, hoping he would land on something soft.

He did not.

He lay for a minute, trying to breathe and trying to figure out if anything was broken. It felt as if everything was.

"This is him, isn't it?"

"I told you he was coming."

The words were spoken in Qunthk, a language that sounded like an all-out battle between a tomcat and a trash can.

Jinx sat up, painfully, and faced the cold stare of three blue-skinned, silver-haired elves.

"I know you," he said, in Urwish. Well, two of them, anyway.

"We should kill him," said the elf who Jinx remembered was named Neza. "I don't know how he got down to the Eldritch Depths, but he must not be allowed to leave."

Jinx scrambled to his feet and backed away.

One of the elves, Dearth, arched an icy eyebrow at him. "You understand the Eldritch tongue, I see."

"I wasn't even trying to get to the Eldritch Depths," said Jinx. "I'm trying to get to the nadir of all things. Is this it?"

Jinx had never heard elves laugh before. It was a most unpleasant sound, like trolls walking on ducks.

"A matter of opinion," said Dearth. "For many humans, it has been."

"My mother," said Jinx. He couldn't remember his mother. But he knew she'd been carried off by elves.

"We should kill him," said Neza.

The third elf spoke. "We should feed him to the Queen."

Jinx put his hand on the hilt of his knife, and the elves laughed again.

"The Queen is asleep, Shatter," said Neza.

"We should not kill him. He's the wick of fire," said Dearth.

"I know that," said Neza. "That's why he would be better off dead."

"I would not!" said Jinx.

"And what happens to our balance, if the other wick wins?" said Dearth.

"Balance happens on its own," said Shatter.

"You're wrong," said Dearth. "Balance requires care and guidance."

"The Bonemaster is already winning," said Neza. "He has nearly won."

"As I've told you before, that is not necessarily desirable," said Dearth, flickering irritation. "The Queen desires balance. Ice in ascendance, yes, but balance. Let this one go down and try to remove the seal. He'll die, of course, but he might succeed even so."

"Where *is* the seal?" said Jinx. "How do I get to it?"

The elves ignored him. They were arguing with each other. "And when he dies, where's your balance?" Neza demanded.

"The Urwald remains," said Shatter. "It's been without a Listener for years. Fire is in abeyance, but enough remains for balance."

"Excuse me, but *I* remain," said Jinx. "And I'm talking to you. Do you mind telling me how to get to the flippin' nadir of all things so I can remove the flippin' seal, and die in the attempt or whatever?"

The elves regarded him coldly. "Goodness, he understands quite a bit of Eldritch," said Neza.

"Doesn't speak it, though," said Shatter.

"It hurts my throat." Jinx wanted to get out of here. Elves creeped him out, even when they weren't talking about killing him. "Where does the path go from here?"

"How would we know?" said Dearth. "It's your path." He turned to Neza. "Take him to the Queen."

"The Queen sees no one," said Neza.

"Then take him to the Princess."

"I will ask the Princess," said Neza.

There was a brief pause.

"Look, all I want to know—" Jinx began.

"Silence," said Dearth. "She is talking to the Princess."

Neza seemed to be listening to the empty air. She nodded. "Very well," she said. "The Princess will see you in the garden."

A garden, down here? "Will she tell me how to get to the nadir of all things?"

"If she desires balance," said Shatter.

"Which she doesn't," said Neza.

"Which she does," said Dearth.

"Come along, human," said Shatter.

Neza and Shatter led Jinx through an ice-glass passageway that opened into a cavern so large that at first Jinx thought he was outdoors.

The garden was dazzling. Clusters of crystals sprouted and spread like shrubberies. There were amethysts blossoming beside the path, and sapphires sprouting from rocks. Jinx stood beside a charming little bed of rubies and topazes, like frozen fire.

"Follow the path. The Princess is waiting," said Neza.

It seemed the elves were coming no further. Jinx walked alone, a narrow path that twisted between outcroppings of emeralds and under an arbor of peridots and pyrite. There was light from somewhere, and the gems and crystals flickered.

"Welcome, Flame."

Jinx had to blink several times before he saw the Princess among the crystals. She was sitting on what he supposed must be a seat hidden in the midst of tall spikes of blue-white crystal—if there wasn't a seat there, she must have been very uncomfortable.

"Hi. My name is Jinx."

"What an unfortunate name."

"I can't help it," said Jinx, staring at the Princess. Putting aside the fact that she was blue, she was the most beautiful lady he had ever seen.

"Do you like my garden?"

"It's, er. There's nothing growing in it."

"If it didn't grow, then how did it come to be?" This was apparently a rhetorical question, as the Princess didn't wait for an answer. "Have a seat on that topaz, and I will tell you about everything."

Jinx would very much have liked to be told about everything, but the Princess in fact only told him about the gems in her garden, and how they'd grown. He learned quite a bit about rocks, and he figured he'd be able to describe the garden now, if he lived long enough to tell anyone about it.

"So much lovelier than those messy gardens in the world above," said the Princess. "Don't you think? No insects, no decomposition." She wrinkled her perfect nose. "Nothing dies down here."

"Nothing *lives* down here." Jinx had meant to be tactful, but it just came out.

"Exactly." The Princess smiled at him, and Jinx couldn't help feeling pleased to be smiled at by such a beautiful person.

But she isn't alive, he reminded himself.

"I—my mother was stolen by elves," he said.

"Was she? And is that why you have come down here, Flame?"

"No," Jinx admitted. "But I would like to know what happened to her."

"Oh, she'll have drifted away by now," said the Princess. "They never stay long."

"You mean she died?"

"Some silly human custom like that." The Princess waved a long, graceful blue hand dismissively.

Jinx was relieved. He had been afraid it might have been possible for his mother to become an elf.

"And for that you came down here? Just to ask me this question?"

"No," said Jinx. "I'm just passing through actually. I'm on my way to the nadir of all things."

"How dramatic."

"I could use some help, actually," said Jinx. "Well, advice."

"Could you? And why do you imagine that I would give you good advice?"

"Well, I expect you know the Paths better than I do . . ."

"The Path of Ice," said the Princess. "And thus far, you have walked the Path of Fire."

"I have?" Jinx was surprised. "But I didn't burn."

"Not yet. You brought your fire with you. But further down, of course, the fire burns hotter. Fire, you know, makes beautiful gems. Would you like a few to take with you?"

"No thanks," said Jinx. "I really need to know how to get to the nadir of all things and—and how to remove a seal."

The Princess half closed her eyes and half smiled. "Ah.

The seal. Yes. We wondered if you would notice that."

"Of course I noticed it!" said Jinx. "He's my friend!"

"Your friend?" The perfect eyebrows frowned ever so slightly. "The other wick is your friend?"

"No, the other wick is the Bonemaster," said Jinx. "The person he's used to make a seal is my friend."

He explained to her about Simon, and what he thought the Bonemaster had done to him. He told her about the threats to the Urwald.

He told her about his people, and about the new free and independent nation of the Urwald. If she privately found all this about as interesting as he'd found her lecture on geology, she gave no sign.

"But I don't understand," said the Princess. "While you're down here, the Bonemaster is up there, in the, er, organic mass, making things difficult for all your other friends, isn't he?"

"Yes," said Jinx. "But if I can remove the seal, then the Bonemaster won't have as much power."

"And you'll have more," said the Princess, musingly.

"Well, yeah, I'll have what I had before," said Jinx.

"If you return to the world above at all," said the Princess. "It's very easy to become lost on the paths."

"To die, you mean," said Jinx.

"Oh, I suppose so," said the Princess. "But also to become lost, which is much more serious. As for your friend, you must realize he won't have . . . kept his shape. It's unlikely there's much left of him that you would recognize."

Jinx felt cold. He thought of how the Simon in the bottle had grown weaker over time. How he'd spoken to Jinx once, but not again. And he'd said he'd stop the Bonemaster from getting at Jinx through him, but he hadn't been able to do that, had he?

"And if he's been made a seal," said the Princess, "there's no way he can escape with his life."

"What about without it?" said Jinx desperately.

"Have you bottled it?"

"Someone else did. The Bonemaster."

"Ah." The Princess smiled. "In that case, it *might* be possible. And then you plan to return to the world above, vanquish the Bonemaster, and reign supreme?"

"I don't want to reign supreme," said Jinx. "I've never wanted to!"

"Never? Not even for a moment?" The Princess's eyes glinted like amethysts. "Not even when the people around you are being impossibly slow and stupid, and you are so much cleverer than they are, and could manage matters so much better, if only everyone would shut up and do as you say?"

Jinx shifted uncomfortably on his topaz. Could she read minds?

"If I ever *do* want that," he said, "I know it's not what I'm supposed to want."

"And you only want what you're supposed to want? What an unusual quality."

"I don't only want what I'm supposed to want," said Jinx. "But I don't want to want stuff that, if I had it, would . . ." He fumbled for the right words. The combination of the Princess and the gems was confusing. "Would mess everything up for everybody. I just want to get Simon out alive, and to stop the Bonemaster. And to save the Urwald."

"I see." The Princess rippled icy amusement. Jinx was surprised that he could see any of her feelings at all.

He was surprised by something else, too. He couldn't help admiring her, because she was, after all, extremely beautiful, and he realized that she was drinking his admiration as if it were a nourishing soup. Feeding on him. It made him angry. He clenched his teeth and looked away, at a thicket of tourmalines.

"You don't want to reign supreme either," Jinx told her. "Not even through the Bonemaster. It's too much work. It involves messy, live things, lots of bugs, and hardly any jewels."

The Princess looked miffed. "You are rather insulting, young man."

"Sorry," said Jinx. "I'm tactless and undiplomatic."

"Very. And since neither of us wants supremacy, I should help you?" The Princess looked around at the gems in her garden, and then smiled down at Jinx. "Very well. I shall tell you the most important things.

"The first is that you must recognize when it is time to make your own path. The path you see may not be the path you should travel.

"The second is that you must travel both paths. No one who travels only one path can achieve knowledge."

"I don't want kn—"

She held up a hand to silence him. "The third is that when you reach the seal, you must touch both paths. This will be difficult for you, because you are so determined to do what's right. But you must touch the paths as your friend would, and not as you would."

"Touch the paths like Simon would? But Simon's . . ." Jinx stopped himself. He didn't think Simon was *evil*, exactly. "I'm not going to have anything to do with death-force."

"Deathforce? Oh, that's what you humans call the ice. I don't know why. It's merely ice."

"It's evil," said Jinx.

"Death is evil? You all die."

"Well, ice, then. I'm not going to have anything to do with . . . ice."

"Then you will not be able to remove the seal."

Jinx started to argue, then stopped. "Okay. Fine. How do I, er, remove him?"

"By touching both paths."

"How do we get out again?"

"If you succeed in removing the seal, you will have already destroyed the Bonemaster's hold on the Path of Fire. Is it to my advantage for you to get out again?" the Princess asked.

"I don't know," said Jinx. "It's to mine, I know that. And Simon's."

"Your friend will be without his life."

"But can't I put it back in him?"

"That depends on what remains of him. You may need to give him something of yourself, and really, why would you want to do that?" She frowned perfectly. "All I can tell you about getting out again is that you can take nothing with you that you did not bring—"

"Can I take Simon at least?"

"—and that it is seldom possible to walk the same path twice."

"So you're saying I can't get out again."

"You seem a reasonably intelligent young man. I have told you all that I feel I can. We side with ice, but we do prefer balance."

She looked up at the distant crystal sky as if listening. "You may go now. Dearth will conduct you to the paths.

Are you sure you wouldn't care for a ruby or two before you go?"

"Something to take out that I didn't bring with me? No thanks," said Jinx.

"Well, you are slightly cleverer than you look," said the Princess. "This has been most amusing. Do drop in again in another millennium or so, if you're in the neighborhood."

"Thanks," said Jinx. "I will."

Dearth met him at the edge of the garden, and led him through a maze of tunnels. They met no other elves, though here and there Jinx heard the distant gargle and snarl of the Qunthk language.

Then Dearth opened a door, and they were standing at the edge of—

—a field. An endless expanse of grass. It was somehow not quite grass, because it was missing the ripe green chaos of life (untidy stuff) and all the grass was just the same height as itself, and no wind stirred it, and no bird-shadows skimmed across it. Still, it was definitely meant to be a field.

Jinx looked up, and the sky was white and sunless. Quartz, maybe.

"Your path begins here," said Dearth.

"Er, where?" said Jinx.

"That I do not know." The elf looked annoyed. "Aren't

you supposed to know these things? It's your path."

"Okay, but which direction do I go? You do want to help me, right?"

"The Princess said you were to be helped. The direction is down, if you seek the nadir."

"Well, the only direction here seems to be across," said Jinx.

The elf shrugged.

Jinx sighed. "Okay. See you later."

He started walking.

The grass was deeper than he'd thought. It parted as his feet touched it. Nothing crawled or buzzed in the grass. No insects hopped, no snakes slithered suddenly at his feet, no baby rabbits scrabbled out of his way. Whoever had made this field had missed the finer points.

The grass grew deeper. Soon it was up to his shoulders. But he didn't have to push his way through it—the path kept appearing at his feet.

Jinx thought as he walked. He thought that what the elves meant by balance was not what Jinx meant. To Jinx, balance meant somehow getting all the creatures—the trees, the humans, the other Restless—to acknowledge each other's right to the Urwald. The elves were talking about a balance between lifeforce and deathforce, fire and ice.

What did it matter to elves, anyway? he wondered. It wasn't like life and death were really things they cared about. A human lifespan—or even a tree's lifespan—must seem awfully brief and fleeting when you were used to farming gemstones.

So why do they bother to steal humans, then?

He thought about the Elf Princess drinking his admiration. Mining it, he thought. They mine us, like we mine iron, salt, and glass. They farm minerals, and they mine life.

He was suddenly very glad to be walking away from them. He walked faster.

Smack into a solid stone wall.

It threw him backward, with a painful shock. It was the same feeling he'd had when he'd touched the slab of ice that the Bonemaster had imprisoned Simon in. Was he getting closer to Simon, then?

He approached it cautiously. The rock was glassy and smooth, like black obsidian. He could feel cold radiating off it.

He looked up. The wall went up further than he could see, into the sunless sky.

One thing was for sure. There was no path through it.

He thought about what the Elf Princess had said.

You must make your own path.

Through that? Unlikely. Jinx walked along the wall, the grass parting for him.

He didn't get really discouraged till he reached a corner.

The wall turned back the way he had come. He had a feeling that if he turned around and went the other way, he'd
eventually run into the same problem. He was boxed in.

So, yes. It appeared he was going to have to make his
own path through that.

He stared at the wall's glassy surface. He saw himself
reflected in it. During his talk with the Elf Princess it had
occurred to him that he had turned into almost the person
he wanted to be. He hadn't been fooled by her beauty or
tempted by the gems. He'd done nearly as well as someone
in a story.

But he didn't look like someone in a story. He looked
tired, dirty, cranky . . . and still too short.

He sat down and ate some bread. It was getting stale,
which was odd because he hadn't been down here all that
long, had he? He put the heel of the loaf back in his belt
pocket, next to the golden aviot. He looked at the little
bird and wondered if Sophie was watching him through
the Farseeing Window.

Well, he had to go through this wall. KnIP? No,
KnIP wouldn't be enough, not when he had only his own
knowledge to use.

Fire, then?

He reached for the fire inside him. It seemed to have
grown a little stronger since his conversation with the Elf
Princess. But strong enough to melt stone? He put his

hand out, and sent fire into the wall. The wall melted, a little bit. Rock ran down in solid-looking rivulets. He had made a slight indentation in the wall.

This wasn't going to work. He saw what he would have to do.

He summoned all the fire he could from inside him, and he walked into the wall again.

It hurt. A lot. There was the ice-hot shock, and there was the solid fact of the stone wall. Jinx remained standing with difficulty. He kept sending the fire into the wall. He took a step forward into solid stone.

He could feel things breaking as he moved—ice and stone. The path was forming as he walked, he could tell that from the emptiness behind him, but all he felt in front of him was stone, ice, and pain.

He wasn't sure how long this went on.

Finally he burst out of the wall, onto a plain of ice. He flopped down on it, exhausted.

And began to slide. The slope was slight at first, then it got steeper and he went faster and faster.

Below him, he could see a bridge of ice. And on either side of it, a drop-off. Frantically he hit at the ice with both hands, trying to steer himself toward the bridge.

He could see he wasn't going to make it. He twisted around onto his stomach, trying to swim toward the bridge with his arms and legs. But he was moving too fast. The cliff edge was rushing toward him.

He kicked furiously, trying to knock holes in the ice. This slowed him down a little, and then a little more. But he was still gliding toward the edge, closer and closer.

He used KnIP and *knew* a hole into the ice, and stuck his arm into it to stop himself. But the rest of him kept sliding . . . over the edge.

He clung to the edge of the cliff, scrabbling furiously at the ice. He was hanging by his bad arm. His hand was freezing, and slipping against the ice. He quickly *knew* a handhold for his other hand. He dangled, hanging over emptiness. He could feel heat rising from below.

He looked down.

Far below him was a river of fire, burbling and flickering red-orange between steep stone banks.

He tried to pull himself up, but couldn't. His bad arm was starting to ache, his hands were freezing, his grip was slipping, and his feet were getting uncomfortably hot. He couldn't work much magic because he didn't have enough fire left inside him . . .

Wait. He knew where there was more available.

Carefully, willing himself not to be sick, he looked down again at the river of fire. And began to draw the fire into himself.

At first it was difficult at this distance, but fire likes to move upward. He kept drawing and drawing, pulling fire from the river, and adding it to the fire inside him.

Then, with more power inside him than he'd ever held before, he looked down at his own boots, and levitated them.

It worked. He felt himself grow light. Gingerly, he let go of the cliff with one hand. He was floating on air.

He let go with his other hand—and instantly flipped upside down. Gah! Now he was stuck in a position that should never happen to a person who is afraid of heights. He tried frantically to work himself right side up again, but there was nothing to grab—he'd drifted away from the cliff. He hung there.

These weren't actually his boots. He'd outgrown his own boots and was wearing an old pair of Simon's, which were too big. He felt his feet begin to slip out of them. Desperately he curled his toes, but his feet kept sliding. He reached up and grabbed the boots, and hung on tight.

He tried levitating his clothes. That worked—sort of. Now he was sprawled flat, high over the canyon, unable to move, and cooking slowly. But at least he wasn't in danger of falling anymore. He began to rise up, up, into the sunless sky.

He could see back to the wall he'd come through, but not over it, because it seemed to go up forever. He could see the ice bridge and what lay beyond it—a field of ice, which ended in a faraway mountain.

What he couldn't do was move. He'd never learned to move things sideways. Simon could do it. Elfwyn could. But Jinx couldn't, and he was stuck.

He kept his gaze focused on the mountain. Looking down might bring on the horrible, rocking, black-edged vertigo. And if that happened, he'd lose his concentration and the levitation spell would break and, well, to put it bluntly: splat.

Jinx hung in the air and thought.

The trees had told him that the Listener had roots that went deeper than the roots of the Urwald. Well, he was deeper than the Urwald, that was for sure.

Dame Glammer had told him that half of him was underground. Like a tree . . . But if he went deeper than the Urwald, then surely that was more than half. After all, some of the Urwald's trees were hundreds of feet tall, whereas Jinx was not really gifted in the height department.

Jinx pounded on his head, in hopes it would make him think better. The movement made him spin around in a circle, slowly. He closed his eyes and hoped he would stop soon.

You must recognize when it is time to make your own path, the Elf Princess had said. *The path you see may not be the path you should travel.*

There was really no point in crossing the bridge, even

if he could get to it. The nadir of all things was going to be *down*. Roots went down. Roots, routes. Jinx opened one eye, just for a second, and looked down at the river of fire below him.

Down was down. If Jinx let the spell go, and just let himself fall . . .

No. Not a good idea. This was not a metaphor. This was real, and he would go splat.

He had to lower himself. All the way down. Into the fire.

Jinx began reversing the levitation spell. He remembered Simon teaching him to do this, snapping, *"Down is just the opposite of up!"*

Slowly he passed the icy edges of the chasm and descended into it. Heat rose from the river of flames below. The heat was part of the fire, and the fire belonged to Jinx, and he belonged to it. He drew it into himself. It was no good thinking he couldn't draw in a whole river of fire—you can't if you think you can't. Anyway, the nadir of all things was *down* . . .

Jinx was low enough now that he could see the shadows of the flames flickering against the canyon walls—which were now stone, not ice. He kept drawing the fire into himself, and he risked a look downward.

He was about ten feet above the highest of the flames. He felt no heat from them. He went further down, and the flames tickled against his skin. He passed through the flames, and drew them into himself, and kept going down, and down, and down . . .

. . . through rock and ice and flames . . .

. . . until he found he could go no further. He had reached the nadir of all things.

At the Nadir of All Things

At the nadir of all things was a box.

It stood in a small, rock-hewn cavern. How Jinx knew he was at the nadir of all things he couldn't have said. He only knew that using all of his power—and he had so much fire inside him now that he felt he might burst into flame at any moment—he could go no further.

There was no sign of Simon. There was only the box, made of almost-translucent white stone. It stood about three feet high, with a neatly fitted stone lid.

Jinx moved toward the box, and was stopped by something inside him.

It was fear. It hit him like a troll's fist. He'd never been so frightened in his life—not even when he'd been a small child who was still afraid of the Urwald.

It was hard to even move against the terror, but Jinx fought it, reached out a hand, and touched the lid of the box. Shock ran up his arm. He recognized it as the same shock that had thrown him across the room in the Bonemaster's house, when he'd touched the slab that had appeared to have Simon inside it. It shook him to the soles of his feet, but he didn't take his hand away. Down here at the nadir of all things, he was stronger than he'd been in the Urwald.

Using a levitation spell to help him, he lifted the lid and set in on the floor. Icy steam poured from the box. Jinx coughed. He batted at the steam to clear it.

He leaned over the box and peered in.

The fog kept pouring out; he couldn't see. He reached inside and felt around. The walls tingled his hands unpleasantly. He leaned further in, balancing on the edge and taking his feet off the floor. His hand brushed something, but it rolled away. He groped for it. His hand closed on it. It was a sphere, slightly squishy and very slippery. It slipped out of his hand. He made a grab after it, and fell into the box.

Shocks rippled through his body. He felt around for the sphere. He touched it, but it slithered away, like soap in a bathtub. Frustrated, he grabbed at it again. He . . .

He wanted to smash it.

Where had that thought come from? He shook his head to clear it. The thing might have something to do with Simon, and there was no way he wanted to smash Simon.

No? Hadn't Simon been rather unpleasant to him? Didn't he *deserve* smashing?

What a crazy idea. Simon had taken Jinx in when Jinx would have died otherwise. He'd taught Jinx to read, and to do magic. How did that work out to deserving—

He'd done dark magic on Jinx, though. Magic that used ghast-roots, and how were ghast-roots made? Well, everyone knew that. Ghast-roots were made by *giving* a human life to the forest, and then cutting down a tree in exchange.

"No, everyone doesn't know that!" said Jinx, scrambling to his feet. "*I* didn't know it."

Terrified, he clambered out of the box.

Something in there had been putting thoughts into his head. He walked around and around the cavern, thinking frantically. Where had those thoughts come from, thoughts he'd never had before?

Except . . . He stopped walking. They weren't thoughts he had never had before. They were thoughts he'd had at one time or another, and rejected.

What about the ghast-roots, though? He really hadn't known . . .

. . . well, yes. Yes, he had. He'd seen something in a book, and the Bonemaster had said something, and Jinx had figured out how it was done. The realization had crept through his mind so quickly and quietly it barely left a memory behind. He'd just chosen not to think about it anymore. Deathforce magic required a human sacrifice. There were ways around everything in magic. Some of them weren't very nice ways. Someone, sometime, had figured out the ghast-roots spell, which exchanged a human life for a tree's life. And the ghast-roots made from one human sacrifice could be used in hundreds of spells. Very efficient.

And Simon had bought some from Dame Glammer and used them to do the bottle spell on Jinx, a spell Simon wasn't even sure he'd be able to do correctly. That thought came from Jinx himself, and not from the thing in the box. Or at least he thought it did. How could he know for sure? He paced furiously around and around the box, not looking down. From here on down there was no reality, so the floor was rather nebulous and springy. It didn't do to look at it too closely.

The box felt like the ice that the Bonemaster had trapped Simon in. These thoughts that Jinx didn't want seemed to be coming from it—coming from the ice. And the Elf Princess had said that to break the seal, he'd have to touch both paths. *As your friend would, and not as you would.*

Very well, he would touch the Path of Ice.

He put his hands on the edge of the box—he still couldn't get used to the slight shock—and spoke down into it.

"I know Simon's not a very nice person," he said. "I know he's got all that stuff behind a wall in his thoughts, and it has to do with the time he was with the Bonemaster, and he saw awful things and maybe did awful things."

He paused. Was there anything else? He knew he had to get this right.

"It's not that I don't care what Simon's done," he said. "It's that whatever he's done, he's still Simon."

He thought hard. That was the best he could come up with.

He waited. No strange thoughts came into his head. Good. So he'd touched the Path of Ice, he supposed, and overcome it. Cautiously, he stepped back into the box.

He felt around for the sphere again, and found it. It slithered away again. Drat. If only Elfwyn had been here, she would have been able to do a summoning spell. Jinx had never learned that. He . . .

. . . wasn't as good at magic as Elfwyn. In fact, he was lousy at it. She was probably telling Wendell, right now, how hopeless he was. They were probably both laughing about it. Figured. Elfwyn thought she was better than him. Despite the fact that he was better at languages, and *much* more powerful. It was just the way Elfwyn was.

And Wendell, well, Wendell would be agreeing with her because she was a girl, and Wendell naturally thought girls could do no wrong. Even if they'd done really horrible things like give a copy of the Crimson Grimoire to the Bonemaster. What an idiot Wendell was. And Elfwyn was deceitful. In fact, it would probably be a blessing to the Urwald if Jinx *didn't* go back to the trolls and they ate . . .

But Jinx was already scrambling out of the box.

He began pacing again. Right. These thoughts were *not* coming from the Path of Ice. Well, they were, but they were his thoughts, nonetheless. He'd had them. Not exactly like that. Not as loudly as that. He'd kicked them away, most of them, anyway, as soon as he knew he was thinking them. But he'd certainly never thought the trolls should eat Elfwyn or, for that matter, anybody. No, he'd never thought anything remotely like that.

He walked around and around the chamber and thought. The things the ice was using were starting with him—little annoyances, little worries—but the ice was twisting them into something lethal.

He stopped, and grabbed the edge of the box, and spoke.

"Right, okay, listen. Wendell probably is kind of stupid about girls. But I think he's learning. He's really smart, even though he thinks he isn't. He's . . ." This was difficult, and he had to take a deep breath and steel himself to get it out. "A lot smarter than me. And . . . and it's true Elfwyn is better than me at magic. It comes easier to her. That's just how it is."

He paused before he climbed into the box again. Who was next? Sophie? He'd gotten annoyed at Sophie sometimes, it was true, but there was nothing big, nothing the Path of Ice could use. Not that he could think of, anyway. Well, he'd soon find out.

He knelt down in the box and groped around for the sphere. His hands closed on it and he quickly clamped his fingers to the floor, trapping it. Right. Now the trick was going to be lifting it. Slowly, he moved his hands together and knitted his fingers together underneath it. It still hadn't escaped. Good. He picked it up. He had it now.

A strong thread of power attached the sphere to the box. It reminded Jinx of the time that he'd taken Simon's bottled life from the dungeon under Bonesocket. There had been a thread of power holding the bottle in place.

Jinx stood up. He pulled the thread until it broke.

The box trembled. The whole chamber trembled. Then it shook so hard that Jinx thought the ceiling would collapse. He fell to the floor of the box, still clutching the gloppy sphere.

Things quaked and swayed. The chamber seemed to have come free from the rest of the world and to be swinging in space. It felt as if great ropes had been unbound and were whipping around like angry serpents. Jinx could hear them smacking into things in the distance. He heard a crash like broken glass, and then the crunch and rumble of breaking rock, and then the roar of fire. He closed his eyes tightly.

The shaking and roaring went on for a long time. Then it ended, and Jinx was still there. He opened his eyes and saw nothing but white fog.

The mist cleared. The chamber was still there, but the box was gone.

Two tunnels appeared, opening out of the chamber in opposite directions. The one Jinx was facing was a hole bored through blue-white ice. He turned around and looked down the other tunnel, which was ringed in flames from top to bottom, as far as the eye could see.

Which was suddenly very, very far. Jinx wasn't sure how it happened, but somehow he found himself able to see both paths, as though from a great distance, winding and twining their way back up to the world. The paths twisted and turned and wove around each other, and sometimes they seemed to be the same path for a while, and then they split again.

"I'm going to have to tell Malthus about this," said Jinx. "He got it all wrong."

If he ever got out again, that was. He looked down at

the slimy thing in his hands. It was a clear, sloppy blob, like a giant frog's egg. Only instead of a little black dot of tadpole, it contained, at the center, an eyeball. An oddly yellow eyeball.

Facing the Ice

J inx had seen that eye before, although not quite so much of it. And there were supposed to be two of them. And there was supposed to be Simon to carry those eyes around.

Carefully, he slipped it into the leather pocket he wore on his belt. Then he searched all around the cavern, in case there were any more bits. But there was no more Simon to be found.

Well, this wasn't enough Simon. So where was the rest?

Where was the last place Simon had been, before this happened to him? The Bonemaster's house, that's where. And there Jinx had seen what had appeared to be a whole

Simon, frozen inside a slab of ice. So Bonesocket was probably the place to start looking.

Except, Jinx remembered, he had an appointment to have his arm eaten off in the Glass Mountains. The thought made his stomach feel as if it weighed ten tons. But he *had* to go back, because if he didn't Elfwyn and Wendell would be killed.

Jinx looked at the Path of Ice. If the Bonemaster was the wick of ice, then did the path lead to Bonesocket? There was only one way to find out. And the Elf Princess had told him he'd have to travel both paths.

After he'd found the rest of Simon—if there was any more to find—then, he thought with a sinking heart, he could go and get his arm eaten. He wondered if they'd eat it while it was still on him.

He looked at the paths. They met here, in this chamber, because of the seal. And Jinx was pretty sure he had just broken the seal.

He took a step onto the Path of Ice.

He looked back at the chamber, and watched it begin to dissolve and sink into the unreality beneath the floor. Probably not a good idea to stick around while that happened.

～ ✦ ✦

The path of ice was slippery underfoot. Twice he walked too quickly and skidded, and once he fell down hard, grabbing his pocket to protect the eye.

But the real trouble started when the path began to climb upward. Jinx stepped up onto the slope, and skidded down it again, barely keeping his feet. He tried crawling. It was no good. The cold burned his hands, and he slid down anyway.

There was no way he was going to get up this. He should have taken the Path of Fire.

Fire! That was it. Jinx sent fire into his boots—not much, just enough to melt the ice. He kicked at the path, and made a foothold. He stepped up. Kicked again.

This was too slow. He needed something faster. He sent fire directly into the ice.

There was a crackling sound, and then a whoosh of water swept down the slope, soaking Jinx to the knees. He braced himself and fought to stay upright as he slid back down the tunnel. After a minute he stopped. . . . There was solid rock under his feet. He waited until the water was gone, and then he started upward.

He climbed for an hour or so, stopping to melt the ice every few minutes. The sphere in his pocket was growing warmer, perhaps from all the fire Jinx was summoning. Finally he came to a level space, and was able to walk on without magic.

Well, good. He'd figured that out. Naturally he had. He was remarkably intelligent, after all. Look how quickly he'd been promoted, at the Temple of Knowledge in Samara. He—

He stopped walking. "I know what you're doing," he said aloud. He thought. "Intelligence is like magic. It's what you do that matters, not what you have."

That seemed to work. Jinx walked on.

He wasn't sure what he was going to do when he got to Bonesocket. He expected to come up in the dungeon. If he was right, then the mysterious bottle-shaped mass of ghostly ribbons that he'd once seen there was the Bonemaster's lifeforce . . . and connected in some way to the Path of Ice.

It's like a wick, Jinx thought, and was suddenly certain of it. The Bonemaster is the wick of ice but that bottle thing, it's part of the wick too.

Then what was the wick of fire? Besides Jinx, that is? Was there anything that stood atop the Path of Fire and channeled its power?

Of course. The Urwald itself.

The Path of Fire, the lifeforce, was channeled into the Urwald, and the Urwald's power was channeled into Jinx.

Jinx wondered how he had been chosen to have all this power.

The wicks choose themselves. The words came back to him from somewhere—where? Oh, he remembered now. Neza the elf had said it to Dearth in the forest near Cold Oats Clearing. They'd put a spell on Jinx to make him forget, but he had no trouble remembering now.

So with all this power, he'd go up to Bonesocket,

and—what? Bearing in mind that he knew only a handful of spells and the Bonemaster knew, oh, probably hundreds?

I'm going to have to kill him, Jinx thought. If I get there at night, I can kill him in his sleep. I can do it. If I have to. And I do have to. The Bonemaster needs killing.

In fact, there were a lot of people that needed killing, when you thought about it.

The Bonemaster, of course. That went without saying. The Bonemaster had killed so many people that he could make a bridge out of their thighbones, cups out of their skulls, and line a tunnel with the rest of them. The Bone-master would go on killing people, and had to be killed himself to prevent it. No question.

And the preceptors. They were evil people who con-trolled all the knowledge in Samara and kept everyone else in ignorance—except for the Temple scholars, whose knowledge fed the preceptors and made them even more powerful. The preceptors deserved to die. And—

Jinx came to another steep, icy slope. He stopped and looked up. His feet were cold, but that was no problem. He'd send fire into them in a minute, when he melted the ice. What was it he'd been thinking about the preceptors? Oh yes, that they should die. They were threatening the Urwald, that was reason enough. Anyone who threatened the Urwald needed to die.

Take King Rufus of Bragwood, for example. Rufus the

Ruthless. Rufus had put Reven's stepmother into a barrel stuck about with nails and rolled her downhill. Rufus would have to go. And that other king, Bluetooth of Keyland. The one who'd murdered Reven's parents. Obviously he would have to die.

And what about Reven?

Well, there was no question about Reven, really. Reven was invading the Urwald. Reven would have to die. There was no way around it.

The cold had crept up from Jinx's feet now to his knees. He tried to take a step, but his feet seemed frozen to the path. That was okay. He'd melt himself free in a minute. What was it he'd been thinking about? Right, a plan. A plan for what? Oh, yeah, to get rid of unnecessary people. People that needed killing.

Pretty much everyone that wasn't an Urwalder, when you got right down to it. Except Sophie, of course. He was fond of Sophie. And Wendell, well, he wouldn't kill Wendell, of course. Wendell was his best friend. But other than that—

Jinx, get a grip on yourself.

Jinx started, as if he'd been caught in a nightmare. He blinked and looked around. No one there. And his legs were encased in ice, well past his knees. He tried to move and couldn't. The ice was real.

And the nightmare in his thoughts was real, too.

"Don't start that with me," said Jinx, aloud. "You can't possibly be getting those thoughts from me, because I've never wanted to kill anybody, not once in my whole life." He stopped, and thought. Being completely honest was the only way to overcome the ice. "All right, maybe I did want to kill Siegfried, when he was cutting down trees. But he didn't die, he just turned into a tree. And if I've ever thought we'd all be better off if someone or other was dead, well, sometimes that's the actual truth, and—"

With a crackling noise, the ice crept a little higher on his legs. It seemed to form out of the air itself, a little mountain of ice with Jinx stuck in the middle.

"So that's it?" Jinx said. "Wanting someone else's death . . . oh, of course. The Path of Ice is the root of deathforce power."

He took a deep breath. "I don't want anybody dead."

Not even the Bonemaster? he wondered. Of course he wanted— Wait. This was important. His feet were numb, and frostbite was undoubtedly setting in, and he had to get this exactly right.

What he *wanted* was for the Bonemaster never to have happened in the first place. Or to have grown up differently, never chosen the Path of Ice, never learned deathforce magic.

And since changing the past wasn't possible, what he *wanted* was for the Bonemaster to stop killing people. Er, maybe the Bonemaster could, let's see, take up an interest in something else—gardening, say? Or poetry?

Jinx said all this aloud. "That's not going to happen," he added. "And so something else is going to have to happen. But I don't *want* him dead."

He tried to send fire into his boots. But nothing happened. He stayed frozen in place.

"And the rest of them, I don't want them dead. In fact, I hope they don't die. That might not be how things work out. We might have to—"

He stopped himself. He had a feeling the words *have to* were especially dangerous when you were talking to the ice.

"Well, it's a war, and we didn't start it—"

The ice crackled upward.

"I'll do whatever will protect the Urwald," said Jinx. "But I'll do it hurting as few people as possible. Because that's what I choose."

He tried again to send fire into his boots. This time he felt the sharp, horrible ache of thawing feet. He kicked out and the ice around him cracked. He looked at the slippery slope in front of him, started to melt it, and braced himself for a flood.

The wall of water rushed down, knocking him off his feet. He had to scrabble at the ground to keep from being washed back the way he'd come. He got to his feet—now his clothes were soaking wet. He unbuttoned his pocket to check on the eyeball.

The sphere had gotten bigger. Much bigger. It strained at the edges of his pocket. Jinx took it out. The aviot was stuck into it like a thorn. That looked painful. Jinx plucked out the little gold bird and stuck it in his mouth, as he needed both hands to hold the sphere, which now had two eyeballs in it. A head was forming around them.

Jinx watched in revolted fascination as the head grew a nose, and then a mouth, and then Simon's twisty brown hair. And then it stopped, while it was a head. There was no more Simon.

"Did you talk to me a minute ago?" said Jinx. "Did you tell me to get a grip?"

The eyes blinked. The mouth worked, trying to speak, Jinx thought, but it was stuck inside this blob of clear jelly.

"Did I make this happen by defeating the ice?" Jinx asked. Then he worried—that sounded conceited, and the ice *liked* conceit. But it might simply be true, he thought. The Elf Princess had said he'd need to give Simon something of himself. What if—

Gently and carefully, Jinx sent a little bit of lifeforce power into the sphere.

The head grew a neck. Jinx fed it more power, and a chest started to grow downward from the neck. Shoulders appeared, and then arms. The sphere was growing heavy.

Jinx set it down on the ground, and fed it more power.

The whole process was really not something you wanted to watch, and yet Jinx couldn't look away. In a few minutes Simon, all of him, was struggling, like a snake trying to work free of its old skin.

The gloop fell away.

Simon coughed, clearing his throat. "You're not the Bonemaster."

"No, I—"

"You're . . . you're the boy. Jinx." Simon brushed gunk off his face. "Why on earth did I name you that?"

"You didn't," said Jinx. "I was already named it when you found me. And now I've found you."

"Hmph."

Jinx was enormously relieved to hear the hmph. It was a genuine Simon hmph.

And Jinx had seldom been so happy to see anyone in his life. Simon really *was* one of Jinx's favorite people. Simon was impatient, disagreeable, and always on Jinx's side no matter what. You couldn't ask for more than that.

Jinx could tell from the warm blue cloud around Simon's head that the wizard was extremely glad to see him too. Jinx thought the least Simon could have done was *say* he was glad to see Jinx. But that was Simon for you.

Then again, Jinx thought, I suppose that's me, too.

"Hmph," said Simon again. "I could use some clothes."

Jinx fumbled in his pack. "Er, there's this blanket—"

"Give it here." Simon grabbed the blanket, wrapped himself in it, and got to his feet.

Jinx started to take his coat off, in case Simon wanted that.

Simon shook his head. "You're shivering."

Jinx hadn't realized he was. "M-my clothes are wet."

"Dry them off," said Simon.

"I d-don't know h—" But fire should do it, right? Very carefully, so as not to set himself alight, Jinx sent fire into his clothes. Just enough. Steam rose from him, and a smell of damp wool, and then he was dry.

Simon frowned. "You're older. You've grown."

"No I haven't," said Jinx. "I don't."

This was rather a sore point. Jinx actually did grow, in small increments now and then. But everyone else his age seemed to grow in large leaps, all the time.

"How old are you?" said Simon.

"Fifteen."

"I thought you were thirteen."

"I was," said Jinx patiently. "But now I'm fifteen."

"Are you sure?"

"Yes," said Jinx. "Completely sure. I was thirteen and then I was fourteen and now I'm fifteen."

"Hm. Where are we?" said Simon.

"On the Path of Ice," said Jinx.

"Nonsense." Simon looked around him. "What would either of us be doing there?"

"It's kind of a long story."

"It can be as long as it wants, but it won't explain that," said Simon. "I don't see any ice."

"I've just melted some of it. The Bonemaster turned you into a seal—"

"What, you mean one of those creatures that swim about in—"

"No, to seal the paths. To bind the fire to the ice," said Jinx. "He was draining the Urwald's power. Drawing it down through you and up into the Path of Ice."

"What took you so long? Why didn't you come before?"

"You told me not to come down here at all," said Jinx.

"Nonsense. When did I say that?"

"Two years ago," said Jinx. "You appeared to me in this vision, after I broke my arm, and you told me not to come down here."

"Appeared to you—" Simon narrowed his eyes. "That really happened, then. I was trying to cast a spell, but—" He frowned. "Things faded out. It was just a couple days ago."

"Nope. Two years."

Simon swore. "I suppose I should be grateful it wasn't a hundred. And I told you not to come down here, and for once in your life you decided to do as I said?"

"No," said Jinx irritably. "I didn't. I'm here. And if I hadn't come down here, you'd still be stuck. Nobody else could have rescued you."

"Right, true," said Simon. "Thanks."

"You knew that?" Jinx was surprised.

"Suspected it," said Simon. "Some sort of nonsense about Listeners and deep roots. Sophie kept going on about it. What about your arm?"

"What?" said Jinx.

"The one you broke."

"Oh. It's okay." Jinx held it up for inspection.

Simon felt it. "It doesn't hurt?"

"Not really."

"Hm. All right. And you think we're on the Path of Ice now?"

"Yeah. The ice talks to you," said Jinx. "Says, um, kind of horrible things, actually."

Simon nodded.

"It's not saying anything now, though," Jinx added. "You have to talk back to it, and tell it what you really think. Which means you have to kind of, um, figure out what you really think."

"Yes, yes," said Simon, making an impatient gesture with the hand that wasn't clutching the blanket. "I know all that."

"Did the ice talk to you?" said Jinx. "What did—"

"Would you mind making it warmer in here?"

Jinx sent a little more fire into the rock, warming the floor. "What did the ice—"

"Did you bring anything to eat?"

Jinx brought out the remainder of his bread. It was very stale now. He broke it and gave half to Simon.

Jinx gnawed at it, but couldn't make a dent.

Neither could Simon. "Hmph." He handed the bread back to Jinx, and started walking, his bare feet pluffing against the stone floor of the tunnel.

"The Bonemaster must've had a spell ready for you," Jinx said. "When you went to battle him. I bet that elf Neza showed him how. He sent you down to the nadir of all things, to seal together the Paths of Fire and Ice, because, um, he could use you for that because you've done deathforce magic. And—"

"So what makes you think we're still on the Path of Ice?" said Simon. "It's not saying anything, is it?"

"I told you. I argued with it."

"You don't argue with the ice, boy. You change paths."

"Oh." Jinx thought about this. "You mean we're on the Path of Fire now?"

"If that's what you chose."

"The fire doesn't—" Jinx stopped. The fire *did* speak to him. It had told him to send fire into the walls. And it had told him to get a grip. "I thought you didn't know anything about the paths."

"Don't take that tone with me. I know deathforce and lifeforce," said Simon.

"But I wanted to be on the Path of Ice," said Jinx. "Because I wanted to come out in Bonesocket."

"What?" Simon stopped walking. "Bonesocket? Are you insane?"

Jinx explained.

"Well, I'm not frozen inside a giant slab of ice," said Simon. "I'm here. And it's a good thing, too, because I can forbid you to go anywhere near Bonesocket."

Says who? Jinx thought. He'd spent the last two years not being ordered around by Simon, and as far as he could tell it hadn't done him any harm.

"Where does this path come out if we don't go to Bonesocket?" said Simon.

"In the Glass Mountains," said Jinx.

"And what season is it out there?"

"Winter," said Jinx.

"Wonderful. We'll both freeze."

"Actually, I can get us home pretty quickly," said Jinx. "But, um, I have to let the trolls eat my arm first."

"What? Nonsense!"

Jinx explained.

"We'll fight them," said Simon. "You can freeze their clothes—"

"They don't wear a whole lot," said Jinx.

"Then you can—have you learned to do an illusion yet?"

"No," said Jinx. "I'm not the sort of person illusions come naturally to."

"And you're saying I am?"

"Actually," said Jinx, "I'm kind of wondering if—I mean, that is. Um." He took a deep breath, and risked Simon's fury. "You can't do any magic at all, can you?"

The Trolls' Dinner

Simon stopped walking, and glared down at Jinx. "What?"

"Well, you didn't—"

"Who's the wizard here, you or me?"

"You," said Jinx. "But you keep telling me to do magic. Um, melt the ice and dry off my clothes and stuff. And—"

"It's this path thing," said Simon. "You have some kind of power down here."

And you don't have any, Jinx thought, with a sinking feeling. At all. "When we get back to the surface—" he began.

"It just takes time to readjust, that's all," said Simon.

"You try being stuck underground for two years and see how much magic you can do when you have to regenerate yourself—"

"I gave you the power for that."

"—and there's nothing to eat."

Jinx wished Simon would stop harping on that. He was starting to get hungry too, although he'd eaten most of the loaf and he'd only been down here . . . had only been down here . . .

"Time is different down here," he said.

"Yes." Simon seemed relieved the subject had gotten off his magic. He started walking again.

"I don't know how long it's been since I came down here." Jinx felt suddenly panicky.

"Best thing to do is come right on up again, then," said Simon. "Can you make this path end at my house?"

"I don't know," said Jinx. "Probably not, because, um, it doesn't go there. And um, about your house—"

"What?"

Jinx didn't know where to start. He thought of Simon's kitchen. The kitchen was where Simon had ruled, even more than in the south wing. And now the big stone stove had dozens of people huddled on it every night . . . laundry hung among the dried pumpkins and strings of onions . . . the cupboard drawers had been turned into cradles for squalling babies . . . *meat* was being cooked in Simon's precious cooking pots. And in all likelihood people were cutting up carrots the wrong way.

Jinx opted for less alarming news. "We're at war."

"Who is?"

"The Urwald against, er, Keyland. And Bragwood."

"Oh yes? Whose idea was this?"

"It wasn't really an—"

"You see? This is what comes of making a nation. I told you not to try to make a nation, didn't I, boy?"

"So, what, I was supposed to just let them invade us?" Jinx demanded.

"The Urwald would have taken care of them."

"It couldn't. The Bonemaster was draining its power. Through you. And anyway, we *are* the Urwald!"

Jinx tried to make the path go to Simon's house. But it twisted and flopped out of his control. It was going, inexorably, back to where he'd started from.

"We're coming out in the Glass Mountains," he said. "And they're going to eat my arm off."

"Trolls are easy to deal with," said Simon.

"They have hostages. They've got Elfwyn and Wendell."

"Who's Wendell?"

"A guy from Samara."

"You brought a *Samaran* to the Urwald?"

"That bothers you more than that I'm going to get my arm eaten off?"

"You're not going to get your arm eaten off," said Simon. "We'll figure something out."

You can't do magic, Jinx thought. Stop trying to reassure me. You can't do any magic at all. It'll just be me and my magic and Elfwyn and Wendell being held hostage and a few hundred trolls eating my arm.

They had reached the bottom of a set of stairs. It was the first familiar thing that Jinx had seen in his journey underground.

Jinx climbed. It was strange—he had a feeling that he had just come down the stairs a moment ago, and then that it had been years and years—longer than he'd been alive. He reached the top.

"This is it," he said. He came to the archway that said

entry not advisable

over it. He was surprised to see it said it on this side, too. Though he supposed it was a good description of the Urwald. He stepped through into the cavern. The sky was a brilliant blue slit peering through the crack in the wall. Jinx blinked.

"It's pretty bright, isn't it," he said, trying to calm himself down and not think about getting his arm eaten.

"Jinx?" It was Elfwyn's voice. "Jinx? Is that you?"

Jinx turned sideways and squeezed through the gap

into white sunshine, which made him blink. He had trouble seeing Elfwyn at first, except as a green glow of happiness. She hugged him, which Jinx would have quite liked if they hadn't been standing on this narrow ledge. And if he hadn't been focused on the immediate prospect of having his arm chewed off. And if Simon hadn't been there.

"Oh, I'm so glad to see you!" said Elfwyn. "I thought you were never coming back."

"I was only gone, um—"

"Two months," said Elfwyn.

"Reall—? Er, oh." Jinx let go of her, with a certain amount of regret. He looked out over the Urwald, and saw, here and there, a yellow wash of leaf-buds on the treetops. He'd removed the seal, and the long, cold winter was over.

A sudden red puff of sadness from Elfwyn. "You didn't find Simon."

"Yeah, I did. He's right here."

Jinx turned around, and Simon was *not* right there. Uh-oh. Jinx stuck his head into the cavern. No Simon. He cursed. "'You can take nothing with you that you did not bring.'"

Elfwyn took his hand, the one that was scheduled to be eaten, and followed him into the cavern. "What does that mean?"

"The Elf Princess said it," said Jinx. "Drat. I thought

it didn't include Simon, because he'd faced the ice and I'd given him something of myself. But it looks like—"

"You're not making much sense," said Elfwyn.

Jinx cursed again. "I'm going to go back for him. Wait here. Please," he added.

He stepped through the archway, and went down the obsidian stair.

He reached the bottom, and found the path very icy and slick. "SIMON!" he yelled.

There was a long silence, and then a call came echoing back to him. "JINX!"

The path went on past the obsidian stair—Jinx hadn't noticed that before. Or maybe it *hadn't* before. Jinx hurried down it, running and sliding on the ice. "Simon! Simon! Where are you?"

"Right here."

Jinx stopped running, but couldn't stop sliding. He smashed into the wizard, sending him flying.

They picked themselves up. "Was that necessary?" said Simon.

"Why didn't you come with me?"

"When? When you vanished into thin air?"

"I didn't," said Jinx. "I just went up the stairway."

"I see. Well, that stairway isn't there for everyone, it seems. It must be your special stairway. Supposing you introduce us."

They went back to the foot of the obsidian stair. "Can you see it?" said Jinx.

"It seems to be escaping my elderly eyes," said Simon.

"Well, um, here." This was awkward. Jinx grabbed Simon's blanket-clad arm, stepped onto the stairway, and pulled.

To his relief, Simon followed. The wizard stumbled onto the first step and looked up, with a little purple blop of surprise. "Why didn't you make this stairway appear a few miles back, and save us all that slogging through tunnels?"

"Because right here is where it actually is," said Jinx patiently.

They climbed the stairs, Jinx holding on to Simon's arm the whole way to keep him from disappearing. When they got to the archway labeled "Entry Not Advisable," Jinx was worried that he might lose Simon again, but he pulled the wizard into the cavern and there they were.

And there was Wendell, jumping up from beside a small campfire and bubbling bright blue joy at seeing them.

"Elfwyn didn't wait for me?" said Jinx.

"She did," said Wendell. "All of that day, and then Sneep and I had to talk her out of waiting all night. We've been taking turns."

"But I only just ran back down there for—"

"Two days," Wendell finished. He smiled at Simon.

"Pleased to make your acquaintance. I'm Wendell."

Simon blinked at him. "From Samara?"

"Angara, actually," said Wendell. "Oh, and don't worry about the trolls, Jinx. I think I've pretty much convinced them that the trial they had for you was all wrong. It's not how we have trials in Angara." He frowned. "Well, it actually sort of *is* how we have trials in Angara, so maybe I lied, kind of. But there's this ideal, obviously, and I told them about that."

"I see," said Jinx, who didn't. "So I'm having another trial?"

"No," said Wendell. "I pretty much convinced them that they weren't allowed to do that."

"You convinced *trolls* that they weren't *allowed* . . ." Jinx trailed off. You really are a lot smarter than I am, he thought. Not just a little bit. A whole lot. But the sort of thing you could say when you were facing the ice somehow wasn't that easy to say to another person, so he just said, "Thanks."

"No problem." Wendell turned to Simon. "Would you care for some, er, warmer clothes? I've brought extras from home."

"You went home?" said Jinx. "But I thought you were a hostage for two months."

"Well, not all of it," said Wendell. "There was the silk market, obviously, and I always have a lot of guiding jobs to do while that's on. Not that I wouldn't have been perfectly willing to be a hostage for two months," he added, in the tone of one anxious not to offend.

"The trolls let you leave?" said Jinx.

"Sure. They're on our side. They've joined the free and independent nation of the Urwald. Elfwyn talked them into it. She's very convincing," Wendell added, a little more admiringly than Jinx cared for.

Simon was being uncharacteristically silent. A heavy gray cloud of dismay hung over him, and Jinx had a feeling that the wizard was trying to do magic, and not succeeding. The thought of a magicless Simon frightened Jinx. He couldn't imagine what the thought did to Simon.

Wendell looked at Simon. "Well, I'll just go get you some of my clothes, then."

❧ ✒ ✒

A couple hours later, after a terrifying climb down the glass mountainside that Jinx never, ever wanted to happen again, they were sitting around a big trollish bonfire, among a crowd of about fifty trolls and five or six humans, eating a vegetarian stew that had been cooked up in consideration of Simon. Jinx sat beside Elfwyn, and ate, and enjoyed the warmth of the fire and of all the life going on around him.

But the overwhelming smell of troll, and the size of them, made him nervous. It made him even more nervous to see a troll and a woman from Deadfall Clearing attacking each other with clubs.

"They're just practicing," said Elfwyn. "The trolls are teaching us their way of fighting."

The troll raised his club high over his head, ready to smash down, and Jinx jumped to his feet.

"It's all right, Wendell keeps an eye on them," said Elfwyn.

"Wend—? But he's just . . ." Jinx trailed off. Wendell had stepped in front of the troll, and said something. The troll put its club down and hooted with laughter.

"No one's been hurt yet," said Elfwyn. "Well, not seriously, anyway. And it is good to have them on our side, even if, well, they're kind of nervous-making."

"Kind of very nervous-making."

"I'm getting used to them," said Elfwyn. "I haven't been home in a couple weeks, actually. I've been here sort of helping them understand what's going on."

Jinx had a lot of questions about this, but stopped himself from asking them. He leaned back on a glass boulder and listened to Elfwyn tell him. She and Wendell hadn't really been hostages after the first few days, and Wendell had spent some time in Samara.

Elfwyn, meanwhile, had brought a deputation to meet with the trolls—Sophie, and Hilda, and Malthus, and Cottawilda—

"Cottawilda's an idiot!" Jinx objected.

"No she's not," said Elfwyn. "I mean, I can understand why you don't like her—"

"Because she let me be abandoned in the forest!"

"But she's quite clever, in a sort of limited way. Actually, she's a lot like a troll. But her coming here didn't work out well, because that troll whose arm you cut off—"

"Bergthold," said Jinx.

"—tried to eat her."

"Well, they used to be married," said Jinx.

"And he's angry because of the little girl," said Elfwyn. "Gertrude, their daughter."

"Cottawilda is supposed to be looking for her," said Jinx.

"She asks people, when she remembers to. 'Did you see a little girl about yea-high in the woods around five or six years ago—'"

"Well, that narrows it down," said Jinx. He was good with faces, but he didn't think he'd recognize Gertrude. She'd been a baby when he'd last seen her, and babies' faces all looked the same to him.

"I don't think she really expects to find Gertrude. But of course she didn't tell Bergthold she was looking for her."

"Why of course?"

"Because she didn't want to give him the satisfaction," said Elfwyn. "That was a question! You're usually so careful."

"Sorry," said Jinx.

The troll and the woman had gone back to battling with clubs.

"In a way they're easier to get along with than were-wolves," said Elfwyn. "I mean, your friend Malthus is really nice, but I think he's probably eaten people, don't you?"

"Yes," said Jinx. "Don't tr—er, I thought trolls ate people."

"They do, but not very often," said Elfwyn. "They don't much care for the taste. Tell me about where you've been."

Jinx thought of where he'd been—miles and worlds away from all the life going on around him now. The Path of Fire might be the source of lifeforce, but only life was life, and Jinx had missed it.

"I'll tell you another time," said Jinx. "Tell me more about the trolls. And the war."

He listened to Elfwyn talk. He couldn't detect the faintest shred of a pink fluffy thought anywhere in her happy green glow at seeing him. But he told himself he shouldn't mind. He was lucky to have friends, and lucky to have people, and enormously lucky to still have a full complement of arms.

Even if, according to what Elfwyn was saying, they were still losing the war.

A Problem with Sophie

J inx decided not to make a doorpath from the trolls' home to the Doorway Oak. Trolls and humans might be allies for now, but there was no telling how long that would last. And KnIP spells couldn't be undone.

"So you're telling me," Simon said, as they walked down the Troll-way, "that you've made a KnIP path that ends at my house?"

"He's made dozens of them," said Elfwyn. "You can get practically anywhere in the Urwald from your house."

"And vice versa, I suppose," said Simon.

"Only if you *know* the doorpaths are there," said Wendell.

"And it's not really *to* your house," said Jinx. "Because I made the ward a whole lot stronger, and I thought the Doorways ought to be outside of it."

"But unfortunately, there are enemy soldiers surrounding your clearing now," said Elfwyn. "Or at least there were when I was there a couple weeks ago."

"I see," said Simon.

"Oh, er, and there's something else I should tell you," said Jinx. "About your house."

Simon glowered in anticipation.

"There's, ah—" Jinx looked at Wendell and Elfwyn, in case either of them wanted to be the one to tell. But they both seemed suddenly very interested in the large chunks of glass heaped beside the road.

"There's, um, a few people staying at your house," said Jinx.

"Oh?" said Simon.

"Yes," said Jinx.

"I see," said Simon. "What sort of people are they?"

"Urwalders," said Jinx. "Some of them are from Cold Oats Clearing, where you come from—"

"And where I left from," said Simon. "I certainly didn't invite it to follow me."

"But it was destroyed by the Bonemaster," said Jinx. "You know that. They didn't really have anywhere else to go. And then a couple other clearings were destroyed by the Bonemaster. Gooseberry Clearing was one. And then some clearings were attacked by—"

"How many is 'a few people'?" said Simon.

Elfwyn and Wendell were still studying the scenery assiduously. "About ninety-four," said Jinx.

"Ninety-four? Ninety-four people in *my* house?"

"About that, yeah."

Purple-gray storm clouds had gathered around Simon's head. "And where are these ninety-four people sleeping?"

"Pretty much everywhere," said Jinx.

"Do you mean to tell me—"

"Not the south wing," Jinx added.

"And how are you feeding all these people?"

"Well, we kind of had to turn some of your clearing into potato patches and gardens and stuff—"

"Some of it?"

"Well, pretty much all of it." Jinx looked at Elfwyn and Wendell to see if they wanted to help him out, but it seemed they did not. They had walked on ahead and were examining the glass as if they shared the Elf Princess's fascination with geology.

"Except for a little bit that we left for the goats and chickens to run around in," said Jinx. "Oh, and Witch Seymour's moved in with them."

The storm clouds grew an angry purple burst. "Witch Seymour? That idiot?"

"He was really helpful to us when we broke Reven's

siege around Blacksmiths' Clearing," said Jinx.

"You what?"

"We had to do it because the blacksmiths are the ones who're supplying all our weapons. Witch Seymour helped us with some illusions that made Reven's soldiers fall back. Actually, Dame Glammer did more than he did, but they both helped."

Simon stared at Jinx. "You really are fighting a war."

"That's what I told you," said Jinx. "Oh, and I've spent some of your money to buy food for people—"

"That was generous of you."

"Sorry, but—"

Simon shrugged. "Doesn't matter. That's what money's for."

"And we've had to buy weapons, and clothes for people, and stuff. I'm not sure how much we've spent, but Sophie's been keeping track."

"Sophie?" The storm clouds dissipated, as if a brisk wind had blown through. "Sophie's there?"

"Yeah. She's left Samara. They sentenced her to death, and I had to help her escape from prison, and—"

"Idiot! Why didn't you tell me this before?"

"Don't call me an idiot!" Jinx looked ahead, hoping Wendell and Elfwyn hadn't heard. "Anyway, I was going to get to it eventually. It takes a long time to tell two years' worth of stuff, you know."

"You start with the important things," Simon snapped,

walking faster. "Sophie's here! Why didn't you—"

"I just did—"

Simon stopped walking suddenly. "She left Samara because they sentenced her to death."

"Yeah. That's what I said. I had to help her escape from prison, and we came through into the Urwald by using KnIP, and that's how Wendell got here—"

"What did they sentence her to death for?"

"For being married to you, more or less," said Jinx. "They didn't know she was in the Mistletoe Alliance. I mean, they accused her of it, but I think that was just . . . reflex, kind of."

"Who told you about the Mistletoe Alliance?"

"Everybody," said Jinx.

"And you broke Sophie out of prison? Out of the prison in Samara? With all those guards and ten-foot thick walls? *You* did?"

"Yeah," said Jinx, annoyed. The trouble with adults was that they never stopped picturing you as six years old and unable to do things yourself.

"How on earth did you do that?"

Jinx told him.

❧ ❧ ❧

They had come down the Troll-way far enough that the ground around them was no longer glass. The forest welcomed Jinx. He felt the Urwald's lifeforce, strong and whole again, and he felt that the fire inside him was part of it.

"Here's the Doorway," said Elfwyn.

They stopped.

"Where?" said Simon.

"Right here," said Elfwyn, pointing. "And you have to *know*—"

"Don't tell me how KnIP works," said Simon. "Just tell me what's there."

"I was trying to," said Elfwyn. "That big hollow oak near your house."

"Right. I see it." He turned to Jinx. "You made this?"

"Well, I used a bunch of other people's knowledge, but yeah." Jinx watched to see if Simon would at least be impressed by that. Most KnIP users could only use their own knowledge.

"Hm," said Simon.

Simon put a foot into the Doorway, and Jinx grabbed his arm. "Hang on. I have to go through and strengthen the ward first."

"You said you did that already."

"The ward tunnel," said Jinx. "It was weak because we didn't have much power. Just wait a minute."

He stepped through, and smelled the rot of the Doorway Oak. He felt the ward tunnel, stretching toward the edge of Simon's clearing. He could feel how weak it was and he could sense that several holes had been scraped in it now.

He poured power into it, filled the holes, and strengthened it.

"Okay, you can come through now," he called over his shoulder.

The others joined him, and they walked up the tunnel to the clearing. Reven's soldiers tried to thrust swords and hands through the holes Jinx had just plugged. There weren't nearly as many soldiers as before.

"Where's Reven?" Jinx asked them. "Or King Raymond, if you'd rather?"

"He's got better things to do than hang around watching you," said one of the soldiers.

Jinx didn't like the sound of that.

He watched Simon as they came into the clearing, which had once been a small green goat pasture and was now all dug up into a patchwork of vegetable gardens. It looked like someone had planted peas and onions already.

There was a pale orange cloud of dismay from Simon, but all he said was "Hmph."

The kitchen was wet with drying laundry and a-squall with babies. People were talking, yelling, quarreling, wheedling, and laughing, but they all stopped when they saw Simon standing in the doorway. Wizards had that effect.

Cats erupted from hidden places, yowling, and rubbed

their heads against Simon's legs.

"Are you the big wizard?" said small Silas.

Simon unhooked a kitten from his leg and nodded.

"He's the big wizard," small Silas reported to everyone.

Simon looked all around the room. Jinx did too. It seemed to him there were a lot more people in the kitchen than there had ever been before. And he could hear voices in the north tower, too. He looked up. Heads peered down from all along the edge of the loft.

"Nobody's gone into the south wing, have they?" said Jinx.

"Of course not," said Cottawilda. "Sophie locked it when she left."

"What do you mean, when she left?" Simon demanded. "Where is she?"

"We thought she was with you," said Jotun.

Jinx had a sudden feeling of foreboding. "Why would she be with us?"

"Because she went to meet you, when she looked in that Farseeing Window thing and saw that you were on your way up," said Cottawilda.

"When?" Elfwyn demanded.

"Must've been about a week ago," said Cottawilda.

Jinx felt rising panic. "Well, she didn't get there!" He turned to Wendell and Elfwyn. "Did the trolls eat her?"

"Of course not!" said Elfwyn.

"Why would there be trolls at the Bonemaster's house?" asked Cottawilda.

Jinx looked at Simon. The wizard's face had gone pale.

"What are you talking about?" said Jinx.

"Sophie went to Bonesocket," said small Silas.

"She looked in the window thingy and she saw you standing there in that cave, holding that blob of glup," said Cottawilda. "We all did, actually. And then you looked at those two paths, and you went up the icy one, and she said you must be going to Bonesocket—"

"What on earth made her think that?" Simon demanded.

"I don't know. She looks in books and things," said Cottawilda.

"Why would a book tell her what Jinx was going to do?" said Elfwyn.

"That actually *was* what I was going to do." Jinx felt awful. He should have realized Sophie would try to interfere—er, help him.

"Right," said Simon. "See you later, then." He turned back to the door.

"Wait!" Jinx grabbed Simon's arm. "You can't—"

Simon shook Jinx off. "I most certainly can." Bright-orange angry lightning bolts leapt around his head.

Elfwyn jumped in front of him and held her arms out to stop him. "You can't go off and face the Bonemaster by yourself."

"I have done so before," said Simon.

"Yes, and look what happened," said Jinx. "And you can't face him now, you can't even do mag—" He caught himself. "*Much* of anything till you've had some rest," he amended.

"You'll go after her, of course," said Wendell. "Obviously. But you really should have a plan, don't you think?"

"I'll kick his—"

"Not that kind of plan," said Elfwyn. "A specific plan. Wendell's right."

The front door opened—nobody bothered to knock anymore. Maud, the nostrilly girl from Blacksmiths' Clearing, came in. Behind her, Jinx was startled to recognize Elfwyn's mother, Berga, from Butterwood Clearing, and her husband, Helgur the Barbarian, behind her. Helgur was carrying a baby, and bouncing it up and down in an attempt to stop it from crying.

"What, more?" said Simon.

"They're traitors," said Jinx, under his breath. "Not the girl, but the other two."

Jinx knew what Berga was going to do. She was going to start asking Elfwyn questions, one after another, bang-bang-bang. Elfwyn hated it. He spoke quickly before Berga had a chance. "What are you doing here? Have you got some supplies to sell that the invaders didn't want to buy? And don't start asking Elfwyn questions, or I'll cast a horrible spell on you."

Elfwyn looked annoyed. "I can cast my own horrible spells, you know."

"They have information," said Maud.

"If you want it," said Helgur, jouncing the baby.

"Why should we trust you?" Jinx shot back.

"What's the information?" said Wendell.

Berga frowned at him. "Where's this one from? He talks funny."

"King Raymond—Reven, that is—is battling his uncle, King Bluetooth of Keyland, southwest of Blacksmiths' Clearing," said Helgur.

"King Bluetooth's got two thousand men in the Urwald," said Berga.

"They're at least eighty miles in," said Helgur. "They haven't come up to Butterwood, because they don't know it's there. They tried to invade a couple of clearings and found them protected by wards, so they probably think all the clearings are like that."

The baby let out a howl. Helgur handed it to his wife. "Your friend Reven's expecting to be joined by King Rufus of Bragwood soon," he went on. "That was the agreement they had—that he'd help Raymond against Bluetooth, and then Raymond would help Rufus conquer his half of the Urwald—"

"Rufus doesn't *have* a half of the Urwald," Jinx snapped. "And neither does Reven."

Helgur made a shut-up gesture. "I'm telling you what they've planned. When the war's over, Keyland and Bragwood will be much, much bigger, and the border between them will be—" He frowned, and looked at Simon. "I'm not sure where exactly—"

"About right here," said Cottawilda.

"We've got a map," said small Silas.

"Don't tell them that!" said Jinx.

Small Silas looked stricken, and Jinx felt bad. "I mean, please don't tell them that. They're not on our side."

"I wouldn't have brought them through the doorpath if they weren't," said Maud.

"We certainly are," said Berga indignantly. "Not because it's *your* side. But we are Urwalders."

"When did you remember that?" said Jinx.

"They knew it all along," said Wendell. "Or, well, that's how it seems, anyway. I mean—" He looked at Berga, then looked away in embarrassment because she was nursing the baby. He turned to Helgur instead. "You sold supplies to Reven so that you could get information from his soldiers, right? So that they would trust you."

It was like Wendell to think the best of people; it was one of his more annoying traits. However, Jinx supposed it *could* be true.

"So when is King Rufus supposed to get there?" said Jinx. "Where is he?"

There were replies from all around the crowded kitchen.

"He was around Mangled Nose Clearing six weeks ago."

"An ogre ate three of his men when they strayed off the path."

"He laid siege to Dovecote Clearing, and they had to come through the doorpaths. They're living in Cold Oats Clearing now. They built huts."

"But where is he right now?" Simon demanded.

"I'll find out," said Jinx. He saw that everyone else believed Helgur and Berga. He supposed he ought to as well.

He went outside to talk to the trees. They didn't pay much attention to the Restless, and usually couldn't tell him where an individual person or werewolf was. But Rufus the Ruthless was a Terror, like Reven and the preceptors. They kept track of Terrors.

Reven's soldiers looked up as Jinx stepped into the ward tunnel. He could talk to the trees here. He used to have to take his boots and socks off and dig his toes into the dirt to hear the trees, but now he heard them as soon as he entered the forest.

Do you know— he began.

FIRE! cried the trees.

An Attack of Wizards

*W*hat—said Jinx.
Death! Fire! Pain! Fire!

It was only partly words. Jinx heard flames roaring up his limbs, felt sap bubbling in his veins, smelled smoke and terror and the loss of all hope.

"Where!" He shouted it aloud by accident. He was dimly aware that the soldiers had gathered beside the tunnel and were staring at him. He ran to the Doorway Oak. The fire was . . . west of here, he thought. It was very hard to concentrate, because the flames were licking at his mind.

He stood in the Doorway Oak and dithered. He could see the Doorways he'd made, dozens of them, as a series of overlapping arches. Which of them was closest to the fire?

Calm down! he said. *Tell me where it is!*

Pain! Where! Agony! Toward the sun, toward the sun and the summertime!

Southwest? said Jinx. He showed them the forest near Gooseberry Clearing in his head.

Yes, and toward summer! Fire!

South of Gooseberry Clearing? he asked.

Flames! Pain! Death!

Jinx found the Gooseberry Clearing Doorway amid the overlapping array, and charged through it.

He strode across the bare ground, clear of any huts since the Bonemaster's attack. He could feel the trees' pain and the enormous power of the fire. He tried to draw the flames into himself, but they were much too far away— miles away. He hurried into the forest.

He ran, and stumbled, and walked, and ran again, tripping over roots and logs and getting scratched by thorns without noticing. Once or twice he thought he heard something following him, but he didn't have time to worry about that. The trees needed him.

He smelled smoke. Then he saw it, pouring through the trees. Trying to block the screams of dying trees, he felt for the leaping flames with his mind. Some of them were close enough to reach, and he drew them into him.

The wind blew more smoke toward him. Choking, he

ran through the surging black cloud, trying to get around to where it wasn't. His eyes stung, his lungs felt on fire. He lurched blindly. Then he found himself free of the smoke at last.

He drew in more fire. But more trees were screaming now. . . . The fire was spreading much faster than he could draw it in. This was too slow.

Reaching out with his mind, he seized the fire and sent it deep underground, down to the Path of Fire, down to the deep tunnels through the rock that led to the nadir of all things.

He grabbed more fire. And more. This was a much faster way to get rid of the flames. The Path had far more capacity to hold fire than Jinx did. Acre after flaming acre of fire went underground.

Twice more, the rolling smoke swept over him and he had to move. Then suddenly the climbing flames burst into life right in front of him. He turned and ran, the flames licking and crackling behind him. He stumbled and fell and saw the flames tower above him. Then a sudden gust blew them back. He got up and ran further from the fire, and sent more flames underground.

Finally there began to be less fire. And then Jinx became aware that he wasn't the only one drawing on it.

With a last heave, he gathered what remained of the flames and shoved them down into the Path of Fire. Then he staggered forward to look at the devastation.

The ground was black and smoking. Red embers crawled among the ash; Jinx sent them underground too. Blackened tree trunks pointed at the sky, their branches gone. The burnt smell was overpowering, and the groans of the trees filled Jinx's ears.

He could see the far side of the charred area—and there were tiny figures standing at the edges. One of them bounced along in giant leaps, as if using a butter churn.

In fact, there were people all around. And one of them was strolling toward him along the near edge. Jinx blinked his stinging eyes and saw Angstwurm's dirty-white robe and square brown beard.

The wizard handed him a goatskin pouch. "First forest fire, eh? Always bring water."

Jinx took the pouch. It sloshed. There was nothing untrustworthy in Angstwurm's square, smug thoughts; not about the goatskin pouch, anyway. Jinx uncorked it and took a long, grateful swig.

He handed the pouch back. "Thanks."

"And never approach from the leeward side," said the wizard. "You look like you've been bathing in soot."

"Uh-huh." Jinx was too distracted by the forest's moans and lamentations to attend particularly to Angstwurm.

"Strange how the fire just went out," said Angstwurm. "We were trying to extinguish it—"

"You were taking power from it!" said Jinx.

"Of course. That's how we extinguish fires. A method beneficial to both the forest and the magician."

"The fire spreads much faster than a wizard can—" Jinx's throat couldn't handle any more words. He reached for the pouch again, and took a long gulp.

With a thump, a butter churn landed in front of him.

"Little chipmunks shouldn't question customs that have been around much longer than they have," said Dame Glammer.

"Witches can't draw power from—" Jinx's voice gave out again.

"Chipmunks don't know what witches can do, do they?" She cackled. "Not a wizard's business to know."

"I'd certainly like to know what you did," said Angstwurm. "A lot of wizards were relying on that fire's power, you know. And it suddenly vanished."

Jinx made a gesture showing his throat was too sore to speak. He could see other wizards approaching, all robes and pointy hats in various colors; beards optional.

There were an awful lot of them. A couple of dozen at least.

"Yes, what happened?" demanded one of them.

Jinx's first instinct was to lie. He opened his mouth to say he didn't know what Angstwurm was talking about. Then an angry impulse overruled him. Lying was what frightened people did, and why should he be frightened? He'd spent too much of his life being afraid already.

"I sent the fire underground," he said.

Angry murmurs from the wizards.

"Pretty high-handed, wasn't that?" said a light brown wizard in a dark brown robe.

"Unhelpful," said a short pink woman in a yellow-orange robe and pointy hat. She looked like an upside-down carrot.

"Wants all the power for himself," said an elderly wizard with a black robe and a beard even longer and whiter than the Bonemaster's. "I've seen his type before."

"Haven't we all," said Brown Robes.

"Mean," said the Carrot.

"Now now," said Angstwurm. "It's nice to see young people with magical talent. Of course, it's also nice to see young people who respect the superior magical knowledge of their elders."

"Right," said the Carrot.

"And if they *don't* have respect, they need to be taught it," said the elderly wizard.

Jinx scowled at them. He could see from their thoughts that they didn't intend to hurt him—no, he corrected himself, they didn't intend to *kill* him. But they certainly intended to put him in his place, and he was likely to get banged up on the way.

Suddenly Jinx found himself inside a purple glass prison. It was a cube about as tall as he was. But then the ceiling began to drop, slowly. Jinx got to his knees and felt his way into the spell. The ceiling dropped still lower. Jinx hunched down, and began to be very uncomfortable. The box was a sort of ward spell, only with an odd element Jinx couldn't figure out, and the moving ceiling was—not quite a reverse levitation, because it had more force behind it, but . . . Jinx felt his way into it and stopped the ceiling from dropping. Then he pushed it up again.

"Clever." The Carrot's voice thrummed through the thick purple glass.

"Simon won't like it if you harm his chickabiddy, dearies!"

"Where *is* Simon, then? Nobody's seen him in years. And this jumped-up apprentice has taken over his house and filled it with his cronies."

Now the ceiling was getting further away. No, wait; the ceiling wasn't moving. Jinx was sinking into the ground. Angstwurm's leaden-legs spell again. Jinx concentrated on reversing it, and thus missed exactly where the screaming goldfishes came from.

There were hundreds of them, darting at his face, biting his ears. Furiously he batted at them, and tried to work his way into the spell, but was distracted by the fact that his purple prison was filling with a nasty, gluey pink liquid that smelled like pickles. It was already up to his waist.

He got out of the lead-foot spell and struggled goopily to his feet, flailing his arms to repel the goldfish. He couldn't get a grip on the goldfish spell at all. It was partly illusion, and he'd never been able to understand illusions, and . . . .

The temperature inside the purple cube began to drop. It grew colder and colder. Jinx sent fire into the cold, and was still trying to work out what to do about the pink goo when it began to rain spiders.

"What's going on here? Stop it! All of you." Simon's voice rang through the glass. "You should be ashamed of yourselves. We're at war, and you have nothing better to do than torment a—"

Don't call me a child, thought Jinx, whacking a goldfish.

"—mere apprentice," said Simon. "It's disgusting."

The goldfishes stopped flying, flopped down into the goo, and dissolved.

"Rats," said the Carrot.

Jinx looked around hastily in case any had appeared. Nope. The goldfishes had been hers—Jinx could feel the short, carroty print of her magic. He brushed spiders off himself and worked his mind into the pink goo spell, which seemed to have come from the elderly black-robed wizard. Jinx gave the spell a little twist and reversed it.

Simon was still haranguing the wizards. Everyone was

shouting at each other, except Dame Glammer, who was merely watching in amusement. The spiders had stopped falling. Jinx looked at the ones scuttling around his feet and decided not to bother with them. The spell he really wanted to undo was the purple prison.

He felt his way into it. It was complicated. It used deathforce, not from a sacrifice, Jinx thought, but from something that was a twist on a sacrifice—perhaps some contact with the ice that had originated in ghast-roots. He touched the wall—it gave a nasty crackle—and pushed fire into it. It began to melt, slowly.

By the time the purple cube was gone, Simon and the wizards had finished yelling.

"We feared for your safety, Simon," Angstwurm was explaining. "After all, it wouldn't be the first time an apprentice has—"

"Not *my* apprentice," said Simon.

"How did you manage to undo my purple prison, Simon?" said the wizard in the dark brown robes, aggrieved. "No one has ever been able to even touch it."

"That's for me to know and you not to know," said Simon. "Now, are we done playing childish tricks? Because we're at war—"

"We know that," said Angstwurm. "We're not fools. We've seen the soldiers."

"And this is the fifth fire in the last month," said the

black-robed wizard. "Where've *you* been, Simon?"

"Absent," said the Carrot.

"Who set this fire?" Jinx demanded. He knew fires were sometimes started naturally, by lightning or firebirds. But not at this time of year.

"One of King Rufus the Ruthless's ruffians," said Angstwurm, sparing him a glance.

"How do you know?" said Jinx.

Angstwurm smiled a thin little smile. "Your apprentice could stand to listen more and talk less, Simon."

Jinx gritted his teeth with fury. Dame Glammer gave him a grin that was like a silent cackle.

"How do you know who set it?" Simon repeated levelly.

Angstwurm shrugged. "The fires follow the army. They always start a few hours after the Bragwood army has passed through. I assume they leave someone behind to set them. We've been running our legs off, fighting them—"

"Fighting the armies?" said Simon, with a little blup of surprise.

"Fighting the fires, of course. Dame Glammer"— Angstwurm nodded in her direction—"graciously guides us through the new magic Doorways."

Jinx worried about this. Every Urwalder should know where the Doorways were. That was the point of them.

But he wasn't sure he liked the idea of all these wizards learning KnIP.

"Why aren't you fighting against the army?" said Simon.

"Well, we've talked that over—" said Angstwurm.

"Discussed it at some length," said the elderly wizard. "Pros and cons."

"The need to preserve the autonomy of the individual magician," said Brown Robes.

"Freedom," said the Carrot.

"The witches, too, have expressed diverse opinions," said the wizard in black.

"The fact is," Angstwurm went on, "we've more or less reached a conclusion that, while wizards don't usually mix with unmagical folk—"

"Too much opportunity for exploitation on both sides," said Brown Robes.

"Mayhem," said the Carrot.

"It probably is time for us to get involved in what appears to be—" said Angstwurm.

"An external threat to our mutual habitat," said Brown Robes.

"Invasion," said the Carrot.

"You mean you've decided to join us?" said Jinx.

"Join you?" Angstwurm burbled surprise. "Goodness no. We've decided to lead you."

Oh, yeah?

"We'll have to have a meeting to decide about that," said Jinx.

Angstwurm sneered. "A meeting? You and Simon?"

"No, all the people at Simon's house. They'll get together and talk about it, and then we'll all vote."

"Vote? Is that some kind of spell?"

"This is a waste of time," Simon snapped. "We can settle all this later. We're being attacked. And it's not just the Bragwood king. The king of Keyland has invaded—two kings of Keyland, in fact—"

"Two?" said the Carrot.

"Seems excessive," said Brown Robes.

"And there's the Bonemaster," said Simon. "And we magicians have to be the ones to deal with him."

"Your old master?" Angstwurm sneered.

"Plan," said the Carrot.

"Right," said Brown Robes. "If we're going to attack the Bonemaster, we need a plan."

"Got one handy, Simon?" said Angstwurm.

"Attack the Bonemaster?" said the elderly wizard. "Magicians don't interfere with each other."

"Didn't mind interfering with the chipmunk, now, did you, dearie?" said Dame Glammer. "Playing with pink goo at your age!"

Jinx was starting to feel smaller by the minute. People

were calling him chipmunk and mere apprentice and all kinds of things.

"Meeting?" the Carrot suggested.

A blue-green wave of consternation rippled through the wizards, and Jinx didn't blame them. He hated meetings too. Still he was relieved when they all nodded.

"Six o'clock," said Simon. "My house."

"Your house, with all those nonmagical people spilling out the windows? I think not," said Angstwurm.

"Cottage," said the Carrot, nodding at Dame Glammer.

"True, it's near one of the Doorways," said Brown Robes. "If you don't mind, Dame?"

She grinned.

"Are you going to teach us this new-fangled 'vote' spell?" said the black-robed wizard.

"I might," said Simon.

Jinx and Simon walked back toward Gooseberry Clearing together. Jinx could hear the trees mourning the lives lost in the fire.

"I hate those wizards," he told Simon.

"Mm-hm."

"They're worse than little kids," said Jinx.

"Well, they're individualists," said Simon.

"And that purple prison thing was deathforce magic."

"No it wasn't," said Simon. "There was vestigial deathforce

there, but it was at several removes."

Jinx was surprised. "You can tell that? I thought you'd lost your magic."

"It doesn't take magic to know what you're looking at," said Simon. "Anyway, I haven't lost it. It'll be back."

Jinx had his doubts about this. "Do you think the other wizards noticed?"

"Why would they?"

"Don't magicians kind of sense—"

"As for Alphonse, I doubt you'll find any of them that haven't done some sort of deathforce magic at some point."

"The Qunthk bottle spell is deathforce," said Jinx.

"Not really," said Simon. "Not entirely. I—"

"You used ghast-roots to do it," said Jinx. "And ghast-roots are made by sacrificing a human to kill a tree."

"Yes, at some point." Simon's thoughts squirmed. "But it may have been done hundreds of years ago, and—"

"The trees don't like it," said Jinx. "It's twisting the Ancient Treaty. And they say the treaty is broken."

"Never mind that," said Simon. "What's your plan for attacking the Bonemaster?"

"*My* plan?" said Jinx.

"That's what I asked, yes."

"You want my plan? So you can go to that meeting and pretend it's your plan?" Jinx was beginning to feel extremely unappreciated. "I got rid of that flippin' purple box and those wizards thought you did it! They wouldn't even listen to me, they treated me like I was some stupid kid and they only listened to you and—"

"That's not important," Simon snapped. "What's important is getting Sophie back."

"I know that!" said Jinx. "My plan is that I go back down through the paths, come up under Bonesocket like I meant to in the first place, grab that flippin' bottle of his, and—"

"Hit the Bonemaster over the head with it?" Simon said.

"Well, I can go up into Bonesocket from the dungeon, he won't be expecting that—"

"You think not? The Bonemaster's no fool, boy. And—"

"Stop calling me boy!" Jinx yelled. He'd had a difficult day, and it had been more than two months long. He'd dealt with trolls, elves, the nadir of all things, a forest fire, and being harassed by a bunch of stupid wizards. And he'd drunk in so much lifeforce and fire he felt ready to burst with it. "You call me boy all the time! I have a name! And I know that's not important, but I don't care!"

"I don't call you boy," said Simon.

"You do too! All the time! All the flippin' time!"

There was a trompling sound of breaking branches, and an enormous ogre burst through the trees. It had gleaming, red-streaked eyes. It opened its snarling mouth and revealed fangs as long as Jinx's belt knife.

Jinx spared it a look. "Get lost!" he snapped.

The ogre gaped, stuck in mid-snarl. It stared at Jinx, its feelings clearly wounded to the quick. Then it turned and slunk disconsolately away into the forest.

Simon glanced after the ogre, and then back at Jinx. "Fine. Jinx. All right, let's say you do go up through the paths and grab that bottle, whatever it is. What are all the other magicians doing meanwhile?"

"Attacking Bonesocket," said Jinx. "Creating a distraction."

"And what's happening to Sophie?"

"I don't know." Jinx thought. "She's not like the bottle; she can move. She can come down to me—"

"And how's she supposed to know to do that? And what will you do then? Take her on the paths?"

"She probably can't go on the paths," said Jinx. "I've been trying to teach her magic—"

"Sophie? Magic?"

"She's not much good at it. Elfwyn's been trying to teach her too. She's better at KnIP, though. Sophie is, I mean. She and Satya have been practicing it. Or they were."

"Little Satya? What is she, four?"

Jinx remembered that Satya had known Simon before

Jinx had. Simon had been in the Mistletoe Alliance in Samara. "I think she's sixteen. And—"

"Sixteen? Are you sure?"

"She might be seventeen. But anyway, she's a traitor." He told Simon about Satya helping the Bonemaster.

"She's not a traitor," said Simon. "She did what someone in the Mistletoe Alliance would do. Knowledge should be free to everyone. How was she to know that the Bonemaster wasn't the right kind of everyone? I doubt he introduced himself as the Bonemaster, or mentioned having killed hundreds of people."

"But—"

"The important thing is whether she *kept* helping him after she found out."

"She asked Wendell to hide a book for him in a tree-house," said Jinx.

"But did she know, at the time, who the Bonemaster was?"

"I don't know," said Jinx. "I kind of haven't talked to her since we found out."

"Because you called her a traitor and chased her out of my house?"

Jinx shrugged. He hadn't expected to be made to feel guilty about it. "Anyway, that's not important right—"

"It's extremely important," said Simon. "Because we need the Company's help to find out what the Bonemaster's mysterious bottle is, before you go grabbing it. Did you find out anything about deathbindings in Samara?"

"Not exactly," said Jinx.

"We have to find that out, too," said Simon. "Because it would be nice if we didn't both drop dead if we do manage to get rid of the Bonemaster. Right, we'll need to get in touch with the Mistletoe Alliance. And Satya's probably the quickest way to do that. I'm afraid you're going to have to apologize to her."

"What?" Jinx was outraged. "*I* have to apologize to *her*?"

"It's always simplest to apologize, with women," said Simon. "The important thing is to get her back on our side."

"Wendell can get her back on our side," said Jinx. "I'm not apologizing. She gave the Crimson Grimoire to the Bonemaster."

"She what?" Simon stopped walking.

"He got into Samara and the Mistletoe Alliance gave him copies of all kinds of books because—"

"Because they would." Simon dispatched the Mistletoe Alliance with a string of swear words. "If he's got his bony hands on a copy of the Crimson Grimoire, that means he can bottle Sophie's life."

Or her death. The thought hung in the air between them.

"But," said Jinx. "He knows she's your wife, and he'll know she's worth something to him as a hostage, and . . ."

He trailed off. It probably wasn't reason enough for the Bonemaster not to kill Sophie. "What are we going to do?"

"Hm." Simon stepped over a beech seedling. "There are obviously a few things we need to figure out."

"Maybe the wizards will come up with a plan at the meeting tonight," said Jinx.

"Oh, of course they will," said Simon. "But we'll come up with a plan first, and then I'll do what Sophie does." There was a little twist of red pain when he mentioned Sophie. "I'll get *them* to come up with a plan, and then I'll nod and listen and nudge the plan around until it's just like my plan, and then I'll get them to vote on it."

Jinx looked at him in surprise. "Sophie's meetings *are* kind of like that."

"They would be," said Simon, with a touch of pride.

"When we go to the meeting—"

"You're not going," said Simon firmly. "They wouldn't listen to you anyway. You just saw that, back there."

"But I could listen to them!"

"And keep your mouth shut? I doubt it. And even if you did, they'd sense that you're sloshing with power," said Simon. "They *may* have been too busy harassing you to notice before, but in a nice quiet meeting—"

"You think I'm overbearing, don't you?" said Jinx.

"You? Overbearing? You're not overbearing," said Simon. "I'm just afraid you'll frighten them all off like you did that poor ogre."

Jinx said nothing and walked on, fuming. It was bad enough that Wendell, Nick, Hilda, and Elfwyn could handle difficult discussions better than Jinx could. But when even Simon thought he was more tactful and diplomatic than you were, well, that was just discouraging.

The Melted Sword

Wendell persuaded Satya to come back, and Satya got in touch with the Mistletoe Alliance. She told them Simon needed every Qunthk book they could find. Books began to arrive in the night in the book room of the Samaran house, brought stealthily by shadowy figures who slipped away silently in the dark.

It was difficult to defeat someone who had a bottled lifeforce. In order to fight the Bonemaster, they had to find out exactly what he'd done to preserve his life, and how they could undo it. And there were the deathbindings, too—people who would die if the Bonemaster was killed. Those would need to be undone. These were Qunthk spells, and somewhere in all these books must be the answer to how to undo them.

Jinx hadn't found these books when he's searched the Temple library; members of the Mistletoe Alliance had hidden them. So much for knowledge being free to everyone, Jinx thought. But no, to be fair, he hadn't asked Satya for Qunthk books during his brief time at the Temple. He'd just asked for the Eldritch Tome, and she'd brought him that.

A committee formed to study the books and the Eldritch Tome. It met in the front room of Simon's house in Samara, all day and sometimes late into the night. Mainly it consisted of Jinx, Simon, Satya, and Malthus. The people in Simon's house got very nervous each time the werewolf passed through the kitchen.

Satya was rather cold to Jinx.

Jinx wasn't much help on the committee. He could read Qunthk better than Malthus and Satya could. But the books were written intentionally to confuse, and Jinx got more confused than anyone. Besides, he hated sitting still for hours on end to study.

Simon took charge of organizing the Urwish army. He divided it into sections, with each section under a leader. Jinx was surprised and offended that one of the leaders was Cottawilda.

"People listen to her," said Simon with a shrug. "And she's experienced in battle."

"She's evil," said Jinx.

"That's really beside the point," said Simon. "If any-thing, it may help."

Most of the men, women, and creatures who made up the Urwish army were away fighting, in their newly established sections. Simon's house was mainly occupied by babies and children, and a few parents to look after them. Things got fairly chaotic. Every now and then Simon would come into the kitchen and scowl, which made silence fall instantly.

Much of the time, Simon was away via the doorpaths, giving orders to the section leaders. Sometimes he took Elfwyn with him. People seemed to prefer getting their orders from the Truthspeaker.

Meanwhile, Jinx went in search of the person setting the forest fires.

It wasn't that difficult. The trees had labeled the fire-starter a Terror, and they kept track of Terrors.

The man was small, slightly built, and dressed in a red uniform. He had a face that put Jinx in mind of an angry rabbit, and pale hair that stuck out like porcupine quills. Jinx found him a few yards off the path, crouched over a pile of dried leaves, twigs, and branches, trying to strike a spark with a tinderbox.

It was one of those times when Jinx probably shouldn't have let his temper get the better of him. There were probably a lot of better things he could have done than charge in and punch the man in the face, which was what he did.

The rabbity man was quick. He whipped out a sword, spun around, and slashed at Jinx, who stumbled over backward in his haste to get out of its way. The man came at Jinx again, and Jinx froze his clothes.

Unfortunately this caused the man to fall toward Jinx, sword and all. Jinx rolled out of the way. Then he made a grab for the sword, but the rabbity man was still gripping it tightly, and had just enough arm movement to take another slash at Jinx. Jinx was barely able to dodge it.

Thinking fast, Jinx sent fire into the sword. The man yelped and dropped it. Leaves began to smoke where it landed. Jinx drew the fire into himself and kicked the sword out of the way.

During all of this, it never occurred to Jinx to draw his belt knife. He hadn't been brought up to stick sharp blades into people. It doesn't come naturally to most folks.

"Who are you?" Jinx demanded.

"Don't have to say." The man's voice was rabbity, too.

"Are you one of King Rufus's soldiers?"

"Don't have to say. Release me, foul wizard!"

"No," said Jinx. "You didn't even ask nicely."

The rabbity man was struggling furiously, trying to get out of his frozen clothes. They had been made for a much bigger man, and Jinx realized he might actually succeed.

And there was still the sword, which only one of them knew how to use.

Jinx picked up the sword and, concentrating very carefully, melted the blade. He'd never done anything quite this fiddly with the fire before. The trick was not to let the hilt, which he was holding, heat up, and not to let the blade melt fast enough to drip its deadly heat onto the forest floor. Or onto his fingers.

Just enough to reduce the blade to a misshapen blob. There. And take the fire out and cool it down and . . . it occurred to Jinx that it would be rather a nice touch to hand it back to the soldier, so he did.

It was very effective. Jinx felt he was getting the hang of this diplomacy stuff. The man gibbered with terror.

"You don't want to end up looking like that, do you?" said Jinx.

The man shook his head, once and emphatically.

"So tell me your name, and who told you to set these fires."

"B-Bagnell of Bragwood," said the rabbity man. "King Rufus wants the forest burned. Says it'll get rid of all the monsters and brigands, and ready the land up for farming by honest folks."

"Well, that shows you how wrong a king can be," said Jinx. "These fires you're setting—they're not even burning for very long."

Bagnell looked disappointed. "You sure?"

"Yes," said Jinx. "They all get put out within an hour or so. You've burned a lot of land, but compared to the size of the forest—hardly anything, really."

"Oh." A crawling purple cloud of trepidation. "That's not good."

"Not from our point of view either," said Jinx.

"The king will kill me," said Bagnell. He thought about this for a minute. "Er, unless you're going to."

Killing Bagnell would be neat and convenient. It would solve the problem of the fires. It would be a long time before King Rufus of Bragwood knew his orders weren't being carried out.

It would also mean touching the Path of Ice. Jinx shuddered, as if the ice were actually climbing his legs again.

Bagnell struggled frantically, trying and failing to sit up in his frozen clothes.

"No, I don't think I'll kill you," said Jinx.

The purple fear diminished, but not completely. "Will you let me sit up?"

And Jinx realized that he'd been rather enjoying watching Bagnell struggle, unable to sit, stand, or lie in his frozen clothes. It wasn't much of an exchange for all the trees killed in the fire, but it was some small compensation. He'd been using magic the way the wizards had used it on him. And that was touching the ice too, in a way.

Jinx undid the clothes-freezing spell and let Bagnell sit

up. Jinx braced himself for the next attack. But Bagnell stayed sitting, and stared at the hilt of his sword and the molten lump on top of it.

"You can go," Jinx decided. "On condition that you go west, and keep going. You're not to rejoin the Bragwood army."

"But that would be desertion! You know what Rufus the Ruthless does to deserters?"

Jinx sighed. "I think I have a general idea, yes."

"He puts them in barrels stuck about with nails and—"

"Well, then don't stop when you get to Bragwood," said Jinx. "Just keep walking."

"Can't I stay in the forest?"

"No," said Jinx. He was starting to feel sorry for this idiot. "Because the forest will probably try to kill you. I'm surprised it hasn't already."

Bagnell's thoughts whirred, as if he were summing up several recent events. His mouth formed an O of surprise.

"Look, I'll try to explain to the trees that you're leaving," said Jinx. "They might let you go, if I ask them. I can't guarantee it, though. Just stick to the path. Keep going west. Don't even sleep off the path. *Especially* don't sleep off the path. Oh, and don't light any fires. Not even to cook with."

Bagnell was nodding frantic agreement. He was still

staring at the lump of metal in his hand.

Jinx was about to ask for it back—it would make at least one ax head, and possibly two. Then he remembered what he'd learned from Witch Seymour about the value of rumors.

"You can keep that," said Jinx. "As a souvenir of the Urwald."

Satya's map of the Urwald was spread out on the workbench, along with various books in Qunthk. Besides the committee, Wendell and Elfwyn were there. Satya listened with the slight frown she always wore when trying to understand Urwish.

"The Bonemaster's bottled life is connected to the Path of Ice," said Simon.

"It's a wick," said Jinx.

"The Bonemaster is the wick," said Malthus.

Jinx remembered what he'd learned on the Paths. "I think they're both part of the wick." Just like Jinx and the Urwald were both part of the Path of Fire.

"Hm," said the werewolf. "At any rate, he's put his lifeforce into the bottle that you saw in his lair."

"His cellar," said Elfwyn.

"His crypt," said Jinx.

The werewolf waved aside these quibbles with a yellow-clawed hand. "The bottle is rooted to the Path of Ice. When you were there, when you saw it before, did it have a cork in it?"

"I don't remember," said Jinx.

"Yes," said Elfwyn.

"Are you su—" The werewolf stopped himself, politely.

"Yes, I'm sure," said Elfwyn. "There *was* a cork, but it's gone now. Or at least, if it's still there, I couldn't see it. It could be hidden in that mess of . . . things."

"What sort—" Wendell began, and stopped.

"They were like ribbons," said Elfwyn.

"Ghost-ribbons," said Jinx. "They were blue, and they looked like smoke."

"And they moved," said Elfwyn. "As if they were alive."

"It was like the bottle was made of them," said Jinx. "We didn't really see an actual bottle at all."

"There may have been an ordinary bottle there at one time," said Malthus. "But it's possible that, at this point, it's made of ice."

"Ice with a capital I?" said Jinx. "As in Path of?"

"Precisely," said the werewolf.

"There's no way you can get to it," said Simon abruptly. His thoughts were orange and blue and worried.

"I'm going to go up the path—" Jinx began.

"And boom, you end up in the bottle," said Simon.

"How—"

"Because it's not corked," said Simon, rapping an open

book with his knuckle. "It's a conduit between the Path of Ice and the Bonemaster himself. He must have uncorked the bottle after you destroyed his other power source."

"When you broke all those little bottles," said Elfwyn.

Jinx winced at the memory. He'd broken most of himself, too.

"The bottle's part of the path now," said Satya, speaking in Samaran and not looking at Jinx. She was still mad at him. "You'll just be drawn into it when you come up the Path of Ice."

"But if I get up there—" Jinx began.

"It's out of the question," said Simon. "I forbid you to go."

Jinx gritted his teeth. He'd missed Simon, but he hadn't missed being bossed around. And he knew that he was more powerful than Simon. Quite aside from the fact that Simon couldn't even do magic anymore.

"If the bottle were corked, however—" said Malthus.

"What, you mean a plain, ordinary cork?" Jinx picked up a bottle from Simon's workbench. The bottle was blue and shaped like a fish. He worked the cork out of it. "Like this?"

Malthus reached for the cork, and held it between two claws. "Not precisely."

"It's a spell," said Satya shortly.

"Could I do it?" said Elfwyn.

"I suppose." Simon frowned at one of the Qunthk books. "The cork spell doesn't look that complicated." (Elfwyn fumed.) "But there'd be no point, because the cork would have to be put in before Jinx got there, and—"

"I can do that," said Elfwyn.

"No," said Jinx and Simon together.

But it was Jinx that Elfwyn chose to fold her arms and glare at.

"Anyway," said Jinx, looking away from the glare, which was rather piercing, "you couldn't even touch the bottle. Remember how it shot sparks . . ."

"I wouldn't have to touch it," she said. "Watch."

The cork floated out of Malthus's hand, flew through the air, and swooped back into the neck of the fish-shaped bottle.

"Very nice," said Simon. "But the bottle is in in the Bonemaster's dungeon. And you are not."

"I'll go there," said Elfwyn. "He'll let me in. He likes me."

"Excuse me," said Wendell. "But you were there for a year, and then you came here. He must know that, surely. What makes you think—"

"No questions," Satya said. She and Elfwyn seemed to have made up their quarrel. In fact, Jinx had seen them earlier, huddled over a bunch of mistletoe leaves and having an earnest discussion.

"He's not going to believe you this time," said Jinx. "If you go back, he'll kill you."

"I don't think he will," said Elfwyn.

"Could you kill him?" Simon demanded.

"N-no," said Elfwyn. "But—"

"Why not?" said Simon.

"Because he trusts me! Stop asking me questions."

"He doesn't trust anybody."

"He's been kind to me," said Elfwyn. "And I know he's evil and I know he's done horrible things, and I think somebody should kill him and—and I wish I could kill him."

"Never wish that," said Simon.

"Anyway, Sophie's there," said Elfwyn. "Somebody has to go in and tell Sophie—"

"The Bonemaster's got the Crimson Grimoire now," said Jinx. "He can bottle your life. All he needs is . . ." Jinx stopped. All the Bonemaster needed was a human to sacrifice. And he had Sophie.

Jinx looked at Simon and decided not to say that.

"The way that werewolves would handle this," said Malthus, "would be to let the person who had the greatest chance of success, try."

"And that would be me," said Elfwyn firmly.

"But we're not werewolves," said Jinx.

"Excuse me. Some of us are," said Malthus.

"That's what the Mistletoe Alliance would do as well," said Satya, with a meaningful look at Simon.

Jinx looked at Elfwyn and saw the grim, green determination that meant there was no point in arguing with her. He looked at Wendell. He looked at all of the others in turn. He saw that everybody had thought about Sophie and the human sacrifice.

"Maybe I could go up the Path of Ice anyway," said Jinx, "and not get stuck in the bottle, even if it is uncorked. I mean, no one knows for sure, do—"

"Yes," Simon snapped. "Someone knows for sure. I do."

"Then we have to let Elfwyn go," said Jinx.

"What do you mean, *let* her?" Satya demanded.

Jinx shrugged. "Well, she's going to go anyway. We can't talk her out of it."

"Fine," said Simon. "Fine. So everybody's going off to get killed by the Bonemaster, in order. Right." He stabbed the workbench with a finger. "Jinx goes first, down the Path of Fire and up the Path of Ice." Another stab. "Then the magicians—"

"I go as soon as Jinx does," said Elfwyn. "So that I can be at Bonesocket and cork the bottle before Jinx gets there."

"Or get killed in the attempt," said Simon. "Fine. Jinx goes"—stab—"then you go"—stab—"then the magicians go—"

"How will the magicians know when to go?" said Wendell.

"Wait." Elfwyn stood up. "Make the plan without me, please. And when you're done, come and tell me, and—"

"Lie to you," said Wendell.

"Yes," said Elfwyn. She left.

"The magicians should attack just before Jinx reaches the dungeon," said Malthus. "Their attack will distract the Bonemaster, enabling Elfwyn—"

"If she's still alive," said Simon.

"If she's still alive, to go down and cork the bottle, leave some sort of signal for Jinx that it's been done—"

"Where's Sophie meanwhile?" asked Jinx.

"I'll go in and get her while the magicians are attacking," said Simon.

"But you can't—"

Simon gave him a look, and Jinx shut up.

"It's just that I don't understand how you'll know when Jinx arrives," said Wendell apologetically.

They all looked at Wendell.

"Oh," said Jinx.

"Because once you get on the path," said Wendell, "time is different for you. So unless there was some way for you to send a signal, like through the Farseeing Window, for example—"

"The aviot," said Satya. "You can have people watch

the window, and Jinx can—I don't know, wave a sock or something when he's arrived."

"And I was thinking," said Wendell, "that maybe we could plant some sort of fake truths on Elfwyn to protect her and Sophie?"

"Like that Simon's done deathbindings and tied the Bonemaster's death to theirs," Satya suggested.

"That's a good idea," said Jinx.

Satya actually looked at him, and nodded an acknowledgment.

That reminded Jinx. "What about the deathbindings? The ones the Bonemaster's done? All the people that will die when he does. Did you guys find anything about that?"

"There's only this," said Malthus.

Jinx peered at the Qunthk words, folded inside each other.

Let death be bound in ice, ever circling. Fly free
to the flame when the tie is undone.

"The usual cryptic stuff," said Simon.

Jinx nodded.

It all seemed settled, then. Except for his part, which he wasn't sure he understood all that well. The Paths, he ought to be able to handle those okay; he'd done it before. But—

"What am I supposed to do with the bottle once I get ahold of it?" he asked.

Malthus, Satya, and Simon looked at each other. They looked at the books spread out on the workbench. They looked at each other again.

"That," said Malthus, "is what we're more or less relying on you to figure out."

Captured by Elves

Jinx was back on the Paths of Fire and Ice. They looked nothing like they had before, but he'd expected that. The Elf Princess had told him he couldn't travel the same path twice.

He had walked for what seemed like forever. He'd stopped to eat several times. He passed through subterranean caves and caverns, fields and mountains, and skirted around the edge of a lake full of glowing silver mist. Nothing lived in it. Nothing lived anywhere.

He was lost.

Before, getting somewhere on the Paths had ultimately turned out to be a matter of knowing where he was going.

But now, even though he was perfectly well aware of his destination—Bonesocket—nothing he did seemed to take him there.

There was no use fighting it any longer. He was going to have to ask directions.

Getting himself back to the Eldritch Depths was easy, and he was once more ushered into the presence of the Elf Princess. This time she sat on a throne made of pink quartz and studded with emeralds.

"Has a millennium passed already?" she asked, amused. "You've kept rather well, for an organic creature."

Jinx explained his problem.

"Ah," said the Elf Princess. "You cannot reach Bone-socket because you cannot travel the Path of Ice. I'd have thought you'd have realized that."

"But I traveled it before!"

The Princess put a finger to the corner of her perfect blue mouth. "If you traveled it, it was the Path of Fire."

"But I touched the ice!"

"Touched it, perhaps. But if you want to travel the Path of Ice to its end, you must embrace the ice."

"What, you mean do deathforce magic or something? I'm not going to do that."

"What happened when you touched the ice?" she asked.

Jinx looked down at the floor, which was tiled in

alternating squares of jade and carnelian.

"You'd rather not say. You humans like to think that evil is something outside of you, don't you? But evil is right . . . here. . . ." She pointed.

"In my stomach?" said Jinx.

She flickered blue annoyance. "In your heart."

"That's my stomach."

"*Anyway,*" said the Elf Princess. "Whatever happened when you touched the ice, you must embrace it, or you cannot walk the path. And that, dear human, is all the help I intend to give you. It's far more than I've given most humans—"

"Well, you kill most humans, right?" said Jinx. "If you meet them, I mean."

"Not always," said the Princess. "In fact, before you go, there's something you ought to see."

The Princess was burbling amusement. Jinx felt a sudden cold terror.

They left the throne room and crossed an agate floor to a deep lake of green glass. Beside it was a crystal waterfall, icy and unmoving. On the shore, amid a thicket of beryls and sapphires, sat Simon.

Jinx stared. "What are you doing here?"

Simon scowled under a lavender cloud of embarrassment. "Ask her."

"You let yourself be captured by elves?" Jinx demanded.

"You wait till it happens to you," said Simon. "Then tell me how much 'let' there is about it."

But I haven't lost my magic, Jinx thought. And you have. And now you can be captured by elves, just like . . . anybody. It was an awful thought.

"I only just left you—" Jinx began, and stopped. Time was different down here. "I only just left you, and you've already gone and gotten yourself stolen by elves! You . . . you . . . you idiot!"

"Don't you call me names, boy!" Simon struggled to stand, and Jinx saw that the wizard's feet were completely encased in the outcroppings of gems.

Jinx looked closer. "Are you stuck to the floor or something? Hold on." He started to feel his way into the spell.

Only there wasn't a spell. There was only rock. Jinx tried to send fire into the gems, and Simon yelped in pain.

"Your magic won't work," said the Princess. "Not without damaging that person."

She was right. He couldn't melt the rock without burning Simon's legs off. Of all the— "I just can't believe you went and got yourself captured again!" said Jinx. "As soon as I turn my back! You know what your problem is? You think you can do anything!"

"*I* think I can do anything?" said Simon. "I'm not the one who thinks he can traipse up the Path of Ice into Bonesocket!"

"I don't walk out of the house and get myself captured

by elves when people are counting on me!" said Jinx. "You—" There just wasn't a word strong enough to express his frustration. Not in any language.

"You care about him very much, don't you?" The Elf Princess sounded merely curious.

Jinx looked away, furious. Urwalders didn't say things like that. "Let him go."

"When you embrace the ice," said the Elf Princess, "you may like it."

"Let Simon go," said Jinx.

"If you found a way to embrace both fire and ice together—"

"It's not possible," said Simon.

"—then you would become very powerful. You would reign supreme. We don't want that. Therefore, we engaged in a very crude, human sort of ploy."

"Jinx, just go," said Simon. "Sophie and Elfwyn are at Bonesocket."

"But—"

"And you have a chance to defeat him," said Simon. "Just make sure that, if you touch the bottle, you're embracing the ice when you do it. I've been thinking about that. It's very important."

"How do I embrace the ice?" said Jinx.

"What happened when you touched the ice?" said Simon.

"I . . . It . . . I . . ." Jinx didn't want to say.

"You wanted to kill people," said Simon.

"It made me *think* that I did," said Jinx. "I don't really."

"Very admirable," said Simon. "Get over it. To get to the Bonemaster's dungeon, you're going to have to want to kill him."

"And then," said the Princess, "you will have ice and be within reach of fire. You could become all-powerful."

"That's not true," said Simon. "To embrace the ice, you're going to have to let go of the fire."

Jinx shrugged. "Okay. All I want is to defeat the Bone-master and—"

"And seize his power?" said the Princess.

"No!"

"But the temptation will be there," said the Princess. "It is the nature of organic beings to want more, when they already have enough. When I see that you have done as you say, and given up the power of ice, I will return this person to you."

Jinx turned to Simon. "I can come back here with an ax—"

"Beneath the gems is adamantine," said the Princess. "Unless you intend to chop off this person's legs, it will avail you nothing."

"Just go," said Simon. "Remember what I said. Let go of the fire. And hurry up! He's got Sophie, Elfwyn, and the Crimson Grimoire. And who knows how long this little conversation has really lasted?"

Oh. Right.

"Okay. But don't eat anything," said Jinx anxiously. "And don't drink anything. And—"

"You think I don't know that?" said Simon. "Go."

～ ✎ ✐

Right. Jinx stood on the path, and looked up a steep slope of ice. He felt as if he'd gazed at hundreds of these in the last few—days? Hours? Months? There was no way of knowing. He had more than enough fire in him to melt it, as he'd done the others.

Instead, according to the Elf Princess, he had to embrace it.

"All right," he said. "I don't want the Bonemaster to take up rose gardening or needlepoint. I don't want him to develop other interests and get out of the skull-and-bones business."

He took a deep breath.

"I want him to die."

And he began climbing.

It was easy. His boots gripped the ice as if it had been granite.

～ ✎ ✐

It seemed like only a few minutes later that he was staring up at the end of the Path of Ice.

He could see the underside of the table that stood in

the crypt under Bonesocket. And, weirdly, as if he were seeing two things at once, the table was both there and not there, and through it he could see the bottle.

Ribbons of smoke writhed around the bottle, as if in pain.

He couldn't see if there was a cork in it.

But he could see, lying under the table, a red hooded cloak . . . Elfwyn's signal. She'd corked the bottle.

Either that, or the Bonemaster had forced her to tell him what she was doing. In which case the signal was a trap.

Jinx took from his pocket a red-and-blue-striped sock. He waved it around. He waved it up, he waved it down. He went on waving it, until it suddenly occurred to him that he had no idea how much time was passing for the people peering into the Farseeing Window. He had to assume that whoever was watching had seen the signal and relayed the message, and that the magicians had leapt through the new doorpath Jinx had made, onto Bonesocket Island, and were attacking.

Jinx climbed up through the floor, and crawled out from under the table. He was standing now in the cavern under Bonesocket. It smelled of mold and graves. He looked up the corridor that was the other entrance to the chamber. It was lined with the bones of the Bonemaster's victims.

Remember that.

Hundreds of victims. Maybe thousands. Over how many years, and in how many places?

Anyway, enough to keep Jinx on the Path of Ice. He had to keep wanting the Bonemaster dead, or he wouldn't be able to touch the bottle.

He turned around and faced it.

The ribbons twisting around it slithered and jerked like snakes in agony. They looped over and under each other; they squirmed. They flailed. They went round and round the bottle in a mad, wriggling orbit.

He was just about to reach for the bottle when he heard the distant grate of stone on stone.

He knew what it was. Someone was opening the trap door that led from Bonesocket to the crypt.

Skeletons and Deathbindings

There were footsteps in the distance, and then the creak of a door opening. Heavy, booted feet thudded down the skull-lined corridor. Jinx stood behind the table and braced himself. *He wanted the Bonemaster dead.*

The Bonemaster strode into the chamber. "You! How did you get in here?"

Before Jinx could answer, more running feet rang in the corridor. Jinx groaned inwardly as Elfwyn burst into the room.

"Leave him to me!" Jinx yelled.

Elfwyn flung a spell at the Bonemaster that was purple and flashed. Jinx ducked. The Bonemaster fell to the ground as the flash hit him. Then Elfwyn spread her arms, flapped them, and began running round and round the chamber clucking like a chicken.

The Bonemaster picked himself up. "I did warn you, my dear."

"Bawk, bawk, bawk!" said Elfwyn, flapping madly. Her head bobbed back and forth as she ran.

Jinx tried to set the Bonemaster on fire, but was too wrapped up in ice somehow to do it. He couldn't find the fire.

Then Sophie came running in, throwing things at the Bonemaster—Jinx saw a clay jar, a candlestick, and a hammer sail through the air. The Bonemaster dodged.

Elfwyn stretched her neck out. "BAWWK! Buckbuckbuck bawk!"

The Bonemaster cast a spell, and Sophie flew to the wall and stuck firmly, struggling like a fly in honey.

"Jinx!" she cried. "Remember what it said in the Eldritch Tome!"

"The Eldritch Tome you assured me didn't exist?" the Bonemaster asked her. "What did it say?"

Jinx tried again to summon fire to throw at the Bonemaster. But Simon had been right . . . the fire was impossibly out of reach now. The ice didn't want fire; fire melted ice.

He tried to think of a language the Bonemaster wouldn't

know—Herwa, maybe? "What did it say?" he demanded in Herwa.

"'Let death be bound in ice, ever circling. Fly free to the flame when the tie is undone,'" said Sophie, in Herwa, and, in Jinx's opinion, unhelpfully.

"It's discourteous," said the Bonemaster, in the same language, "to speak a language that everyone present doesn't understand." He raised a fist to cast a spell at Jinx. "I doubt Elfwyn knows Herwa."

"Anyway, I don't know what you mean!" Jinx yelled, diving behind the table as the Bonemaster sent a flash of black lightning at him. The bottle on the table rocked dangerously. Jinx looked up at the circling ribbons.

"*Those* are the deathbindings!" Sophie said. "As close to *his* life as possible! But no one can touch them and live!"

"You mean—oh." Jinx made sure he was still firmly fixed on the Path of Ice. "I think I—" No, there was no time to argue. Hopefully she was wrong about that last bit. He held his breath, and reached out and grabbed a ribbon as it sped past.

He caught it, just for a moment, then it jerked and squirmed out of his grasp and went on circling the bottle. But in the second he'd touched it, an image of Simon came into his head—not a face, but the things that were really Simon, the jagged flashes of orange, the warm blue cloud.

Sophie was right. Each ribbon was a deathbinding. One

of them was Simon's. One was probably his own. Elfwyn and Sophie were sure to have ribbons. Reven would have one . . .

The Bonemaster, meanwhile, had been readying another spell. A green flash hit Jinx, a shock worse than touching ice-glass. It threw him across the room. Jinx hit the stone wall and everything went wavery and gray for a moment.

He was surprised Sophie even knew the words she called the Bonemaster.

"Don't overestimate your value as a hostage," the Bonemaster told her.

Elfwyn charged at the Bonemaster, neck out, squawking rapidly.

Jinx took advantage of the distraction to get up and stagger back to the table. He grabbed a ribbon and held on tight. Remembering that he wanted the Bonemaster dead—Path of Ice, Path of Ice—he wrenched the writhing, squiggling thing free of the mass.

It leapt away from him, and for a moment they all watched it twist and spin in the air before it burst into blue flame and vanished.

"That was Reven," said Jinx. "I guess you bound his death to yours when you held us captive."

"I didn't need that young fool anyway," said the Bonemaster. "Rufus and Bluetooth will take care of him for me. You realize that—"

"None of those kings would have been able to get so far into the Urwald if you hadn't sealed the Paths of Fire and Ice," said Jinx.

"Precisely so," said the Bonemaster.

Jinx could feel Elfwyn frantically trying, between flaps and squawks, to undo the spell that held Sophie. She seemed to be doing the magic right, but couldn't match the Bonemaster's vast deathforce power, drawn from the Path of Ice. Jinx felt his way into the spell. But power was giving him trouble. He was used to fire, and it was still *there*, but it was hard to find it through the deathforce ice. And as for the fire inside him, it was barely there at all.

Sophie let out a muffled gasp and began to turn purple. Jinx recognized the spell—the Bonemaster was shrinking her clothes, squeezing the breath out of her. Angrily Jinx reached into the spell and tried to reverse it. The trouble was he couldn't get ahold of the lifeforce power, because he seemed to be stuck in the deathforce ice: The more the Bonemaster hurt Sophie, the more Jinx wanted him dead.

So Jinx used deathforce and undid the squeezing spell.

He was feeling his way into the stuck-to-the-wall spell when the Bonemaster spun around and cast a spell that sent Jinx flying through the air. Jinx hit the wall hard and slid to the floor. He lay there stunned, and watched Elfwyn free herself and Sophie. Jinx frantically tried to use KnIP to dig a hole under the Bonemaster's feet, but it was too slow.

"Bawkbawkbawkbawk!" cried Elfwyn warningly.

There came a ripping, rending sound from the corridor. Jinx watched, transfixed, as the bones and skulls tore themselves free of the walls and moved toward the chamber, clanking and assembling themselves as they came.

Then the chamber was full of skeletons, hundreds of skeletons, dancing and rattling, kicking and swinging. They were all coming at Jinx. Sophie, meanwhile, was stuck back to the wall.

Elfwyn gave another squawk of warning. There was a swooshing sound, and the Bonemaster's hired ghoul flew into the room, its tubular greenish-white mouth flexing, its huge eyes searching for victims. Ghouls sucked people's brains out through their eyeballs. The ghoul swooped toward Sophie . . .

"Set the ghoul on fire!" Jinx yelled. He couldn't do it himself, he was nearly buried in skeletons and he couldn't find the fire. They clawed at his eyes and encircled his throat with bony hands. Their horrible cold arms and legs battered at him. He punched and kicked, and they flew to pieces, but there were always more coming at him.

Through the crowding skulls and vertebrae, he could see that the ghoul was aflame. Its low, moany wails filled the chamber. The Bonemaster was turned toward Sophie, ready to cast a spell, and Elfwyn was flapping and squawking and trying to summon a spell of her own.

Jinx charged through the skeletons, sending bones flying everywhere, and grabbed the bottle from the table.

It was like grabbing an armful of ice-cold electric eels. Jinx had to cling to the Path of Ice—plant his thoughts firmly on it—to keep the bottle from sending horrible shocks through his body, and at the same time he had to fight to keep the bottle from wriggling out of his arms.

He kicked over the table. He could see the gaping hole in the floor that led to the Path of Ice. He just hoped the Bonemaster could see it too.

"Hey, Bonemaster!" he yelled. "I've got your life!"

He jumped down the hole.

Jinx hit the ice and slid, clutching the bottle. He grabbed a ribbon of smoke and pulled it loose as he fell, set it free, and watched it flame. It was someone he didn't recognize, a person with soft, bewildered purple thoughts.

He pulled another ribbon loose—where was the Bonemaster? He was supposed to follow Jinx, not stay behind and keep attacking Elfwyn and Sophie—

The ribbon floated free with shocking-pink splashes of joy. Another stranger. The ribbon flamed and vanished. The next ribbon—

Something slammed into Jinx, almost knocking the bottle out of his grip. It was the Bonemaster. Jinx and the Bonemaster zipped down the slope, tumbling over and over as they wrestled for the bottle. They fought as if they weren't magicians—they kicked and punched, and meanwhile Jinx managed to wrest another ribbon free with his teeth. This one was brown and blue, wreathed in silver—Sophie! So that was one less person he had to worry about. (If you didn't count that he'd left her being attacked by skeletons and a burning ghoul.)

Jinx managed to wrap himself around the bottle. The Bonemaster's fists and feet hammered every part of Jinx that they could reach. Jinx was able to free two more ribbons—both strangers to him—as he kicked back.

He tried to set the Bonemaster on fire. But it was impossible—not a flicker of flame came to his call. He was too firmly on the Path of Ice. And he didn't dare leave it while he had the bottle in his hands.

He felt a squeezing sensation—the Bonemaster was shrinking his clothes. Jinx undid the spell, and turned it back on the Bonemaster. The Bonemaster undid it, and slammed Jinx's head against the wall.

Jinx saw stars and black flashes. He could feel the Bonemaster tugging at the bottle. Jinx kneed him, hard, then kicked him away with both feet. The Bonemaster slid until he reached a flat space in the corridor.

Put up a ward, you idiot, Jinx told himself, and did so . . . a quick, messy ward that stayed with him as he slid.

He skidded down the last of the slope and bowled ward-first into the Bonemaster. The ward knocked the wizard flying.

The Bonemaster picked himself up. He stood there for a moment, his thumbs twitching, and Jinx could see from the whirring and slashing of the knives in his thoughts that he was working up a big spell.

Standing inside the ward, Jinx frantically grabbed handfuls of ribbons and threw them into the air. Colors and lights twisted and flashed in the air, then flamed out. One of the ribbons was orange and jagged on one side, warm and blue on the other—Simon. He'd freed Simon and Sophie from the deathbinding curse. That left only—

The Bonemaster threw the spell at Jinx.

It was a whole storm of spells. The first one froze the ward and shattered it, sending shards of magic flying every-where. The second froze Jinx so that he couldn't move. It wasn't the clothes-freezing spell; it was Jinx himself, cold and frozen and unable to blink or breathe. He could see, though—the Bonemaster's tight, pleased smile. And he could hear—a crackling sound as the ice of the corridor grew inward, from the ceiling and walls, toward him. And he could hear the thud of his own heart, which hadn't stopped yet, but would soon, and the swish of something coming down the steep slope behind him—

Which smashed into him, hard. If he hadn't been

frozen, he would have dropped the bottle. He crashed into the Bonemaster, and they zoomed the length of the flat space.

"BAWK! Buckbuckbuck BAWK!" cried Elfwyn, flapping her arms and stretching her neck. The three of them skidded and screeched down the next slope, Jinx frantically working his way into the spell the Bonemaster had cast on him. As soon as he'd undone enough to move his hands, he tore wildly at the last few ribbons on the bottle. He got Elfwyn's ribbon free—it was green woven through with blue. That was everyone he knew who'd been held captive by the Bonemaster, except himself. There were four ribbons left, and then three, and two, and one—

The last ribbon, deep green with angry red streaks, zipped free of the bottle and burned out in a bright green flash.

Jinx hadn't seen his own ribbon, which meant the Bonemaster had probably deathbound him somewhere else, in some other way. Drat!

Elfwyn pointed and clucked wildly.

The Bonemaster, fighting to regain his feet as he slid, was readying another spell. There was no time for Jinx to worry about his own deathbound life. Killing the Bonemaster was likely to prove fatal to Jinx.

So was not killing him, though.

There was nothing else for it. Concentrating hard, he

did three things at once.

He let go of the ice and reached for the fire, hard. He threw the bottle at the Bonemaster, harder still. And he sent all of the flame, all of the vast lifeforce of the Path of Fire into the bottle with all his might.

The bottle burst into flames and shattered into a million pieces.

Blue, ice-cold smoke washed over Jinx and Elfwyn. Flames filled the corridor—red flames, pale blue flames, deep green fire that crackled and rippled over Jinx's skin.

When the smoke cleared, Jinx saw the Bonemaster engulfed in an ice-blue column of fire. Then water from acres of ice came rushing down the path, sizzling. The flames around the Bonemaster fizzed and spat.

For a moment a cold white skeleton stood there. Lightning streaks of blue and green flame rippled up and down it, and then flickered out.

Then the skeleton flew apart, and, with a surprisingly quiet clatter, the bones slid away down the Path of Ice.

Bonesocket from Within

The second thing Jinx noticed was that he was still alive.

The first was that he was holding on tightly to Elfwyn. They were standing on a stone slope from which all ice had vanished.

"Sophie!" said Jinx. "Is Sophie—"

"*Bawk! Bawk! Bukka-bukka,*" Elfwyn replied.

Jinx felt his way into the spell. It was a nasty thing, and full of power. But he was able to undo it by drawing on the fire.

"She's okay," said Elfwyn. "I shrank the bones to the size of pins, and I put up a ward to keep her from coming after us, because I knew she couldn't walk the Paths."

"Neither could you," said Jinx.

"I had this." Elfwyn nodded at a sprig of tiny leaves pinned to her dress.

"Mistletoe?"

"It's supposed to connect lifeforce and deathforce. Satya told me it might work."

"It might not have!" said Jinx. "You could have been killed! You—"

"Oh, shut up," said Elfwyn. "I have just as much right to get myself killed as you do. Ouch! What are you doing?"

She pushed away from him.

"I just thought, if I could take the chicken curse off you, then maybe I could get rid of your truthspeaking curse as well." But he couldn't—it wasn't like the Bonemaster's spell. It was so completely intertwined with Elfwyn that he could hardly see where Elfwyn ended and the curse began.

"You can't," said Elfwyn flatly. "It's a witch's curse, and it's old. You heard what my grandmother said. It's part of me, like my skeleton."

At that they both looked down the corridor, to where the last bits of the Bonemaster had rattled away.

"That was weird," said Jinx.

"Yes," said Elfwyn.

"Do you think—" Jinx caught himself. "I hope he's really gone now."

"I think he is," said Elfwyn.

"I thought I was going to die," said Jinx.

"When he froze you. It was awful. You turned blue, and bits of you looked like ice. I was trying to—"

"No, well, that too," said Jinx. "But also because I didn't undo my deathbinding. Maybe he didn't do one on me."

"The ribbons?" said Elfwyn. "You did, I saw you. You undid me, and a woman who used to live in Butterwood Clearing, and a couple other people, and then you undid yourself last of all."

Jinx thought of that last ribbon he'd pulled off the bottle. Did he really look like that? The deep green was okay. When he did magic, it often seemed that color. But what were all those jagged red slashes? "Was I—" Jinx caught himself in time. "I wonder if I was green and red."

"No, you just looked like you," said Elfwyn. "I mean not you on the outside, but you the way you are."

She flopped blue-white embarrassment.

"Overbearing?" said Jinx.

"No, of course not," said Elfwyn. "That was a question. You're not overbearing, you're just . . . forthright."

"That almost sounds like a good thing," said Jinx.

"Of course it is." For some reason Elfwyn's face turned red. "You're really . . ."

She trailed off.

"Really what?" said Jinx.

"Nice," said Elfwyn, turning even redder. "But that was a question, and that's not nice."

"Sorry," said Jinx.

He was grateful for his ability to see feelings. Because right now, if he didn't know better, he might have thought she was thinking pink fluffy thoughts about him. And then he might have made a horrible mistake, and said or done something that would not have turned out well. Possibly even stuck his face at her and gotten bitten.

"Did the Bonemaster—" Jinx had a ton of questions, but this was Elfwyn. "Um, I'd like it if you told me what happened while you were at the Bonemaster's house."

"He put the chicken curse on me as soon as I got there," she said. "He told me it would be triggered if I acted against him. And he'd done something to the doors and windows—there was no way out of the house at all. He'd already done it when I got there, so that Sophie wouldn't escape. She tried, of course."

"Why— I mean. He didn't bottle your—"

"No," said Elfwyn. "He doesn't use ghost-roots, so he would have had to kill Sophie to bottle my lifeforce, and he wanted her as a hostage. For now, anyway."

"How long—" Jinx began, and stopped.

"It's been about two months since you went under-ground," said Elfwyn. "Or it had been, anyway."

They didn't know how much time had passed since they'd left the Bonemaster's crypt, of course.

"When the magicians attacked Bonesocket—"

"Oh, yes. That went all right," said Elfwyn. "At first. They were wonderful, all flying pink goo and dragons. The Bonemaster rushed outside to fight them, but he left us locked up in the house of course, and then after a minute, he came running back in, and . . ." Elfwyn trailed off into a deep blue cloud of embarrassment.

"He asked you if the attack was just a distraction," said Jinx.

"Pretty much," said Elfwyn.

"And he asked you what was really going on."

"I'm sorry," said Elfwyn. "Unfortunately, I'd figured most of it out."

Jinx shrugged. "It came out all right in the end."

"*And* I saved your life," Elfwyn pointed out. "When I came down that icy slope and knocked you both down."

"Oh, right," said Jinx. "Thanks."

"You're welcome," said Elfwyn. "Thank you for taking the chicken spell off me."

"No problem," said Jinx.

"It was horrible." She shuddered. "I couldn't stop flapping. I must have looked like an absolute idiot."

"No, you looked nice." The color of her thoughts told Jinx this was the wrong thing to say, so he hurried to fix it. "I mean, you always look nice, even like right now when your face is dirty and your hair is—"

The color of her thoughts was not getting any pleasanter. He shut up.

"Shall we go back up?" she asked.

"First we have to go get Simon," said Jinx, and explained.

"Oh, no," said Elfwyn. "I hope she'll give him back."

"She said she would."

"*If* she was sure you weren't going to take over the Bonemaster's power," said Elfwyn. "But why would she be sure of that now? It seems like she'd think just the opposite."

Suddenly Jinx remembered something. "She said people drift away. We'd better hurry."

Simon glowed bright blue relief when he saw Jinx and Elfwyn. He struggled to his feet, tottering inside his prison of sapphires. "Where's Sophie?"

"At Bonesocket," said Elfwyn. "She's— I think she's all right."

"We defeated the Bonemaster," said Jinx.

The Elf Princess arched her beautiful eyebrows. "Defeated him? Does he know he's been defeated?"

"I don't know if he knows or not," said Jinx. "He's dead."

The Elf Princess looked startled. "Are you sure?"

"Pretty sure," said Jinx. "He turned into a skeleton and then he went all to pieces."

"Tell me everything that happened," said Simon.

Jinx did, with Elfwyn filling in the parts he hadn't seen.

Simon looked worried. "You didn't kill the Bonemaster. You understand that? You broke a spell that he'd created himself."

Jinx shrugged. "Anyway, it's done." He turned to the Princess. "So now you have to let Simon go."

"I don't think so," said the Princess.

"But I confronted the Bonemaster, and I, well—killed him—"

"You didn't kill him," Simon said firmly. "His own magic killed him."

Jinx knew Simon was trying to make him feel better. But Jinx didn't actually feel bad about killing the Bonemaster. Not yet, anyway. He hoped he would, later. Right now what he felt about it was a sense of accomplishment, and this bothered him.

"And I didn't seize his power," said Jinx. "I had to embrace the ice, and as soon as I was done, I let go of it. No more ice."

"As I said, you are young," said the Princess. "You may change. You have walked both paths now, and achieved knowledge. You may decide to embrace the ice later on."

"And how long will it take until you realize I won't?" said Jinx.

"Not so very long." The Princess thought, prettily. "Perhaps a couple of centuries."

"What?" said Simon.

"You can't do that!" said Elfwyn.

"No way," said Jinx. "You're going back on what you said before."

"I didn't say how long I'd keep your friend hostage," said the Princess. "However, I am not an unreasonable elf. Let's say one hundred years."

"Let's not," said Simon.

"Let's say one hundred seconds," said Jinx.

"Elves are creatures of ice, aren't they?" said Elfwyn.

The Princess's perfect face was impassive, but Jinx caught the silver flicker of nervousness in her thoughts.

"That's right," said Jinx. "I don't need the Path of Ice to be dangerous to you, do I? All I need is fire. And I've got plenty of that."

The Princess had aeons of practice in controlling her expression, and it didn't falter. But her thoughts were definitely tending toward alarmed.

"Let him go," said Jinx. And then, because he didn't like the idea of himself as someone who barged in and threatened people, not even if they were elves and not even if they were holding his friends hostage, he added, "please."

"As a favor to you," said the Princess. "And as a reward for a job well done."

There was a crackling sound. Gems cascaded to the floor. Simon kicked them away, stiffly. He stomped his feet; Jinx supposed they must be all pins-and-needles.

"Thank you," said Jinx. And then he remembered that elves had taken his mother, and had *not* given her back. "And if you ever take anybody of mine again—no, if you ever take anybody of *anybody's* again—"

"*If* is a big word," said the Princess. "It is our tradition to take people."

"Well, make it a tradition not to," said Jinx. "Please. Or I'll make it a tradition to come down here with all the fire I can find."

The Elf Princess gave a tiny shudder. "How rude and importunate you organic beings are. If it's really that important to you, then I suppose we can agree to that temporarily. For *your* lifetime."

Jinx was surprised she'd conceded that much. "That'll do to start with."

"After all, you won't live long," said the Princess.

"In elf terms, she means," said Simon.

It was night when they reached the cave above the Glass Mountains—a warm, summer-smelling night.

"Can't you make a doorpath from up here?" Simon demanded.

"No. Not with just our knowledge," said Jinx.

"Then down below. With the trolls' knowledge."

"We don't want the trolls to have a doorpath to the clearings," said Jinx.

There was the horrible glass stairway to get down. Jinx hugged the mountainside and was grateful for the darkness that hid the drop.

Jinx and his companions picked their way through the sleeping, snoring troll town. Then they hurried down the Troll-way in the dark.

"We don't know how long we were down there," Jinx pointed out. He and Elfwyn were jogging to keep up with Simon's rapid strides. "Sophie might not be at Bonesocket anymore."

"Then we'll go home," said Simon. "You can go home now, if you want."

But Jinx didn't want. He wanted to see Bonesocket, devoid of the Bonemaster.

And Elfwyn didn't want to go home, either. So they stepped through the Doorway into the dark shadows of the Doorway Oak, and then through another arch and onto Bonesocket Island.

All the windows in Bonesocket were alight. People were strolling around the island in pairs and groups, talking. In the moonlight Jinx recognized some people from Simon's house, and some from Blacksmiths' Clearing. There were a few witches and wizards, too.

The front door stood open. Several butter churns were parked beside the steps.

There was a fire crackling in the great hall, and people were sitting around the Bonemaster's big table, eating and drinking. Jinx was glad to see that they weren't using the skull cups.

"Elfwyn!" someone called. It was a woman from Butterwood Clearing. Elfwyn went over to her. Jinx and Simon went looking for Sophie.

They found her upstairs, in the room where Simon had been imprisoned. The slab of ice was gone now. Instead there was a table spread with maps, and a chair, and Sophie, who jumped up when she saw them.

She stared at both of them. Then she stared at Simon. Then she hugged Jinx, embarrassingly. "Jinx, you're all right! I thought, when you vanished into that hole in the floor . . . Where's Elfwyn?"

"Downstairs," said Jinx. "She's fine. And this is Simon, you remember Simon? You must've married him at some point."

Sophie looked at Simon. Simon looked at her. Jinx hadn't really thought about it, but if he had, he would have expected that they would cry out in delight and rush into each other's arms. After all, they hadn't seen each other in three years.

Instead, there was this staring, and not a word or a smile. And their thoughts rippled with trepidation, and worry, and resentment.

And guilt. Jinx had no idea at first what the guilt was about, but then he remembered that Sophie had told Jinx to destroy the seal if he had to, and that Jinx had rescued Sophie from prison, instead of Simon doing it.

These feelings were knotted like cords, holding back the old silver-sweet stuff. The silver stuff glowed, as if it was trying to burn the cords away.

They both looked horribly dignified.

"I'm sorry you had to come here," said Simon.

"Oh, are you?" said Sophie.

"To the Urwald, I mean," said Simon.

"I'm sure you must be dreadfully sorry," said Sophie tightly.

"I mean," said Simon, "I know it's not what you wanted."

Really, Jinx could have shaken both of them. "You're both thinking the same things, if that's any help," he said.

They glared at him.

But the silver glow brightened anyway, and one of the cords holding it back snapped.

"What I wanted was to be with you," said Sophie.

"Oh," said Simon.

More cords snapped.

They smiled at each other tentatively.

Jinx got out of there before they could get any more embarrassing.

～ ↗ ～

He went down to the kitchen and found leftovers—part of a roast chicken, some bread and cheese, and some sort of applesauce made of dried apples. There was no sugarplum syrup or cinnamon in it, and it was sour. Jinx wondered how long it would be before Simon was ready to start baking pies again.

He filled a plate and took it into the Bonemaster's laboratory, where he suspected he would find Elfwyn. He was right. She had a map spread on the workbench and was staring at it, leaning on her elbows. Heavy gray gloom enfolded her. Jinx pushed the plate at her.

"Oh—thank you." She avoided the chicken, but took a piece of cheese and nibbled at it disconsolately. "Did Sophie and Simon find each other?"

"Yes," said Jinx, assembling a chicken-and-cheese sandwich. He felt like he hadn't eaten in months. He probably hadn't. "Have you—I mean." He nodded at the trapdoor under the sink, which led to the crypt where he, Elfwyn, and Sophie had fought the Bonemaster, the ghoul, and the skeletons.

"No," said Elfwyn. "I don't exactly want to. Do you?"

"No." The full horror of his battle with the Bonemaster hadn't really caught up with him yet. He wasn't ready to revisit the crypt. And he had no desire to see the skeletons again.

"The ghoul's not dead," said Elfwyn. "It came back, but when it found out no one was going to pay it to patrol the island, it left."

"Oh." Jinx thought that was weird, but then he didn't know much about ghouls.

He looked up at the Bonemaster's collection of books. There were more than there'd been before—gifts to the Bonemaster from the Mistletoe Alliance. Well, the Urwald needed more books. It was too bad so few Urwalders could read them.

He looked at the extremely neat, extremely straight rows of bottles and jars that lined the shelves above. He felt suddenly sad at these signs of a carefully arranged life interrupted.

"He's got dried elf livers," he said. "But elves don't *have* livers. I don't think they have any kind of . . . guts and stuff."

"Elf liver is a type of mushroom," said Elfwyn.

"Oh." Jinx started to reach for the jar, and then wondered if he could do a summoning spell. He'd seen Elfwyn do it. He ought to be able to.

He raised his hand, and summoned the jar of elf livers. It leapt off the shelf and smashed on the stone floor.

"Oh well," said Elfwyn. "Anyway, you can see they're just mushrooms."

There was a broom in the corner, and a tin dustpan hanging neatly beside it. "How long . . ." Jinx began, as he swept up the fragments. "I mean, did anyone tell you . . . I mean—"

"How long we were gone?" Elfwyn knelt to hold the dustpan for him. "Three weeks. It's really weird; it feels like just a few hours to me. And it took you two months to come up through the floor, so neither of us had really heard any news in almost three months . . ."

"And now you've heard some," said Jinx.

And she was going to tell him, and he could see that it was going to be bad.

"Let me show you what's happened."

Elfwyn gathered up a handful of elf livers that Jinx had managed to rescue from amongst the broken glass.

"Reven's headquarters is right here." She picked up the lid from the shattered elf-liver jar and set it down on the map, in the Storm Strip.

"That's his fort," said Jinx. "Where he's got walls built out of logs and stuff."

"Right," said Elfwyn. "But his soldiers are here"— she dumped a little cluster of elf livers at the fort—"and here"—the next cluster went near Butterwood Clearing, and Jinx wished he'd had time to build a ward there. "And here"—by Blacksmiths' Clearing. "And here"—she dropped more elf livers for the soldiers that were guarding Simon's house—"and—"

"Wow," said Jinx. "How many—er, he must have a lot."

"Fewer than he did before, I think," said Elfwyn. "Because there was a big battle with Bluetooth's men and it didn't go well. Reven had to retreat to the Storm Strip for a while, except for his men around Simon's house, because Bluetooth probably didn't know about them."

She summoned a red bottle from a high shelf, and shook something like black marbles out onto the map.

"What are—"

"Nixies' eyeballs," said Elfwyn. "These are King Rufus's men. Some of them are here—drat!"

Jinx cupped his hands to catch King Rufus's men as they rolled off the workbench. "Maybe you should use something else."

A jar of tiny, luminescent snail shells drifted down from the top shelf. Jinx watched carefully—he really wanted to learn the summoning spell.

"All right, *these* are King Rufus's men," said Elfwyn.

"Have— I wonder if they've been setting more fires."

"Not that I've heard of," said Elfwyn. "But I haven't

asked the wizards. They'd know. Anyway, King Rufus of Bragwood's men are right here, and along here. And King Bluetooth—"

"The king of Keyland that Reven's trying to over-throw." Jinx could see the bad news that Elfwyn was holding on to, like a large blue-gray bubble, and he wished she'd hurry up and tell it.

"—is here. Do you see what's going on?"

"No," said Jinx.

"King Rufus of Bragwood is positioned so that he can switch sides at a moment's notice. Right now, he's allied with Reven. But if Reven looks like losing, King Rufus will go over to Bluetooth, and they'll finish Reven like *that*."

"Oh," said Jinx. "That must be what you're so upset about."

"Doesn't it bother you?"

Jinx shrugged. "I guess." He supposed he didn't really want Reven to be killed, but he also didn't want Reven invading the Urwald.

"I don't think that's what you're upset about, though," he added.

He watched her eyes. Her gaze slid from the Storm Strip to the Edgeland, from the Edgeland to Keyland, from Keyland to her home clearing, Butterwood.

"Butterwood Clearing," he said, carefully not making it a question.

Elfwyn took a deep breath. "A party of Butterwooders were coming back from selling cheese to Reven's troops. And they were captured. It's not clear who captured them. But whoever it was"—she took another deep breath— "murdered them all and left them in the forest."

There was a long, heavy, blue silence.

"Oh," said Jinx.

He was dreading the next part.

"And—and what I heard was—what I heard was that my mother was one of them," said Elfwyn, all in a rush.

She looked down at the map and at the piles of dried mushrooms and gently glowing snail shells. Her thoughts were a rolling mass of blue clouds, like a storm blowing in.

Jinx patted her on the shoulder, awkwardly. He knew she hadn't gotten along with her mother at all, but he was aware that now wasn't a good time to mention that. He remembered Berga coming with her husband and baby to Simon's house, and he wished he had been a little more welcoming.

"There were eight of them," said Elfwyn. "Eight Butterwooders. And it could have been King Bluetooth who did it, because they passed near his camp." She traced a line on the map with her finger. "And it could have been King Rufus, because he's called Rufus the Ruthless."

She opened her mouth as if to say something, then closed it again.

"And it could have been Reven," said Jinx.

"No," said Elfwyn.

"I'll find out," said Jinx grimly.

"That's not even—" Elfwyn spread her hand over the map. "It's not just that. You see how it is?"

"Yes. There are three enemy armies inside the Urwald," said Jinx.

"And any one of them outnumbers us," said Elfwyn.

⌒ ⌒ ⌒

Jinx could tell Elfwyn wanted to be left alone. He wandered outside. There was still the line of butter churns beside the steps. A fierce-looking little girl was standing in one of them, up to her armpits, thrusting ineffectually at the ground with a stick.

"I don't think you're going to get anywhere," said Jinx, amused. "You need a smaller churn."

"I know what I'm doing," said the girl. "You don't. Boys can't churn. *I'm* a witch."

The girl did have magic, Jinx sensed. Pretty strong magic, of an unformed, witchy kind. "An apprentice witch, maybe," he suggested. "Whose apprentice are you?"

"Dame Esper's," said the girl. "She's a very mighty, powerful, superb witch and I'm going to be even better."

She made another thrust at the ground, and dropped her stick. She reached for it, swarming up out of the churn, which started to tip over. Jinx grabbed it and righted it.

"Give me my stick, please," said the girl.

Jinx shook his head. "You're going to hurt yourself. Come on, get out of there." He tried to pick her up. She ducked down into the churn.

"I know who you are," said the girl, peering over the rim. "You're Jinx. You have tons of power but you're not a wizard, and you never will be. You can see feelings better than the trolls can, and sense magic better than werewolves and ogres can, but you're not one of them either. Dame Glammer said."

Jinx wasn't going to argue with the kid about his wizardly prospects. "Trolls can see feelings?"

"Yup. It's deep Urwald magic. Dame Glammer said. Do you know Dame Glammer?"

"Yes," said Jinx. "And if you don't get out of that butter churn now, I'm going to go and get her."

The girl shot upright. "I don't believe you," she said, and allowed Jinx to lift her out.

Elfwyn Tells the Truth

A lot of the people from Simon's house had moved to Bonesocket. More refugees kept arriving at Simon's house, and Sophie was kept busy sorting them out. Simon was usually off somewhere directing the army. Jinx was relieved that Simon and Sophie seemed to be friends again—although they quarreled a lot.

It was also a relief that, in the midst of the war, Inga dropped all pink fluffy thoughts of Jinx and turned them on a refugee who arrived from Churnbottom Clearing. Jinx wondered if he should warn the Churnbottom guy about the pig muck. No, probably best to let things take their course. Anyway, Jinx had other things to worry about.

He went to Butterwood Clearing to set up a ward. But when he got there, he found the clearing swarming with Reven's soldiers. He left in a hurry, without making the ward.

⌐ ⌐ ⌐

It was four o'clock in the morning. Jinx stepped through the doorpath into Reven's fort in the Storm Strip. He carried a white flag, because Wendell had told him that was the thing to do in these situations. But just in case Reven didn't know that, he also put a strong ward around himself as soon as he arrived.

Nobody even noticed him at first. This was very annoying. Jinx flapped his white flag vigorously, making it snap.

A couple of bleary-eyed soldiers came over to him, swords raised.

"Woodrat," said one. "Should we kill him?"

"No, it's the Werechipmunk. Take him prisoner."

"I want to talk to the king," said Jinx. "Don't you see this?" He flapped his flag again.

"A nightshirt?"

"You brought your nightshirt? We supply all that."

"Right, King Raymond treats his prisoners like princes. Everybody wants to be taken prisoner by us."

"It's a flag of truce," said Jinx. "I want to talk to your king."

"You're surrendering?"

"No," said Jinx patiently. "I'm parleying."

The guards looked at each other, confused. Then one of them made a lunge at Jinx. "Ouch! He's put up one of those invisible wall things."

Jinx frowned at the soldier, who was sucking his bruised knuckles. "Go and get Rev—King Raymond, please."

"I'm here," said a voice from the shadows.

The soldiers instantly looked more alert, and stood up straighter.

"Good morning, Jinx," said Reven. "If it is morning, forsooth. Have you come to surrender?"

"No, I've come to parley," said Jinx. "Which means talk."

"I know what it means." Reven's eyes glinted in the darkness. "Are you asking for terms?"

"Terms for what? Surrender?" said Jinx. "No, but I might be offering them. It depends on how you answer a couple of important questions."

The guards rumbled red and black anger that anyone would dare speak so disrespectfully to their king.

"I am not interested in your terms. However, you may ask your questions," said Reven, regally.

"Not in front of your soldiers," said Jinx.

Reven made a small motion with his head, and the soldiers backed away, burbling resentment, their hands on their sword hilts.

"Also," said Jinx, "there's something I want to show you."

"Very well," said Reven.

"I need you to come with me."

"Oh really?" said Reven. "Through your magic door-way, you mean? And what will I find at the other end?"

"A patch of burnt land," said Jinx. "That's all."

"You seem to expect me to trust you," said Reven. "Whereas you've chosen to show up here surrounded by a magic ward."

Good point. Jinx took the ward down. "Fine. It's gone. Now, will you come with me?"

Reven reached out and touched where the ward wasn't. He patted Jinx gently on the head, which Jinx didn't much care for.

"I want to show you what your ally King Rufus has done," said Jinx. "Unless you're afraid."

This had the effect that Jinx expected. "I'm not afraid."

"Good," said Jinx. "Then come on." He grabbed Reven's sleeve, and pulled him into the Doorway.

❧ ❧ ❧

It wasn't yet dawn, but it was just light enough that the trees stood out black against a deep-blue sky. Jinx and Reven crunched over the burnt ground, the smell of char-coal sharp in their nostrils. It made Jinx feel ill and irritable.

"So there was a fire here," Reven observed.

"It was set by one of Rufus's soldiers," said Jinx.

"Hm," said Reven.

"This was the last of several," said Jinx.

"And there's something you want me to do about it?"

"No," said Jinx. "I only want to know whether it was your idea."

"It was not. It seems very wasteful to me. There must have been good timber here."

"Are you *trying* to annoy me?" said Jinx.

"Of course not," said Reven. "That would be no kind of challenge at all. I'm simply pointing out the truth. The Urwald has to be cleared eventually. You must realize that."

"I don't realize it," said Jinx. "Sorry."

"It can be done reasonably," said Reven. "As I said before. Reservations can be set aside for you and your monsters. I mentioned that we might preserve an area of a hundred square miles. I could probably be more generous than that, provided—"

"Wait." Jinx held up a hand to shush Reven. There were footsteps crunching over the charcoal behind them. He turned around. He could just make out Elfwyn's face in the slowly growing light.

Reven smiled. "Good morning, Lady Elfwyn. How surprising to find you here."

Elfwyn gave him a curt nod. "Hello, Reven. Did you kill my mother?"

The calculating blue and green squares of Reven's thoughts turned to red, angry surprise. "What?"

"Did you?" said Elfwyn.

"I'm astonished that you could think such a thing of me, my lady."

"You haven't answered me," said Elfwyn.

"No," said Reven coldly.

"I think he's telling the truth," said Jinx. "At least as far as he knows it."

The coldness was turned on Jinx. "At least as far as I know it? Am I supposed to have killed the good lady in my sleep?"

"Your men could have done it," said Jinx.

"Somebody murdered eight people from Butterwood Clearing," said Elfwyn. "As they were returning from taking butter and cheese to your camp."

"I had heard of this," said Reven. "I did not know that your mother was among them. I am sorry to hear it." He bowed. "Please accept my condolences."

Elfwyn waved his condolences aside angrily. "So you didn't know one of them was my mother. But did you have them killed?"

"An unarmed party of traders?" said Reven, going cold again. "No. Why would I?"

"Because you found out they were spies," said Elfwyn.

"If that was to have been my reason, I would have

killed them months ago," said Reven. "Since I always assumed they were spies."

"Why did you let them into your camp if you thought they were spies?" said Jinx.

"Because we needed the goods they were selling, of course," said Reven. "And also because it was to our advantage that you understand the superiority of our forces."

"I think he's telling the truth about that, too," Jinx told Elfwyn.

Elfwyn pursed her lips and nodded.

It occurred to Jinx suddenly that the last time the three of them had been together was when Jinx had turned Siegfried the Lumberjack into a tree.

Elfwyn turned to Reven. "Why don't you ask me about *our* forces?"

"Hey!" said Jinx. This wasn't what they had agreed to. At all.

Elfwyn smiled at him, then turned back to Reven. "Or whatever else you want to ask me," she added coldly.

Reven looked from Elfwyn to Jinx, calculating, and then back at Elfwyn again. "I don't believe I have Jinx's permission to do so, my lady."

"You don't need his permission," said Elfwyn. "It's me you're asking. Go ahead. Ask."

"Which clearings are defended by wards?"

"All those that have people living in them," said

Elfwyn. "Except for Butterwood Clearing, which you've already captured."

"And how many men do you have under arms?"

"About five hundred," said Elfwyn.

"That's not very many," said Reven.

"And four hundred women," Elfwyn added. "You didn't ask. And about eighty big kids. And that's not counting a few thousand trolls and werewolves, of course, and the magicians."

More like a few hundred. "You're telling him everything?" Jinx demanded.

"Yes," said Elfwyn. "That was a question."

"You told *him* he could ask—"

"Yes, but not you."

Jinx subsided. He understood what she was doing. She was hiding lies in with the truth. But she could have discussed it with him first.

"Aren't the magicians men and women?" said Reven.

"Of course," said Elfwyn. "But they're not armed, because they don't have to be. They're dangerous enough as it is. They can turn men to stone with a glance."

Now that just wasn't true at all.

"And where is everyone?" Reven asked.

"Hey!" Jinx said, more loudly. "Enough's enough. Elfwyn, stop. You can't just tell him everything. I mean it. Seriously. Shut *up!*"

He was shouting, trying to drown out Elfwyn, who was telling Reven everything.

"Well, great," said Jinx, when she had finished. "You're providing him with all the information he needs to completely wipe us out."

"He can try," said Elfwyn. "If he's that stupid. You notice he hasn't asked me the important questions."

Silence greeted this, as both Jinx and Reven tried to figure out what these might be.

"What are the important questions?" Reven asked her.

"How much magical power we actually have," said Elfwyn, "and what we can do to you with it."

Reven looked thoughtful.

"We have more power than all the magicians in the world put together," said Elfwyn.

"Then why haven't you used it yet?" said Reven.

"Because the results would be too terrible," said Elfwyn.

"Forsooth, my lady," said Reven. "You have been surprisingly generous with information. All I can tell you in return is that you are facing the united forces of my own army and that of King Rufus the Ruthless—"

"The guy who killed your stepmother," said Jinx. "You sure can pick allies, can't you?" He felt an unpleasant twinge of guilt at the gray twist of pain that his words caused Reven. "Rufus is going to change sides as soon as he thinks it's convenient."

"I doubt that he will find it convenient," said Reven.

"If he does, then *you'll* be facing the combined forces of Rufus and Bluetooth," said Elfwyn.

"And us," Jinx added.

"Alas, Dame Fortune might leave me with no alternative," said Reven.

"Here's an alternative," said Jinx. "You could just leave, and let us deal with them."

"And go where?" said Reven. "In Keyland, I'm a criminal. I've been banished from Bragwood. That leaves the Boreal Wastes, and I understand they're even colder than the Urwald. No, I'm quite happy where I am, thank you."

Jinx felt an unwanted qualm. "You're invading the Urwald because you can't turn back? Look, if you need to get away, I can help you with that."

Reven looked at him coldly. "Really? Myself and all my thousands of followers? I do not need to get away. Now, I have seen your burnt ground, and I have been accused of murder. . . . Was there anything else you wished to say to me?"

Jinx and Elfwyn looked at each other. They shook their heads.

"Then it seems only common courtesy," said Reven, "for me to return the offer. Join forces with *me*, before Bluetooth and Rufus wipe *you* out."

"Without you, we wouldn't even have them in the Urwald," said Jinx.

Reven acknowledged this with a curt nod. He turned to Elfwyn. "Some of my men think that King Bluetooth was responsible for the murders."

"Why?" said Elfwyn.

"To terrify the populace into submission, I suppose."

"I thought King Rufus the Ruthless did things like that," said Elfwyn.

"Most kings do such things," said Reven. "Even, if you read your history, kings who are called 'the Good.' King Bluetooth, you'll recall, murdered my father. Now, if you would be so kind as to show me the way back to my fort. . . ."

Elfwyn offered to do it, but Jinx managed to edge her out of the way. She looked quite nice, really, with the dawn light reflected on her hair. He was pretty sure he didn't look nice at all, at least not to Reven and his soldiers.

He delivered Reven at his fort, and then came right back to the scorched ground, because he had a feeling Elfwyn would be waiting for him there. She was.

"Why did you—" he began. "You shouldn't have done that! I don't see the point!"

"He's much more powerful than us, you know," said Elfwyn. "But he came out of that conversation thinking that *we* were more powerful."

Jinx thought about this. It was true.

"Which in a way we are," Elfwyn added. "Because we've got you."

"Yes, if you need anything levitated or set on fire, I'm your man," said Jinx.

"Is that really all you can do?" said Elfwyn.

"Don't rub it in," said Jinx.

"It's just that I don't think it is," said Elfwyn. "We need to think about it some more."

"You told him we were more powerful than all the magicians in the world, and that if we used our power, the results would be terrible!" Jinx accused.

"Well, I'm pretty sure that's the truth," said Elfwyn.

Magic Battle

Elfwyn went back to Simon's house. Jinx needed to think. He walked across the charcoal field in the gathering dawn. High shoots of fireweed with bright purple blossoms surrounded him. Birds called to each other in the forest, announcing the day.

He walked for a long time before he reached the edge of the burn and leaned against a cedar tree.

He looked out at the burnt space and imagined the whole Urwald like that—the tall trees gone, the lifeforce gone. Branches curling as they burned, fire spreading through the tree roots underground, the porcupines and bears and squirrels gone, the werebears and werechipmunks and ogres gone, the nixies boiled out of their underground pools.

Then what? More Keyland, more Bragwood, or maybe a wasteland, a desert like Samara, only colder.

No magic, anyway. The Urwald's magic came from its lifeforce. And without the Urwald, the lifeforce would retreat back down to the Path of Fire, back to the stone. It would spend itself making mountains and rockflows and pretty gems.

Terror, said the trees. *Terrors.*

Yeah, said Jinx. *I know. They're everywhere.*

You must drive them out, Listener. We must drive them out.

Yeah, well, we've tried to do that, said Jinx. *We haven't had much luck. They're armed, they know more about fighting than we do, and they outnumber us.*

They do not outnumber us. No, not them. Not any of the Restless. We outnumber them.

What, you mean . . . Jinx thought about this. *All right, so the trees outnumber them. That's not going to help.*

We will fight them.

How? said Jinx. *By falling on them?*

There was a murmur among the trees, a long ripple and hum of thought, a quiet conversation that spread outward. It seemed to Jinx that it extended to the very edges of the Urwald. And after what seemed a very long time—it was full day now, and the sun's rays slanted into the purple mass of fireweed—the ripple of talk came back.

We have shown you the way before, Listener, said the trees. *Perhaps you have forgotten.*

Shown me what way? said Jinx.

Again the conversation spread far away, along the inter-twined roots of the mighty lifeforce that was the Urwald. Thousands of trees, millions of trees, discussed and dis-coursed. Jinx couldn't hear most of it, except as a distant sense of something happening. It made him feel very small.

And then, in the blackened land before him, amid the fireweed, a tree appeared.

It was a copper beech, and it was bigger around than Jinx was tall, and taller than the tree he leaned against. It looked as if it had grown there for hundreds of years. But a gentle wind blew through it, onto Jinx's face, and he knew it wasn't really there at all.

A young woman walked through the fireweed—literally through it, Jinx noticed, as he watched a tall spear of purple flowers disappear into her dark brown face and then reemerge behind her head. She wasn't really there, of course. Jinx knew who she was.

The last Listener, he said. *You showed her to me before.*

The Listener, yes. The last Listener.

It felt odd to hear the trees calling someone else "the Listener." The Listener was supposed to be Jinx. *What was her name?*

Name? Name. Listener. Her name was Listener.

She must have had a name, said Jinx.

Listener. Listen.

I suppose you're not going to remember my name either, said Jinx.

The trees would not understand why this bothered him, of course. Trees didn't have names. They didn't need them. Nobody ever had to ask where they were. No one ever had to distinguish them from some other tree so that they could be paid or fed or put in jail or married. They never went to a new place where they'd have to explain themselves to anybody.

My name is Jinx, said Jinx.

The trees paid no attention to that.

The young woman stopped, under the spreading branches of the mighty beech. She was about Jinx's age.

She reached up a hand, and a branch bent down. The grace of its motion reminded Jinx of Reven bowing to kiss a lady's hand.

The last Listener took hold of the end of the branch as though she were shaking hands.

She's making the branch move? said Jinx.

The Listener has deep roots, said the trees.

The Path of Fire, you mean, said Jinx.

The branch bent lower still, and the last Listener sat on it and was lifted gently as it rose. High in the air, she looked off into the distance, as if searching for something. The beech bent some branches aside to give her a clear view.

So she used the power of the Path of Fire to move the trees, said Jinx.

The trees murmured. *Move? No, we did not move. We are rooted deep into the earth.*

To move their branches, then, said Jinx.

He thought he saw what the trees wanted him to do.

No, he said.

~ ✧ ~

The enemy armies moved inexorably inward.

By now it was probably clear to Reven that the Urwald's magicians could *not* turn a man to stone with a glance. But they could make things explode—rocks, fallen trees, and nearly anything except people. They could levitate anything that wasn't alive, and drop it on the invaders.

The goldfish were useless, but the wizard Alphonse could put his purple prison up around two or three invaders at a time, and maintain up to ten purple prisons as long as his eyes didn't get tired. Spiders rained down on the invaders. Here and there an unfortunate soldier's boots became mud, and his clothing turned to leaves and fell rustling to the ground. But it wasn't enough. Whenever one soldier was hit by a spell, two more seemed to take his place. Many of these wore the red uniforms of King Rufus.

Reven's men were almost (but not quite) used to having illusory dragons and firebirds dive-bomb them from the sky.

"If only we could get real dragons and firebirds," said Elfwyn. "But dragons are rare—"

"And firebirds aren't thinking creatures," said Jinx.

Simon had divided the magicians up among the Urwish army sections, making each one responsible for casting spells to protect a group of humans, werewolves, and trolls. Jinx was surprised that the wizards and witches deigned to take orders for Simon, but then, no one could deny Simon was turning out to have a talent for war.

Simon kept the Truthspeaker near him, ostensibly so that people would trust him. Jinx suspected it was also so that Elfwyn could do spells now and then and people would think Simon had done them. She used the purple flash spell a lot. It knocked enemy soldiers down, or sent them flying.

Hilda and Nick were in the army section commanded by Cottawilda, along with Gak the Troll, a number of humans, and several werewolves.

Sophie, meanwhile, had taken charge of treating the injured, because she knew more about that than anyone else did. She insisted that everything she used had to be boiled—bandages, thread, needles, knives, and weird-looking implements that Wendell and Satya bought in Samara. If you came near Sophie, she'd dump a heap of stuff into your arms and say, "Boil that, please."

At first she had the idea that it would be quicker to have Jinx sterilize things by magic, but after Jinx accidentally set a pile of bandages on fire and melted an expensive and nasty-looking hooked knife, she went back to boiling.

Jinx had learned the pink goo spell. Using the Urwald's power he could make big lakes of it. This slowed down the attacking soldiers, but it slowed down the Urwalders too, so it had to be used carefully.

He could use the clothes-freezing spell too, of course. He rather hated this one. It enabled Urwalders to disarm and capture the invaders. It also enabled Urwalders to slaughter the invaders, which happened a few times.

"He said it was an accident," said Wendell, after one of these incidents.

"He *ate* the guy," said Jinx. "How could that be an accident?"

"Well, trolls are . . . trolls see things differently," said Wendell.

"Bergthold wasn't born a troll," said Jinx. "He knows the difference between disarming someone and eating them."

"He sees it differently now that he's a troll," said Wendell.

The situation was even worse with the werewolves. With them it wasn't just a matter of forgetting; they seemed to regard the invaders as their lawful prey.

"That's the way werewolves fight," said Malthus, when Jinx complained. "We're not in this war to help you humans, you know. We're fighting to defend our territory."

"Yes, but—"

"And as we seem to be losing anyway, perhaps it's time you became a little less squeamish. I feel certain you could be doing more than you are."

Jinx looked away. "I'm in every battle. The same as everyone else."

The werewolf tapped his lower lip with a claw. "Yes. The same as everyone else. And yet you're *not* the same as everyone else. Where is the Path of Fire when we need it?"

Jinx didn't pretend he didn't know what Malthus meant. "I can't use the Path of Fire. People would get hurt."

"And what do you think will happen if you don't use it?"

❦ ❦ ❦

The battle was not going well.

Reven's and Rufus's armies were massed along a line a mile wide, just east of Simon's clearing. The Urwalders had abandoned Blacksmiths' Clearing the week before, along with the other eastern clearings. Butterwood Clearing was held jointly by Reven and Rufus the Ruthless. A few Butterwooders had managed to escape, but the rest were prisoners or dead.

"You should go home," said Jinx to Wendell, as they prepared for yet another attack.

A little orange blurp of surprise. "Why?"

"Because," said Jinx, "we're losing. You should get out while you still can."

"I can always get out through Simon's house," said Wendell. "They won't be able to get into Simon's house because of the wards."

"You won't be able to trust the wards once we've lost," said Jinx. "All the kings need is a few magicians to go over to their side. And once we've lost the Urwald, I think they'll get that. If they manage to break through the wards any- where . . . I won't be able to fix them once the forest's gone."

"Well, that can't happen quickly," said Wendell.

"It can if they set fire to it," said Jinx.

"Ah." Wendell thought about this, then turned to look at the advancing forces of Rufus the Ruthless. "I'll stay till things get to that point, anyway."

He went off to join his section.

The wizards had floated logs, rocks, and branches through the air and piled them between the Urwish army and the invading forces, forming a huge barricade. Jinx climbed a maple tree so that he could see where to throw his spells. His fear of heights never bothered him when he was in a tree. He felt at home in trees.

The invaders began climbing over the barricade.

The battle cry "The Urwald!" rang out among the trees, accompanied by werewolf howls and troll bellows. The Urwald's human soldiers, armed with axes, drove forward in a line, with werewolves moving in to harry the invaders from the side. The trolls were interspersed with the clearing folk, armed with clubs.

Jinx stood on a branch with one arm wrapped around the maple's rough trunk and, with his free hand, cast clothes-freezing spells and threw pink goo.

He could see the other magicians' spells—illusions to distract the invaders, and clothes-freezing and leaden-foot spells to freeze them in their tracks, wards to keep them from advancing. Then several wizards cast a spell together. A large chunk of the barricade exploded, sending the invaders flying. Logs and stones thundered down on them.

The elderly wizard in black robes, whose name was Frank, threw green thunderbolts which struck like lightning. The Carrot made the ground roll and ripple under the invaders' feet.

And still the invaders poured through the forest toward Simon's clearing.

Some of them suddenly found themselves wielding swords the size of pins, and Jinx hoped that meant that somewhere in the boiling mass of battle, Elfwyn was alive and doing shrinking spells. But the invaders dropped the pins and grabbed up the swords of their fallen comrades.

Witches bounded amongst the trees in their butter churns, making illusions and doing a few nastier spells. Witches, unlike most wizards, could do magic directly on people. Led by Dame Glammer, they'd worked out ways to combine their power. They made the invaders stand on their heads. They curled them up into balls and sent them rolling back the way they had come. They made the soldiers climb trees and then jump out again.

Jinx could only work magic against the soldiers he could see. He froze their clothes. He heated their swords till they dropped them.

And still there were more enemy soldiers, and still they came.

The Urwald talked, telling Jinx that just beyond this battle, another Terror lay in wait.

I know, said Jinx. *King Bluetooth of Keyland's forces. When we're driven back to Simon's clearing, they'll attack.*

Jinx had to pick out individual struggles and figure out who to freeze. Below him, he saw Hilda's friend Nick battling two invaders. Jinx froze their clothes. But one of them toppled and fell behind a tree, out of Jinx's line of vision, and the spell broke. Nick swung his ax at that invader, not seeing another who was coming at him from the side. Jinx froze that one's clothes.

The Terror is elsewhere, said the trees. *Everywhere. Here. Afar.*

I know. You've told me. They're outside every one of the clearings, said Jinx. *They're ready to move in once we fall.*

More invaders were moving through the trees. Jinx mired their feet in pink goo. He could hear the clang and cries of battle around him, but he didn't dare take his attention off Nick.

Three more invaders were attacking Nick. In freezing their clothes, Jinx lost control of the first spell he'd done, and that man was up again. Nick was surrounded.

Listener, you must be willing to kill, said the trees.

Shut up, said Jinx. *I'm busy.*

Carefully not letting the clothes-freezing spells slip, Jinx started leaden-foot spells on Nick's attackers. At the same time, he sent fire into their swords, making them cry out and drop them. One of his spells slipped by accident, and the invader's clothes burst into flames. The man yelled in anguish and tried to fall to the ground and roll, but couldn't because of the leaden-foot spell. Meanwhile Nick's ax connected with another soldier, and someone stabbed Nick in the leg. Nick went down. Then Gak the troll rushed in, clubbed each of the invaders, and casually bit the head off one of them.

Jinx felt ill. He was about to levitate Nick into the tree when the troll threw Nick over his shoulder and ran back toward Simon's clearing.

"Don't worry about me!" Nick yelled as they thumped out of sight. "There's a whole battle!"

Nick was right. And Jinx hadn't kept up with it. While he'd been trying to keep the invaders from killing Nick, they'd taken over the ground below Jinx. The Urwalders had fallen back, and below Jinx there were only enemies.

And where was Wendell, and where was Simon? And—well, where was almost everybody Jinx knew and cared about?

He spread more pink goo across the ground. It slowed down the attackers, but others were getting past.

He heated the invaders' swords. But in the time it took him to make one soldier drop his sword, twelve others would struggle free of the goo.

Jinx tried to send more goo after them, but they were quickly out of sight.

The sound of battle had moved further west. Then came a green flash in the sky. It was Elfwyn's signal: Retreat.

And Jinx was trapped. There were invaders all over the battlefield; he couldn't descend. He climbed from the maple into the branches of a neighboring hemlock, and from there to a pine. But after the pine, there were no branches close enough to reach.

He stood there with pine pitch all over his hands and

wondered what to do. In the gathering dusk he could hear voices beneath him, speaking in un-Urwish accents. If he climbed down, he'd be captured by Reven's men or killed by Rufus's.

He could levitate himself, but he couldn't fly.

Listen, said the trees.

The image of the last Listener appeared below him. A branch of the pine, a branch that wasn't there in the present day (it had broken away in a storm, the pine remembered) bent down at the last Listener's beckoning, and she climbed onto it and rode it upward.

Let us move, said the trees.

Okay. It was the only way he could get home.

I'm not really sure, he said. *But I think this must have been how she did it.*

He touched the pine's sticky trunk and felt down the tree, into the roots, into the root network that spanned the Urwald. He felt down deeper, deeper than the roots of trees, into the Path of Fire. He felt the source of lifeforce and he drew it upward, and as he drew it he put himself into it, so that when the force reached the pine tree he was able to give it something that he had and it did not: the ability to move.

The pine branch swung gracefully around until it mingled with the branches of an oak tree. Letting go of the trunk, Jinx walked along the limb and stepped into the arms of the oak. Then he edged out onto a branch on the other side of the oak, and helped it reach a neighboring beech.

And that was how Jinx got home, handed from branch to branch by the trees, sailing above the heads of the enemy.

"Must be a storm coming," said a Keylish voice far below. "Listen to those branches creaking."

"I don't like this forest," said another voice. "It's creepy. Sometimes I think it's listening."

Double Green Flash

Sophie did not think Nick would be able to walk again. Jinx found this out from Hilda, because Sophie was tending the wounded, and Simon was busy amid his section leaders and a mass of detailed area maps that Satya had drawn.

"Sophie said there are surgeons in Samara who might be able to do something, but otherwise . . ." Hilda trailed off in a blue cloud of gloom.

"I shouldn't have been up in the tree casting spells," Jinx said. "I should have been down there with an ax and—"

"Stop, please, sir," said Hilda. "It doesn't do any good to talk about it."

"Sorry," said Jinx.

He was ashamed of his outburst of guilt. It really didn't help, and he was glad Nick had been too unconscious to hear it. Jinx still hadn't seen Elfwyn or Wendell. He went in search of them. The house was more crowded than it had ever been. Jinx pushed his way through the mob, stepping around the injured and the people tending them.

He finally found Elfwyn outside, serving soup to masses of people. They were sitting and standing all over the garden beds, which were a total loss as far as Jinx could tell.

Elfwyn glowed bright-green delight at seeing him. She handed him some soup, in a cup with a broken handle.

Jinx drank it straight down. He hadn't realized how hungry and thirsty he was. He would've liked more, but he suspected there were more potential soup eaters on hand than soup.

"Have you seen Wendell?" he asked her.

"No." Elfwyn turned to someone nearby. "Could you take over, please? I need to talk to Jinx."

"Sure, Truthspeaker." The man took the ladle from her.

Elfwyn and Jinx walked out of the clearing, into the ward tunnel, and sat down in the hollow Doorway Oak.

"The invaders aren't here yet," Jinx observed. "I thought they'd be surrounding us by now."

"No, I expect they don't think they need to," said

Elfwyn. "They're staying out of reach of our spells. Jinx, you've got to—"

"Are you sure you haven't seen Wendell?" said Jinx. "When was the last time you saw him?"

"Yes. I don't know, before the battle sometime. I'm sure he's . . ." Elfwyn trailed off. "Jinx, how did you get back here?"

Jinx told her.

"You mean you moved the trees?"

"Well, helped them move. Yeah."

"I *thought* you could do that. Grandma said something once that made me think so."

"I only just found out myself."

"Jinx, you've got to get the trees to fight."

"Get them to—I'm having trouble *keeping* them from fighting," said Jinx.

"They can't fight without you."

"It would mean lots of people would get hurt," said Jinx. "Including lots of us, because the trees can't tell people apart."

"We could warn our people in advance. We could tell them to get down when they see—I don't know, a double green flash."

They sat and thought. Elfwyn rested her chin in her hands as she always did when she was thinking. Jinx picked at the sawdust on the ground.

"I don't think it's your decision to make," said Elfwyn suddenly.

"What!" Jinx was so outraged that he only just managed to make it not a question. "I'm the one who—"

"We could all be dead by tomorrow," said Elfwyn. "If there's a weapon that we haven't used yet, then everyone has a right to know about it. Everyone should decide."

"Do you—you realize how many everyones you're talking about! You can't run a war by vote."

"You can't win a war by refusing to use what you've got!" said Elfwyn.

They had gotten to their feet and were almost yelling at each other.

Suddenly Jinx became aware of another presence in the darkness. Someone had just come through a Doorway.

"Sorry. I didn't mean to barge in," said a familiar voice.

"Wendell!" cried Elfwyn. "Are you all right?"

"Yeah," said Wendell. "Just a little banged up."

Jinx could only just make out Wendell's form in the dark. "What happened?"

"I'm not sure," said Wendell. "I was fighting this big red-bearded guy, and then something hit me on the head from behind, and then I think I was unconscious. A little after that people were running on top of me, and then they were gone and I got up and there was this Keylish guy who was kind of seriously injured, so I found a

Doorway and took him home."

"Home where?" said Jinx.

"Keyland," said Wendell. "He was from Keria."

"You took an enemy *home*?"

"To his mother. She was awfully glad to see him."

"Wendell, tell Jinx how wrong he is," said Elfwyn.

"Sure." Wendell turned to Jinx. "You're wrong, man."

"No, wait," said Jinx. "Listen to what she wants me to do."

Wendell listened. Then he listened again as Elfwyn told him.

"Well, Elfwyn has a point," said Wendell. "It's not entirely your decision to make."

"Right!" said Elfwyn. "It should be put to a vote."

"Wars aren't usually run by vote," said Wendell.

"But this is the free and independent—" Elfwyn began.

"Because if they were, nearly everyone in them would vote to go home," said Wendell.

"But we're going to lose if he doesn't do it," said Elfwyn. "We've pretty much already lost."

"Not while we still have the Urwald's lifeforce," said Jinx.

"What good is that if you won't use it?" Elfwyn shot back.

"You don't understand how it is," said Jinx. "It's not you that would be killing everybody."

"Jinx has a point," said Wendell. "He shouldn't be

forced to do something he thinks is wrong."

"Men," said Elfwyn furiously, "always stick together."

"He said *you* were right before," said Jinx.

"Well, you're kind of both right," said Wendell.

"*I'm* going to go warn everyone," said Elfwyn. "Then if *you* manage to catch up to your conscience before we're all dead, at least they'll know to duck."

She marched off. They watched her go.

"I kind of think she has a point," said Wendell. "Really."

"Oh, shut up. You think everyone has a point," said Jinx.

"Well, they do," said Wendell equably.

The injured were moved to Bonesocket, where Sophie had set up a hospital. Everyone who couldn't fight had gone there to help her.

Witch Seymour and Dame Glammer directed the witches in constructing a phalanx of illusory dragons around Simon's clearing.

Hilda and several other women were practicing their ax swings on the firewood.

Jinx went around to the back of the house, hoping for a little privacy to think. There were people back there sharpening axes.

He leaned against the wall. There was no privacy anywhere.

A window creaked open above Jinx. Simon stuck his

head out and made a come-here gesture.

"Not around the house," Simon snapped, as Jinx started to walk away. "I mean levitate."

Jinx levitated his clothes until he was standing in the air beside the window. The noise of ax grinding stopped, and everyone stared.

"Go back to your sharpening," said Simon, and the grind wheel started again reluctantly. People were still staring.

Jinx climbed onto the window ledge. The workroom was full of magicians, arguing and muttering and poking around in Simon's stuff. Jinx could see that Simon's patience, such as it was, was being stretched very thin.

"Come into the other room," said Simon.

By which he meant Samara. They seized a second when no one was looking, and slipped through the KnIP door into the Samaran house.

The table and desk in the front room were piled high with things from Simon's workroom, things Simon was hiding from his visitors. Calvin the Skull perched atop a stack of books.

"I can't hold those magicians much longer," said Simon. "There's a lot of grumbling. They're for the Urwald, but they're for themselves more. I give it another day before Angstwurm or Frank slips out and goes and offers his services to king-boy."

Jinx nodded. This was more or less what he thought. "Or the Carrot."

"The—? Oh, you mean Magda. She's hard to read—"

"Because she never says more than one word," said Jinx.

"But it's mainly those two that worry me," said Simon.

"It's not just them," said Jinx. "*Anyone* could bring Reven and his men through the wards."

"I know that," said Simon. "So either we wait for that to happen, or we attack."

"Listen, about Nick—" said Jinx.

"What about him? You want to know if there's a surgeon in Samara who can help him? Maybe, maybe not. Next time someone's attacking one of your friends—" Simon picked up Calvin and hefted him thoughtfully. "Do what you have to do."

Jinx looked from Calvin to Simon, and then back at Calvin. "Embrace the ice?"

"No," said Simon. "Don't be an idiot. Use what you have."

He tossed the skull to Jinx.

Jinx caught it. He looked at Calvin. The skull grinned. Deathforce power radiated from it.

Jinx set the skull back on the stack of books. "I don't need that kind of power."

"Use what you have," said Simon. "But use it *now*.

There isn't going to be a battle after this one. What happens next is up to you."

Jinx looked at the skull. It winked an eye socket at him.

"Yeah," said Jinx. "Okay."

⁓ ⁓ ⁓

"Did you warn everyone?" Jinx asked.

"Almost. There are still people out warning the guards we left in the clearings," said Wendell.

"And Leisha warned the werewolves," said Elfwyn. "The cubs and their mothers have all gone to ground in Salt City."

"And the trolls know," said Wendell.

"And they're telling the ogres," said Elfwyn. "And the werewolves are telling the werebears."

She drew a deep breath, and looked at Wendell.

"We haven't told Reven yet," said Wendell.

"You don't tell him," said Jinx. "He's the enemy."

Wendell and Elfwyn exchanged glances. They'd been talking about Jinx. He could tell.

"We thought you might like to do it," said Wendell.

"If not, I could," Elfwyn added.

Jinx started to say something, and then had a feeling that he was being maneuvered. Rather carefully, which hurt his feelings. It wasn't like he was the kind of person that had to be *managed*. They could just say what they meant, couldn't they?

"I don't see why we have to warn him," said Jinx. "He told me once that I shouldn't let my enemy know I'm going to hit him until I do."

"You're going to take his advice?" said Wendell.

"Remember when we were prisoners in Bonesocket?" said Elfwyn. "Remember how Reven found a way to climb down? He could have just run away. But he came back for us."

"I died anyway," said Jinx.

"But that wasn't his fault."

"And besides, Reven would make a better neighbor than King Bluetooth," said Wendell. "Unless you're planning on starting an Urwish Empire and ruling Keyland yourself."

~ ✦ ✦

Jinx took a white napkin to wave this time, because he didn't want to hear any more nonsense about nightshirts.

Reven's army was less than a mile from Simon's clearing. As Jinx walked among them, he realized how terrified they were. They hadn't bargained on fighting magicians, trolls, and werewolves. They didn't like it that Urwalders could appear out of thin air. It horrified them to think that witches might take control of their bodies. These things loomed so large in their thoughts that Jinx could almost taste them.

Reven folded his arms. "Yes? What now?"

Jinx folded his arms too, and glared back. "Your soldiers are very frightened."

"Oh really? And am I?"

"No. But you feel guilty, now that I've told you. So maybe you're a better person than I think you are."

"I certainly hope so," said Reven. "Is that what you came to say?"

"No," said Jinx. "I came to tell you this. If you see a double green flash in the sky, hit the ground. Lie flat. Close to a large tree trunk if possible."

"Why?" said Reven.

"Because," said Jinx. "We've talked it over, and we've decided that we'd rather have you as an ally than an enemy. I don't mean me personally. And I don't mean Elfwyn personally, either. I mean we, the free and independent nation of the Urwald."

Reven opened his mouth to speak, and Jinx held up a hand to stop him.

"King Bluetooth's army is lying in wait for you," Jinx said. "They're planning to attack you as soon as you finish us off."

"Do you imagine I don't know that?" said Reven.

"When this is over, whatever happens, don't stay to fight them. You'll have ten days to get out of the Urwald. I can't guarantee your safety after that."

"It would take us two weeks to get out of the Urwald," said Reven. "Assuming we wanted to go."

"Ten days," said Jinx. "If you're not out in ten days,

we'll take whatever steps we have to to get rid of you."

"Some people might say, under the circumstances, that you are delusional," said Reven.

"Just remember what I said. Double green flash; lie down. Tell your men."

Jinx cast a look around the camp, and then at Reven, and wished he hadn't. It was better not to have to look at people.

He nodded, and turned, and walked quickly out of the camp.

Deep Green Magic

Simon was right. The wizard Frank Magus went missing in the night. The Urwalders set out to attack Reven's forces at dawn.

They advanced cautiously, hiding behind the trees. Jinx moved forward with the rest. He sensed werewolves creeping in from all sides. He heard the stomp and crunch of trolls behind him.

The whole forces of the Urwald were here today . . . they'd been coming in from the remaining clearings, from the Glass Mountains and from Salt City. If they lost today, there wouldn't be another chance.

Ahead of him, Jinx sensed Reven's soldiers, lying in

wait. He sensed their feelings—worry, fear, excitement. Loyalty. They were all very loyal to Reven. It was that king thing.

They were eager to fight. And they were afraid to die.

Terror, said the trees. *The Terror has reached the heartwood.*

It was different with the Urwalders. They were angry. Much more angry than afraid. But afraid, too—each of them. Jinx saw clouds and blobs and swirls of fear all around him, purple and green, blue and pink, yellow and orange.

Elfwyn was sticking close to him. Jinx was annoyed. She was waiting for him to . . . He didn't think he could. Not with all these terrified people.

Let us fight, Listener. Let us strike the Terror.

"Just let me know when to send up the—" Elfwyn began.

"I don't think I can do it," said Jinx. "Everyone's so afraid and—"

FIRE! Pain! Listener! FIRE!

The forest's agony and terror almost knocked Jinx over. He had to stop and clutch a tree for support.

"Jinx, what's wrong?"

Vaguely, through the cataclysm of fire and fear, Jinx felt Elfwyn's hand on his shoulder. And vaguely, he was aware that there was no actual fire where he stood.

"The Urwald's burning," Jinx said. "They're . . . everything."

"Where?"

"Around all the clearings," said Jinx. "They've . . . set . . ."

"You mean the soldiers they've left there have set fires?"

Jinx barely heard her. Flames were roaring in his ears, climbing his bark, crawling along his roots. His sap boiled and crackled.

Wait. Stop, he told himself. The fire isn't everywhere. He needed to concentrate.

He reached through the root network, mile upon mile, and found the burning trees. He drew the fire to himself. He could do this now; he was the Urwald.

He felt the forest's lifeforce all around him, beneath him and above him. It flowed through the trees, branches, leaves, and roots. It flowed through the undergrowth and the moss beneath the trees, and the vines that climbed the trees. It flowed through the Restless—the worms and the birds and the bugs, the porcupines and the bears, the squirrels and the bats. It flowed through nixies and werewolves, trolls and ghouls, humans and vampires and firebirds and dragons. Everything that lived in the Urwald was part of it.

And it reached down, deep down, deeper than the roots of the trees, down onto the Path of Fire, though Jinx was the only one that could sense it there.

He reached down and touched the Path of Fire, and he drew its power up, up through the paths, up into the trees' roots, up into the trunks and . . .

. . . and he was forgetting something.

"Double green flash!" he yelled to Elfwyn. "And get down!"

And he didn't know if she obeyed or not, because he wasn't really seeing at that point. Not with his eyes. He was feeling, power coming up through his roots and into his trunk, through his xylem and phloem, along his branches . . .

. . . except that he didn't have branches. Because he was one of the Restless, and that meant he could *move*.

He moved.

Not his feet. That wasn't possible, because they were rooted too deeply into the earth. But his arms, his hands, his head—these could move. As he'd been yearning to do for a hundred years, he moved his branches.

And then he could see. He could hear. He smelled the smoking remnants of the fires, and it made him angry.

He was a tree. He was a forest. He was the Urwald. And he could move. The Terror was attacking, and finally he could fight back. He swung his branches. There was scurrying and skittering as squirrels and chipmunks scrambled for safety. A million birds took to the air as the great branches thrashed out, lashing at the invaders. Thousands upon thousands of limbs whipped and tore at anything within reach.

From the east to the west, across hundreds of miles, the forest fought back. The towering giants had few branches that could reach the ground, but the younger trees bent, swayed, and struck. The sprawling old oaks swept their thick branches inexorably across the forest floor. The spiny spruces slashed at the intruders. The Terror that had tormented the trees for so long finally ran, screaming. It ran onto the overgrown paths, it fled into the Storm Strip, it leapt into canyons. It tried to hide in the clearings, but the wards stopped it.

In one part of his mind Jinx saw that it was *people* running, and he tried to save them from the trees' anger by pulling down the wards. He tried to stop hitting them, once they'd dropped their weapons and were running away. But his ability to move belonged to the trees now, and the trees were striking the Terror as hard and as often as they could.

Some of the Restless stood their ground and tried to fight, broke their swords against the branches and trunks that felled them.

The trees didn't hear the screams like Jinx did. They heard noise, running, the usual sort of desperate, impetuous churning in which the Restless spent their lives. They didn't care. They gloried in the ability to move, to *see* the enemy, to chase him, to strike back, to exact revenge for the chopping and the Terror and the fires.

It must have gone on for a long time.

Then it stopped, and the motion slid out of the trees, and back down through the roots, and down, down, down into the Path of Fire, and Jinx went with it. He left his body behind. He found himself walking along, between high glass walls that were so narrow his shoulders and elbows brushed them on either side.

There was none of that zapping shock that Jinx remembered from the Ice. And yet he couldn't feel the fire anywhere.

"He can't seem to find his way back," said a voice he thought he remembered, but the memory didn't seem attached to anything, nor did he.

"He'd better. If he knows what's good for him." An anxious voice, warm and blue, but Jinx didn't know anything about that voice, either. There were a lot of voices, and they bothered him, so he walked on until he couldn't hear them anymore.

Then a voice was right in front of him.

"What do you think, now, about good and evil?" it asked sweetly.

And then Jinx knew where he was. He was standing

on a broad agate floor, beside a crystal waterfall that didn't move, that didn't really have water in it and didn't actually fall. A beautiful, slightly glowing blue lady stood beside him, and looked at him with deep amethyst eyes.

"Uh?" he said.

"Or more specifically, evil," said the lady. "What do you think about evil?"

Jinx had to think hard just to remember what thinking was. Once he'd got that in order, he had to remember how to speak, and who he was talking to.

"I think it depends on what you actually meant," he said.

The Elf Princess looked beautifully puzzled. "Oh?"

"I mean, what you meant to accomplish. When you did the thing. Whether your intentions were evil."

"That may be part of it," said the Princess. "But it is also very much a matter of what you've actually done."

"I guess." Rearranging his thoughts into words that came out of his mouth felt strange. He felt as if he would rather speak with his roots.

"You can't stay here," said the Elf Princess. "But you can go on from here."

Jinx frowned. A vague memory pushed at him. "I think I'm supposed to go back."

"If you go on," said the Princess, "you need never face what you've done."

"Are you sure about that?" said Jinx.

The Elf Princess frowned. "It's not really my concern."

"Yeah, but it's mine." Jinx collected his thoughts, which seemed to have scrambled off in thousands of differ-ent directions, like leaves in a sudden October whirlwind. "I . . . um, I at least have to find out. And there's people. I'm pretty sure there's people I want to check up on. I can't remember who they are, but it'll come back to me, and . . . I don't really know what happened, but I'd better go find out."

There was a purple cloud of irritation from the Elf Princess . . . that's right, Jinx remembered. He could see stuff like that. He could probably do other stuff, too. He had some memory of that. And he had memories of other people, orange and brown, blue and green, and he wanted to talk to them more than he wanted to talk to the Elf Princess.

"Right, I'll be seeing you," said Jinx. "Or not."

And he walked away from the waterfall that wasn't, and found himself back on the path.

A Spell for Simon

Everybody fussed far too much. Especially Sophie. It was days before Jinx was allowed to get up, and he could feel people carefully not telling him things.

Of course, it wasn't as if everyone spent *all* of their time fussing over Jinx. There were flurries of activity away from the south wing, in the main part of the house, and much coming and going through the big front door, and even some coming and going through the secret door to Samara.

When he could finally escape, Jinx didn't feel like going into the forest. He wasn't ready to talk to the trees. He went to Samara instead.

He walked the moonless streets at night. He could tell there were people following him, on the rooftops and in the shadows. They could follow him all they wanted; he wasn't going anywhere.

He almost wished someone would attack him. It would have distracted him from his thoughts. But no one did.

On his third night of wandering, he let some of his stalkers catch up with him and surround him. They were Elfwyn, Wendell, and Satya.

"You shouldn't be doing this," said Elfwyn. "There've been all kinds of people following you."

"That's their problem," said Jinx.

"There was a spy for the preceptors," said Satya. "It took us hours to lead him astray last night."

"And you know we can't keep doing that," said Wendell. "What if the preceptors started having Satya followed?"

That was a point.

Jinx let himself be led to the Twisted Branch, down near the Crocodile River, after Satya and Wendell had scouted the rooftops to make sure no one was following. Inside, the inn smelled of spices and cooking. The place was cheerful with torchlight, and full of people eating, talking, and shouting in different languages. Wendell bought some spicy chicken pies from a barmaid. Then he led them all up several flights of stairs, past halls that rang with laughter, music, and argument, to his room in the attic.

Jinx ate his pie in six large bites. He had a feeling he'd spent weeks or months without eating again. It suddenly occurred to him that after all his journeys underground, he no longer knew how old he was.

He got up and paced back and forth, running his finger along the rooftiles that formed the slanted ceiling. Elfwyn, Satya, and Wendell sat on the bed and watched him with their different colors of worry.

He turned to them. "Is someone going to tell me what happened?"

"Yes. The trees fought," said Elfwyn. "With their branches."

"I know that," said Jinx. "I was there."

"Well, you asked. A lot of people survived, though," said Elfwyn.

"Great."

"Reven survived," she said. "In fact, he's the King of Keyland now."

"Really?" said Jinx.

"Yes." Elfwyn didn't say anything about that being a question. That was how delicately people were treating Jinx these days.

"King Bluetooth of Keyland was killed," said Wendell. He looked at Jinx as if anxious to see how he would take this.

"By a tree?" said Jinx.

"Yes," said Wendell.

"Well, he was a murderer anyway," added Elfwyn hastily.

"How many—"

"We don't know," said Elfwyn.

"But enough of Bluetooth's followers were killed that the rest thought they might as well change sides and follow Reven," said Jinx bitterly.

"Well, he *is* a king, obviously," said Wendell. "And that means something to people. I think there were a lot of people who, if they couldn't have Bluetooth, would just as soon have Reven. Royal blood, you know. Grandpa's arse, would you quit sulking?"

Jinx couldn't help smiling, despite his mood. It was a relief to have someone lose patience with him. "Sorry. But I . . . well, I guess I'd just feel better if I knew that every one who got killed was a bad person."

"That's not really how wars work," said Wendell.

Satya stood up suddenly and dusted her hands off in a businesslike manner. "The Urwald's going to need to make terms with Reven. There'll be a dispute over the Edgeland—"

"They're not getting the Edgeland," said Jinx.

"—but really, it seems like you could have worse neighbors than Reven."

"Like King Rufus the Ruthless," said Elfwyn.

"Did he die?" said Jinx.

"No," said Elfwyn. "That was a question."

"He did retreat though," said Satya. "All the way back to his own capital in Bragwood. You'll have to make terms with him, too."

"I bet I killed a lot of his men, didn't I," said Jinx.

"Look, I know how you feel—" Wendell began.

"Really? How many people have you killed?" said Jinx.

"You didn't kill them," said Elfwyn. "The trees—"

"Couldn't have done it without me," said Jinx.

"So?" said Elfwyn. "Didn't they have the right to defend themselves?"

Jinx looked at her in surprise.

"I don't really see what else you could have done," said Wendell.

"Except nothing, and let the Urwald be conquered," said Satya. "Now, there will be treaties that have to be made, and agreements that have to be reached. Who's going to do that?"

"You're talking about diplomacy, right?" Jinx thought about Simon, and himself, and Urwalders in general. They were probably going to need help with that.

By the time Jinx was able to bring himself to go and talk to the trees, summer was brightening into autumn. He walked through the forest for a long time. It knew that he was there, and it murmured to itself, telling itself that the Listener was back. And it waited for him to speak.

We're not going to do that again, said Jinx.

If it becomes necessary, if the Terrors return, if.

Well, we'll just have to make sure that doesn't happen, said Jinx. *Now, can we talk about the paths?*

The ancient agreement was broken.

Yes, and you told me I had to unite all the thinking beings of the Urwald and get them to agree to a new treaty. I think I can do that now. At least, we've got the werewolves and trolls, and that's a start. We'll get the nixies and ogres and the werebears and werechipmunks. The vampires . . . I don't know about vampires. But I need to tell them all what you're offering.

Jinx had never made such a long speech to the trees before, and he wasn't sure how they'd take it. They murmured and muttered to each other for a long time, discussing his words along the root network.

Offering? they asked at last.

As your part of the new agreement, said Jinx. *They'll want the paths back, of course. And possibly some of the Storm Strip, for new clearings. I don't know about the burnt area—*

No. Not the burned ground. It is ours, the burned ground. Fire builds the forest.

It sounded like they might concede the new Storm Strip clearings. Jinx didn't press them. He'd give them time to think.

There are a couple other things I need, he said. *If you don't mind. I need to use the lifeforce power for a couple of spells. Kind of big spells.*

It is your power. We are only part of it. You are only part of it. We are the Urwald. The Urwald is only part of it. Your roots are deeper than ours. You will use the power. We will allow it. We will help.

He'd figured they would. It was to their advantage to help him when he asked.

The Urwald knew how to look after itself. And it knew it needed a Listener to explain it to the Restless. And it would do what it could to . . . . hm. Come to think of it, Jinx wondered if his being found by Simon, all those years ago, was quite the accident it had seemed.

It was no good asking the trees. They'd pretend not to understand the question. They'd say they couldn't tell the Restless apart.

He couldn't always tell when they were lying.

Jinx turned and started homeward, watching the ground to avoid trampling small seedlings. He saw a row of hemlocks growing along a fallen, rotted trunk, their roots wrapped around it. When the old trunk was gone, they'd stand as if on stilts, reaching down to the ground and into the Urwald's root system, and the Fire.

He heard a crunch of footsteps and looked up. Elfwyn was coming toward him through the forest. Nobody would leave him alone for a minute!

"I just came to see—" she began.

"I'm fine," said Jinx. "Stop fussing."

A large blue glow of hurt. Really disproportionately large—he hadn't exactly snapped, had he?

"Sorry," said Jinx. "I didn't mean—"

"I wasn't fussing." Elfwyn shrugged. "I just thought maybe you'd like to talk."

"Yes," said Jinx. "I would like to talk."

They looked at each other and didn't say anything.

Elfwyn was surrounded with a warm green glow, which was very Elfwyn-like and had been there for a long time. And maybe the green glow was also coming from Jinx, now that he really looked at it. And maybe that unreliable pink fluffy stuff (which still hadn't shown up, and never would) was completely irrelevant, when you had a green glow.

Sometimes, Jinx thought, he really was a little slow on the uptake.

He was right about one thing, though. Sticking your face at someone was extremely awkward.

Jinx was glad that it wasn't going to be his job to restore Simon's life, after all. He knew he wasn't very good at spells, and this was a horrendously difficult one. He'd dreaded messing it up, which would result in Simon being either 1) dead or 2) very angry or possibly even 3) both.

Elfwyn and Sophie were in charge. They had studied the Crimson Grimoire while they were captives at Bone-socket. Sophie seemed to understand the spell perfectly in theory, and Elfwyn might actually be able to do it.

There were other people there to help—Dame Glammer, and Dame Esper. And Wendell and Satya had come to help carry torches.

"Are you sure this is a good idea, Simon?" asked Satya. "After all, you're not dead, like Jinx says he was when you put his life back—"

"He wants to do it anyway, dear," said Sophie, before Simon could snarl.

"Yeah. Having your lifeforce missing makes things feel . . . weird," said Jinx. He remembered how the Bone-master had described the feeling: not quite whole.

"But no one's ever done it this way before—" said Satya.

"And now they're going to," said Simon. "Right, are we ready?"

"Yes," said Sophie. Her thoughts were all jittery brown-and-blue nervousness. Jinx wished they weren't.

"Better lie down, dearie!" Dame Glammer said.

Simon stepped in amongst the carefully chalked figures. He had drawn most of them himself, with Elfwyn's help, on a patch of dirt that Jinx and Wendell had carefully swept free of leaves and humus. Because they were doing it in the forest, of course. They were going to use lifeforce power instead of deathforce power. And they were going to use a lot of it.

Simon propped himself on his elbows and glared around at them. He had acquired a jagged scar over one eye in the war. It had definitely improved his glaring skills.

"Just trust us, dear," said Sophie, sounding as tense as Simon had when he'd done the spell on Jinx. She even managed to make *dear* sound like *idiot.*

Simon lay down, sat up suddenly, dug a sharp rock out of the ground, and tossed it into the forest. He lay down again. "Right. Let's get this over with."

Jinx was relieved that all *he* had to do was provide the power. He would have felt very nervous if he'd had to stand there holding a torch with the others. They were now marching around Simon widdershins, and Elfwyn was chanting the Qunthk words that Jinx had helped her learn.

Jinx reached down deep into the Path of Fire. He drew power up through the tree roots. The flames on the torches flared higher. They became a tower of fire— higher and higher, as Jinx drew more fire from the Path. But the fire didn't touch the trees. Jinx was controlling it. When Elfwyn knelt to put the bottle to Simon's lips, Jinx brought the fire down into the spell.

Flames leapt and scurried along Simon's still form.

And then the spell was finished.

Simon lay there with his eyes closed. They all gathered around. Simon's eyes remained closed. Why didn't he open them?

It was Jinx's fault. He shouldn't have suggested using lifeforce for a deathforce spell. He shouldn't have insisted on not using ghast-roots. There was a way around *most* things in magic. But not everything.

Jinx leaned down, anxious, and then jumped as Simon's oddly yellow eyes flew open.

Simon blinked. He sat up. He looked around. He stood up. He shook his head furiously. Then he shook it again. Jinx wondered if a bug had crawled into his ear.

Simon blinked some more. He looked around at all of them.

"Thank you," he said.

Everyone exchanged worried looks. They weren't used to hearing Simon say such things.

Simon put out his hand, and experimentally, cast a spell. Jinx could see it was a levitation spell. Simon was trying to levitate a fallen log.

And he did. The log flew high into the air. They all looked up as it became a stick in the distance, then a twig, then a dot against the deep October sky.

Then it came plummeting down again. They scattered as it hit the earth, nearly burying itself. It boinged into the air again, then careened off at an angle, smacked into a tree, ricocheted, and flew toward them. They threw

on the ground as the log whizzed overhead. Jin

twigs snap as it crashed into another tree.

"Stop it!" said Sophie.

Dame Glammer cackled.

Dame Esper grinned and waved her hands, and the log

fell harmlessly to the ground.

"Hm," said Simon. "Well, I'm sure it will all come

back to me eventually."

Everyone gathered up the bits of magical paraphernalia

and headed back to Simon's clearing. Simon and Sophie led

the way, arm in arm, with Simon looking preternaturally

cheerful and agreeable. Jinx assumed it wouldn't last.

He stayed behind to thank the trees for their help, and

to remind them that there was one other important spell

he needed to do.

When he got back to Simon's clearing, where the goats

and chickens once more wandered freely, he saw the fierce-

looking little apprentice witch eyeing the butter churns

parked beside the door.

Dame Glammer and Dame Esper were talking to Witch

Seymour outside his shed. Dame Esper turned around.

"Gertrude!" she screeched. "Get away from those

churns or I'll turn you into a toad!"

The girl scowled. She went into Simon's house, slam-

ming the door behind her.

ent over to the witches. "That girl, Gertrude.

find her abandoned in the forest?"

ind?" Dame Esper frowned at him. "And what if I

Finders keepers. Anybody that *left* her in the forest

had better not think they're getting her back!"

"I agree," said Jinx. "I just wondered, that's all."

Dame Esper gave him a mistrustful look and hurried into the house, perhaps to guard her apprentice against any sudden claims.

Whitlock the goat wandered over and chewed thoughtfully on Jinx's bootlace.

Jinx smiled to himself. Well, good. He'd found Gertrude. And she might well be the oldest Urwalder with two living parents. But Jinx didn't intend to tell those parents, because they were Bergthold and Cottawilda. He'd tell his stepsister that they existed. Just in case she wanted to know.

He turned to Dame Glammer. "Why did you, um—"

The two witches were staring at him. Jinx hated being stared at by witches, because it always made him feel that he was being weighed and found ridiculous.

He plunged on. "Why did you say I'd never be a wizard?"

"Not that sort of magician are you, chipmunk?" said Dame Glammer. She tried to chuck him under the chin, but Jinx was ready for that and took a hasty step backward.

"More of a Listener than a wizard, aren't you?"

"I suppose," said Jinx.

"Why would one want to be a wizard, anyway?" ask.
Witch Seymour.

Jinx shrugged and went into the house. He might
become a wizard. You can't if you think you can't, and Jinx
rather thought he could.

Where the Path Begins

J inx had been avoiding it. He knew he had. But you have to face up to what you've done, including turning people into trees. He shouldered a shovel and walked out into the Edgeland, among the silver-blue stumps and the blackberry canes, until he came to a slender green sapling.

Ash trees grow very fast. The tree was already as tall as Jinx. He curled his fingers around the smooth green trunk and felt the tree's lifeforce. Its roots just touched some of the outer roots of the Urwald, and Jinx's power wasn't as strong here as it would be in among the tall trees.

I'm going to need to dig you up, said Jinx.

The tree murmured in protest. It liked where it w.

Just to make sure the spell works, said Jinx. *I want to car
you to where the lifeforce is stronger.*

The lifeforce is strong here. I am alive.

I know, but . . . look, Siegfried—

I remember Siegfried, said the tree.

Well, I've come to turn you back into him. I—

No.

I'm pretty sure I can do it, said Jinx. *It should just be a
matter of—*

I refuse, said the sapling. *I remember Siegfried. I do not
wish to be him.*

Well, he was kind of obnoxious, Jinx agreed. *But—*

Siegfried always wanted *something*, said the ash. *And as
soon as he had it, he wanted something else. He was never happy
with what he had. I am happy. I have everything, and I am the
Urwald.*

I see, said Jinx.

He argued a little more, for form's sake. But it was
quite clear that Siegfried wished to remain a tree.

～ ✌ ✌

Meetings happened. They went on all through the fall and
into the winter. There was a lot of shouting, several knock-
down-drag-out fights, and a prodigious amount of voting.
Then people realized that it was almost time for spring
planting, and that new huts were going to have to be built,

that they generally had other things they'd rather do
than stand around arguing.

"We could have a council," Sophie suggested. "Each
clearing could elect someone to the council—"

"What about the werewolves?" said Malthus. "Someone needs to represent werewolves."

"Yes, of course," said Sophie. "Each werewolf pack
should send someone, and—"

"Trolls," said Sneep.

"Oh, yes," said Sophie. "Of course, each, er—"

"Clan," Sneep supplied.

"Clan of trolls, yes—" said Sophie.

"Magicians," said the Carrot.

"Right," said Sophie. "Magicians can, um, send a representative, and—"

"One scarcely cares to be represented by a wizard," said
Witch Seymour.

"Yes, all right, a representative for wizards and a different one for witches, then," said Sophie.

"Trees," said Jinx. "The trees need to be represented.
There's more of them than of anyone else."

"Nobody can talk to them except you," said Sophie.

Jinx sighed. He did hate meetings, but there seemed to
be no avoiding them. "All right. So I will."

"We need to write this all down," said Malthus. A
notebook had appeared in his hand. "We should have a

written document that tells how the council's going to be constituted, and then how the laws are going to be constituted—"

"Who said we need laws?" someone asked.

"We do," said Malthus. "To protect the rights of the individual."

Somehow, looking at Malthus's fangs, you did sort of want your individual rights protected.

"For example," said Malthus, "I was thinking of something along the lines of 'A well-regulated diet being necessary to the health of a werewolf, the right of the people to eat each other shall not be infringed.'"

"We need a law," said Jinx, "saying that people can't abandon their children in the forest."

"Why?" said Cottawilda. "*You* did pretty well out of it."

"That doesn't matter," said Jinx. "Most of the kids get eaten."

"The Urwald hasn't gotten any bigger," said a woman. "What are people supposed to do when they've got more children than the clearings can hold?"

"Maybe they shouldn't *have* more children than the clearings can hold," said Jinx.

"Oh, now you've done it," muttered Simon, who was standing nearby. And the whole meeting dissolved into screaming and shoving, with Elfwyn and Jinx hastily evitating all the dishes up to the loft so they wouldn't get broken.

Sophie was determined to start a school. Jinx agreed with her. He figured the Listeners had died out partly because Urwalders seldom lived long enough to pass on any kind of knowledge—and Listeners needed knowledge. Knowledge was power. Future Listeners shouldn't have to figure everything out for themselves, as Jinx had.

Besides, it would be nice if people learned to read, and learned about the world outside, and learned to be just a little less afraid of everything.

"I myself would like to teach a course on Urwish history," said Malthus. "I've done considerable research on the subject."

"Er," said Sophie. Jinx could see from the shape of her thoughts that she didn't wish to offend. "I'm not sure werewolves—er—"

"Oh, you can't have a school without werewolves," said Malthus. "Werewolves can be very helpful in dealing with problem students."

"What was the last Listener's name?" said Jinx. It bothered him not to know.

"Matilda," said Malthus promptly. "She closed the portals to Samara."

"How did she do that?" said Jinx. "A KnIP spell can't be undone."

"I have a treatise on it in my library," said Malthus. "I can lend it to you, if you're interested. And if you're careful not to spill anything on it."

"Thanks," said Jinx.

"It was the great battle of her time, as this"—Malthus waved a claw vaguely at the forest—"was the great battle of ours."

"So at least someone remembers her," said Jinx.

"Oh my yes. She was a hero. There's a song, too. The chorus goes 'O, Matilda was a brave woman/And she would have been crunchy to eat.'" He tilted his head at Jinx thoughtfully. "It makes sense if you're a werewolf."

Sophie insisted on calling the school the University of the Urwald. But everyone else called it Bonesocket, because that was where it was.

～ ✲ ～

The Wanderers had come back. Jinx showed them the doorpaths, and explained how their merchandise could be passed through from one Doorway to another.

"What's the point of that?" said Tolliver.

"It saves a lot of time," said Jinx.

"Yeah? And then what?" said Tolliver.

"Wandering is what Wanderers *do*," Quenild explained.

Jinx hadn't realized that before. But now he did.

"If the Urwald no longer needs our services—" Quenild began.

"We do!" said Jinx hastily. If nothing else, he realized,

the Urwalders needed to see outsiders regularly. Urwalders were in constant danger of becoming too . . . Urwish. "But we might want to trade through the doorpaths ourselves, just to move the sugarplum syrup to Keyland," he said. "Because we can sell that for a lot more than you've been paying us."

This remark set off a hubbub of remonstrance from the Wanderers, which eventually led to meetings, arguments, more meetings, and an enormous amount of voting.

And Satya was right. There had to be treaties. The first one was with Reven—King Raymond of Keyland, rather. And that was mostly a matter of getting Keyland to give up all claim to the Edgeland. Wendell, Sophie, and Hilda—and Nick, on crutches—went to King Raymond's palace in Keyland and worked this out. Jinx didn't really understand how it was done, but for some reason it involved the prices of glass and sugarplum syrup.

The treaty with King Rufus the Ruthless had yet to be made. It was still in the shouting stages.

The preceptors let it be known, via a note posted in the hallway of the Samaran prison and visible through the KnIP portal Jinx had made, that Samara would like to establish diplomatic relations with the free and independent nation of the Urwald. Jinx was almost 100 percent against this. Except that there was the matter of Nick's leg. If a Samaran surgeon could help Nick—and all the other Urwalders who'd been injured in the war—then maybe it was worth thinking about.

And then he remembered how the preceptors had looked at the trees in the Urwald and calculated how much money they were worth, and he was back to being 100 percent against it.

Well, the new Urwish council would decide the matter. Eventually.

And, of course, there was the treaty with the trees, which was the most important one of all. Jinx told the council what the trees wanted, and then he told the trees what the council wanted. He did a lot of running back and forth. People listened to him. People did listen when you had the ability to turn millions of trees into deadly weapons.

And that was the wrong reason. But it would have to do for now.

And with all of that, a year had come and gone in the free and independent nation of the Urwald. The paths had been restored, for those who needed them. Unfortunately, that seemed to be a lot of people—some folks just couldn't get the hang of the doorpaths. Jinx had taught a course at Bonesocket in how to use them, and he'd be teaching another one soon. He'd found he was pretty good at teaching, except that he tended to lose patience with his students now and then.

At least people weren't quite as bound to their own clearings as they had been. The war had shaken them up a bit. Jinx and Elfwyn sat in an ancient maple tree a little way off the path, and watched through the leaves. There was actual traffic. A party of Wanderers passed by, their wagon wheels creaking.

"So this Presider they're talking about having, to stop the fights in the Council meetings," said Jinx. "I guess people want it to be you."

"I know," said Elfwyn. "I'm not sure if *I'd* like it, though."

"Having people ask you questions all the time," said Jinx.

"Yes," said Elfwyn. "Although they do that anyway, so in a way . . ." Her thoughts went green and blue and mused around each other. "I might like it."

"They wouldn't want me to be Presider," said Jinx.

"Of course not," said Elfwyn. "You're the most powerful magician in the Urwald. That's kind of scary. Not to me," she added hastily. "But to people."

They watched the people walking along the path.

"I hate my curse," said Elfwyn. "Even if I have learned to use it." She sighed. "If this was a story that was coming to an end, then my curse would be magically fixed because everything would have to come out exactly right for every-body. But real life isn't like that, and sometimes you just live with things."

Jinx looked at her fingers intertwined with his. No, this wasn't a story, and it wasn't coming to an end. If it were a story, he supposed, then the evil King Raymond would have been vanquished along with the other evil kings. Instead, the probably-okay King Raymond owed his throne to the Urwald. And the peace with Keyland might last for years, as long as Reven remembered what the Urwald could do to him.

King Rufus of Bragwood was a bit more of a problem, of course. But at least he was out of the Urwald for now.

And Wendell was still trying to get Satya to quit the Mistletoe Alliance, and Satya was clenching her teeth and refusing. Jinx couldn't guess how that story would end.

"And what about Simon's magic?" Jinx forgot himself and made it a question.

"I don't know. He still might get it under control. And if not, he can just keep busy with his cooking, and bossing people around. And he can look after his baby, once it's born. It's not just Sophie's job, you know."

"I never said it was," said Jinx, amused. "But any kid Simon looks after will have to be awfully good at looking after itself."

"Don't leave the path!"

A tiny child about two years old came careening down the path. Behind it, its mother was yelling.

But the child did leave the path. It veered off into the woods, where it tripped over a tree root and went sprawling. It stared around, stunned, but didn't cry. Urwish children seldom cried.

Jinx jumped down, and went over and picked the child up. Its mother, who had stayed on the path, looked absolutely horrified to see her baby in the arms of a powerful magician.

"Don't leave the path!" she cried again.

Jinx took the child back to its mother. But first, he told it a secret.

"You'll never get anywhere unless you do."

Acknowledgments

I would like to thank the people without whose patience, wisdom, and kindness Jinx and the Urwald would not have seen the light of day.

For reading various drafts and stray bits and making suggestions, my eternal thanks to Deborah Schwabach, Aaron Schwabach, Jon Schwabach, Caitlin Blasdell, Joel Naftali, Lee Nichols, Nancy Horgan, and my late sister, Jennifer Schwabach.

I am grateful to everyone at HarperCollins and Katherine Tegen Books for brilliant editing, and for being so understanding and patient. Many thanks to Anne Hoppe (who helped me understand the monsters and, even more importantly, the paths), Sarah Shumway, Katherine Tegen, Laurel Symonds, Katie Bignell, and everyone else there.

Many thanks to those whose help gave me time to finish the middle book, *Jinx's Magic* . . . James and Cynthia Vail, Gabrielle Vail, Lindsay Vail, Ty Giltinan, Qienyuan Zhou, Martha Scott, and Yingfei Zhou.

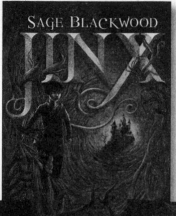